Waking Up Dead

By Zabe Truesdell

This book is available in eBook format at most online retailers

Table of Contents

Special Thanks to my beautiful wife Crystal for inspiring me, as well as Deanna, Greg, my Moms (all three of you!), Dad, Misty, Charlie, and all of my other friends and family who helped make this book possible.

The soul is the same in all living creatures, although the body of each is different. - Hippocrates

Prelude

Jack had little doubt that if the metallic monstrosity landed a clean blow it would kill him again. As a hulkish metal fist exploded a tree next to the spot Jack had just vacated a split second before, he lost any remaining doubt. There was no reason to let his opponent know this, however.

"Aye, close mate but still too slow." Jack spun quickly out of the way once more as the clenched steel hands cratered the ground where he had stood. "Last chance lad. Give up or we will destroy you. I can keep this up all day."

That was a lie. The oddly metallic rogue soul swinging at him still drew power from the sanctuary. Unless Jacob and Heather managed to help the sanctuary's real owner regain control quickly, this was going to end very badly. Jack rolled out of the way of another sloppy but powerful punch. He came back to his feet wielding a cricket bat he had willed into existence, which he slammed into the back of Mr. Metal's legs. It felt like connecting with a telephone pole; the jarring recoil slowed him just enough to get clocked by a powerful backhand.

Jack rolled backwards across the metallic grass to reduce the impact of the blow. Luckily the grass still retained the texture of real St. Augustine despite its new sheen, but even the softened landing didn't detract from Jack's fast depleting energy stores. He flipped back to his feet with near lightning speed, hoping to keep up the bluff that he was doing well.

"Seriously, lad? That the best you've got? You fight like you decorate. Which is badly, by the way. I mean really, you could have turned this place into anything you wanted when you took it over, but you just cover everything in metal? Who does that?"

The stoic figure lunged at him again. Jack ducked, but not as fast as he would have liked, and this time the rogue soul came away with a chunk of his Hawaiian shirt.

Jack just broadened his smile. "Thought you might want something to remember me by on your way into the River."

He was prepared to evade once more when the metal man's near expressionless face suddenly connected with a large flying metal baseball bat. The bat bounced off, but Jack noticed it made more of an impact than his own swing had earlier.

Heather had obviously found the real owner of the sanctuary, freeing her partner up to come join the fight.

Jack smiled as the bat flew backwards into the hands of a tall bald man with near obsidian colored skin.

"Bout time you got here, Jacob."

The man named Jacob rushed forward, ducking under a heavy punch and slamming his bat into the metallic stomach of his opponent. "Thought you had this one."

Jack rushed forward using his cricket bat to knock the metal man's fists off guard before they could connect with Jacob's head. "Aye, well, don't like to claim all of the fun, you know."

Jack slammed the cricket bat into the rogue soul's stomach and was rewarded to see it stumble backwards. Heather was doing her part in taking back control of the Sanctuary and severing this soul's link to it; with a bit of luck and skill they might actually pull this off. He ducked a much slower but still obviously potent swing, and then had to half fall, half roll backwards to avoid a second. Jacob took the attention once more with a well-placed swing to the back of the thing's head. The metallic soul stood and turned slowly back towards him.

Jacob stepped back and shook his head. "Man, this dude makes Huang seem talkative. River job?"

Jack nodded. "Aye, fraid so." A slight tug at Heather's connection gave him a welcome piece of good news. She was ready.

Jacob obviously felt it too. He stood up and motioned to the metal figure. "Come on, big boy. Try your best."

Without a word the steel statue looking soul charged forward. Jack knew the plan, and quickly rushed forward himself. As the opponent reach for Jacob the tall black man ducked at the last possible minute, swinging his baseball bat into the metal man's thick legs. Jack leapt up and kicked the rogue soul in the back almost simultaneously, sending him stumbling ahead.

Jacob scrambled away yelling "Now, Red!"

The sanctuary shifted, and where once there was metallic ground the shift now had their opponent stumble over the edge of a cliff. Without a word the figure plummeted down. Without a splash it disappeared into the River, ceasing to be.

Brilliant fall colors exploded in place of the monochromatic metallic sheen that had, till a moment ago, covered everything.

Jacob dismissed his baseball bat, then turned to observe the newly decorated realm with an approving whistle followed by a sigh. "Man used to be these dug in souls were rare. They're getting way too common. And this guy was not the subtle type. Leo should have had us here a long time ago."

Jack nodded. "Aye. Should a would a could a. Fact is, there's getting fewer of us to go around and they seem to be getting dug in more quickly. Leo can only do so much, and we can't keep up with the work he gets us. He's got another job waiting already."

Jack felt a strange summoning. He realized who it was as Jacob shrugged his shoulders "No rest for the weary then."

Jack smiled "Nay lad. For the wicked neither. Have Heather point this soul to Willy then head to the next job." Before Jacob could object, Jack raised a hand to stop him. "Aye lad, I know he's a scoundrel but he does well in what he does. You don't have to talk to him, just give the soul his card."

"Fine. What are you going to do?"

"Just got a summons from Dan."

Jacob winced. "Ug. He's worse than Willy."

Jack smiled and nodded. "Aye. But good at what he does as well. If he's calling then he may have a recruit. Can't turn that chance down right now."

Jacob shrugged an agreement. "Good luck with that.

One

Thomas tried to scream, but whether he succeeded or not was beyond him. The pain seared his entire being. He couldn't remember where it came from. He could no longer even imagine life without his every nerve ending crying out in tormented misery.

Relief offered itself up at the edge of his awareness. A warm nothingness exhibited itself as an alternative to the torturous agony. Thomas welcomed it, letting it wash away all hurt. The release was sweet, sudden and soothing. The comforting warmth then faded slowly to a heavy cold. For a brief moment Thomas felt the pang of fear; then he felt absolutely nothing at all.

Thomas opened his eyes to a brilliantly blue cloudless sky. He sat up, trying to identify his surroundings and how he had come to be there. He wasn't sure where 'there' was, though he recognized that it was definitely not where he had been. After further thought he realized that he wasn't entirely certain where he had been either. The fogginess of his memory disconcerted him.

"Where am I?" As soon as he vocalized his question the answer came to him, though that answer was so patently ridiculous that he immediately dismissed it.

"Thomas, lad, I'm sorry to break the news... but you're dead."

Thomas ignored the absurdity of the statement and continued to take in his surroundings.

He stood at the edge of a cliff face. A couple of hundred feet below, a dark forest stretched out to the horizon like an emerald blanket. A sense of comfort washed over him. Wherever this was, it bore an amazing resemblance to his favorite family camping grounds of his childhood.

Except… it was quiet… and something about that was strange. There should have been birds, wind, any number of animals. No sound existed; not even the annoying whistling his eardrum often made when no other sound remained to break the silence. It was as if someone had pushed the mute button on a TV.

In the distance, a large river twisted its way along the horizon as far as he could see in either direction. That too made the scene different from his childhood camping spot. The River had an odd shimmer to it, a color Thomas had never seen before. It struck him as being completely strange and yet something about it comforted him as well.

Next to Thomas, a man in a Hawaiian shirt stood admiring the view. He had been the one to speak before, and Thomas now realized that he had done so with a slight European accent. Scottish maybe? The man's words finally began to register.

"So umm… Dead?" Thomas didn't feel dead. Then again he didn't seem to feel much at all. He did vaguely remember the surge of adrenalin as the car slipped out of control. He should have known better than to take that corner in the rain, but wanted to make it home to see… "Shari. My God, I have to…."

"Do you love her?"

"Of course I love her. I'm engaged to her for god's sake."

The man smiled with a tint of sadness. "One doesn't equate the other. But if you love her, I recommend waiting awhile before you go see her. You can do what you want, but you'll only cause more pain, and trust me, you don't want to be there when she finds out."

The scene played out before Thomas's eyes. The knocking at the door. Her long brown hair shining with the reflection of the setting sun. Her wonderfully inquisitive look fading to concern as the she noticed the officers in front of her. The dawning of understanding at their first few words turning to horror as she realized what they were telling her.

Thomas stopped, dropping to one knee, staring out in the distance. The man in the Hawaiian shirt put a hand on his shoulder. "I told you lad, you don't want to go there."

"My god." There was no denying the truth of it. He knew it to be fact, despite the impossibility of the idea. "I'm…I'm really dead."

"Aye. Take as long as you need, lad. Soak it in. It's a big change, I can tell you that."

"I'm dead."

Thomas's other knee crumpled and he slumped into a seated position on the edge of the precipice. He sat lost inside himself without seeing anything, trying to rationalize the unacceptable. *"I'm dead.... I'm... oh Shari, I'm sorry. I'm so very sorry. I'm....But.... I'm here.... I'm.... Where?"*

Suddenly there were so many other things to think about that Thomas didn't know where to start. He looked around at the quiet but majestic scene below. It was breathtaking.

"Or would have been," he thought wryly, *"if I had breath to take."*

The sky was cloudless but pure blue, the forest a dark majestic emerald green. The cliff had a beautiful mix of earth tones, browns and reds and oranges mixing into each other. The colors were more vibrant than he had ever witnessed before. The River in the distance was…. Beautiful… *"How can there be a color I've never seen?"*

Whatever expectations Thomas held for the afterlife, this wasn't it.

The man in a blue and white Hawaiian shirt was definitely not what he had expected. At around five-foot ten, he stood roughly the same height as Thomas. But where Thomas's half Hispanic heritage gave him brown hair and dark eyes, the stranger at his side had blue eyes with more dirty blonde, slightly balding hair. He was also a lot pudgier and at least twenty years older than Thomas. He didn't look like any relative Thomas could remember. Maybe he could be one of his mother's relatives, but definitely not from his father's Hispanic side.

"Umm… so uh… is this Heaven?"

"Where you Christian?"

"No. Not really."

"Subscribe to any other major religion?"

"No. I would have to say I was more agnostic. I didn't really know what to believe."

"Good. Then you'll be a bit less disappointed. I was Catholic meself. Let me tell you that was a shocker." The man gave a hearty laugh as if there were a joke there that Thomas missed. He then continued, slightly more seriously. "The answer to your question is basically, yes. This is the afterlife. Though not exactly as any of the major religions would have you believe."

"And you…" Thomas studied the man closely. No, definitely not a relative he recognized. He certainly didn't look like an angel or ferryman either. In fact, he looked like a middle-aged tourist at some beach resort.

"I'm Jack. Least I was last time around. And since ye look like you're wondering, no, I'm not a relative, nor am I an angel, crow, Valkerie, demon, or any other guide religion and folklore have come up with. I am exactly what you are. A projection of my last life. A… a soul you could say."

"Then why are you here? Not that I don't appreciate answers, but…"

"Someone told me you'd be here. I've got a job offer for you."

Thomas shook his head, still trying to come to terms with his situation. This was to too much to wrap his mind round. "Wait. I'm dead and you want me to work?"

Jack shrugged. "People get bored."

There was no arguing with him there. "Um… what kind of job?"

Jack smiled and clapped him on the shoulder. "Patience lad. We'll get to that. There'll be more you'll want to be knowing first."

Thomas stood up and took a deep breath. The air had no feel to it. It wasn't cool, it wasn't warm. It wasn't dry or damp. It had no odor whatsoever. "*Of course, being dead, I probably don't even need air.*" An odd thought, but low on the list of many odd thoughts and questions. "So. Where do we start?"

Jack put a hand on Thomas's shoulder and pointed out to the horizon. "Ye see that river there?"

"I don't think I could miss it."

"It's the best place to start."

*****

They were standing on a beach made of pebbles. The loud roar of the River created a violent juxtaposition to the complete silence Thomas had experienced up to a split second ago. It wasn't necessarily the sound of rushing water that he had expected, but more a combination of howls, screams, whispers, chirps, barks, and more. There were laughs, there were cries, and there were moans. There were many elements he didn't recognize at all. It sounded as if someone had recorded all of the sounds of life, be they human, animal, insect or other, and put them into one soundtrack, then pumped the volume up to impossibly high levels. It was extremely disconcerting.

Equally disconcerting was the fact that it was suddenly there. Or rather, they were suddenly there. One moment they were on the cliff top, the next they were here. "*I guess the dead can teleport?*" That seemed sort of cool, he guessed, though he would have traded it in a second to still be alive. He started to drift back to Shari but quickly shut her out of his mind. Thomas didn't know much, but he knew instinctively that Jack had been telling him the truth on at least one thing. He didn't want to be there, standing by completely helpless, as Shari went through the initial stages of grief over his…. loss. He couldn't do that.

Jack put a hand on Thomas's shoulder again and shook him from his thoughts. When he spoke to Thomas he had to lean close and still talk at near a scream to be heard over the noise.

"The first thing you need to know is that being dead does not make you omnipotent. There are things you will know because they're instinctual. There are things you will know because somebody 'll tell you, and there are things you just figure out for yourself. In that respect, afterlife mimics life. This existence, however, it's much more fluid. The realms you find yourself in will be a sanctuary created by one or more Souls. Each will have its own laws or rules, and they're subject to change depending on the point of view of that soul. That's how we were able to travel between your canyon top view and here so quickly. Somewhere in each sanctuary, however, there is always one thing constant and that's this."

Jack stretched his finger out towards the River in front of them. Thomas suddenly realized that it did not, in fact, contain water. The roiling, bubbling flow before them appeared much more ethereal than any liquid. It really looked closer to a gas, though strangely it still moved and behaved like a liquid. It stayed within its bounds, had a steady, if constantly shifting, surface, and a murky quality that made it impossible to see down into. Looking down into it reminded Thomas of looking over the edge of a boat into a deep lake.

The shimmer easily explained itself from here as well. Everywhere up and down the length of the River, circular portals opened and closed at a rapid pace. As Thomas stood studying it, he realized that there were, in fact, two sets of portals opening and closing.

The first kind were vertical, and they always opened just above and perpendicular to the River before dipping into it and then disappearing. The others were horizontal. Those always opened slightly above and parallel to the River line, dropped something into the River, then closed. The whole thing happened so quickly that you barely had time to focus before it was over and starting somewhere else, but as he watched he began to get the feeling that the things being dropped in might be bodies of all manner of size and shape. Some might even have been human.

Whatever fell into the River, however, never resurfaced. There were no splashes. There were no arms, legs, paws or claws poking out. There were no rocks and no debris. There was only the River and the portals.

"This," Jack continued to yell, "is the Alpha and the Omega. For all practical purposes this is bloody God."

*****

Thomas stared into the campfire. Silence blanketed the world again, and that startled Thomas more than the sudden scenery change.

"Sorry, lad." Jack smiled from his seat next to him. "I thought this would be an easier place to talk. You can never hear yourself think around the River. Don't be worrying, transitions will get easier as you learn to move around yourself."

Thomas looked around the area. They were back on the cliff face, sitting back in a recess. The sky above disappeared into a deep black devoid of light. The firelight flickered as if it were real, but offered no heat or sound. Late evening bathed the forest below in a twilight emanating from no discernible source. Off in the distance, The River was once again a silent border. The whole thing seemed eerie and unreal. "This is all so strange."

"You can change it if you like."

"Really? To what?"

Jack shrugged. "Anything you want. This is your sanctuary, lad. Everything here is part of your memory. Like I said, there aren't many real rules. Once I walked into a sanctuary of a guy who loved the arctic but hated the cold. I tell you, everything was snow and ice, but the bloody temperature was tropical. It was extremely disconcerting, I can tell you that for sure."

"I don't even feel a temperature here."

"Well, you haven't gotten practiced enough to control the details, have ye? Here, I'll show you." Jack closed his eyes and appeared to be concentrating. Suddenly it felt cool, as the night temperature appeared and dropped to around fifty degrees. The fire began to crackle, and gave off a nice cozy warmth. As Thomas looked around he noticed the twinkling of stars pop into view, and suddenly a full moon appeared over the horizon, giving source to the light below. Jack opened his eyes and smiled. "Oh, wait…" He looked down at the forest below and suddenly the sounds of exotic birds and monkeys filled the night's background. "You'll um… have to forgive me. Me mum and dad liked the tropics, so that's where I spent most me life. Seems more natural to me than a proper forest would.

Even with the odd monkey howls in the background, the world felt more real and comfortable to Thomas than it had since he had arrived. It brought a smile to his face. "Thanks. So I can do that too?"

"Aye. Easier than I can to be sure, this being your sanctuary and all. As you get more practiced it'll become harder for others to adjust what you've created. Get good enough and it'll be pretty bloody impossible to change."

Thomas sat back and studied the fire for a moment, trying to figure out which of the many questions banging on the door of his mind he should ask next. He finally settled on one. "So, you said 'my last life'. Does that mean you've had others?"

"Oh, aye. Without a doubt."

"How many?"

"I dunno. One complete one, of course. Jack Macintyre. Me dad was Scottish, me mum , she was from Australia. They both liked to travel so they sorta met in between. They spent most of me own life traveling too, and when I got out on me own I kept that up. Least till a few years after I'd gotten married, and then I caught myself a bad case of dengue fever. Thought I could beat it on my own. No need for a third world hospital, no sir. Turned out… well… I fell asleep, had some weird, fever induced dreams, then woke up here. That was probably twenty years ago, now. Since then I've remembered pieces of maybe six other lives." Jack shrugged. "Could be 10 times that though for all I know. "

"So I might have been someone else before this?"

"Oh, aye. And something else too no doubt. Let's see if I can explain this in a way that makes sense. Now keep in mind, some of this is supposition while other pieces are facts, but as far as I can tell it's all true, every word of it. You remember the River down there?"

Thomas shuddered. "Yes. I don't think I'll be forgetting that anytime soon."

"No, you wouldn't, would you. The River is life. It is the source of us all. Now picture a soul as being an ice cube, made of up of, let's say, five thousand particles of water for a human. Now, say ye were to take one of those ice cubes and drop it in a lake. When it melts completely, then you scoop out enough to make another ice cube. How much of the original five thousand particles do you think you might have?"

"Uh. I dunno. It depends I guess. Probably not a lot though."

"Exactly! The horizontal openings you saw, they were returning ice cubes to the River. The vertical ones, now they were scooping out new ones. Now add to that the fact that all living things have souls, though a bird's maybe only has 500 particles, a grasshopper maybe 50. A cat might have two thousand particles. All of it goes into and come out of The River. Any one of us may be made up of hundreds or more lives. Hells, you and me may even have parts of the same lives, and not all of them even human. A bloke in Brooklyn dies, he may reincarnate into two dogs, fifty grasshoppers, a lion, and 1/100 of a little lass in Nigeria."

"Um… Wow. That's…" The concept danced around the edge of Thomas's mind. He struggled to grasp it. "That's just weird."

The two sat in silence for a time as Thomas let some of this new information sink in. The fire gave off a comforting crackle.

"So let me see if I understand this. Before I was Thomas Salazar, I might have been a field mouse, a hawk, a butterfly and a host of historical people?"

"Aye lad. Personally I think most everyone has a mosquito and a cockroach or two in 'em, though it's such a right tiny portion it's hard to access any of those memories without a hell of a lot of meditation and practicing. I do actually remember being a pigeon once, which has come in handy more times than I care to admit to you. Understand that we aren't really as we appear. Just like the sanctuaries, we're constructs based on our memories of how we looked when we were alive. The more lives you can remember, well…"

"You can actually shape change into a pigeon?"

Jack nodded. "Aye. Though it's not always an entirely comfortable experience I'll tell you. You'd be amazed at how many pigeon memories are based on being afraid of everything around you. For others… well, I know a man who claims to be 80% of Leonardo de Vinci. He was also a barn owl once, and spends most of his time looking like it."

"80% of De Vinci?"

"Aye. Is he telling the truth? Who the hell knows, but he definitely makes a compelling argument. I've heard people say that stronger personalities 'melt' slower, so more of them stick together going into new lives. That'd explain why everyone remembers being someone famous when they claim to have past lives.

For all I know most people may have someone famous in 'em. Let's say Cleopatra breaks into 50 parts, 100 hundred particles each by what we said earlier. 50 people at a time could have significant memories of her life buried in their psyche, and every time one of them dies and enters The River another person might be born with those memories. "

Thomas struggled to wrap his mind around the idea that all of this was reality; that life and death could exist in this fashion. He had no reason to doubt Jack, but then again he had no reason to trust him either. For all Thomas really knew he could be feverishly hallucinating in a coma somewhere. For Shari's sake he hoped that was true, but it didn't feel like it. Somewhere deep down he felt certain that at least a large portion of what Jack was saying was based in truth. Questioning reality in a world that responded to your thought sounded like a quick and dangerous path to insanity. Thomas decided that, at least for now, he would just trust Jack.

"So, what makes creatures return to the River? Or, maybe I should ask 'why didn't I return to the River'?"

Jack shrugged. "The best idea I've found is that you didn't want to. Most of those that really had a proper hate of their life don't seem to make it beyond the River. Hells, most just appear directly over it. The rest appear in their own sanctuary like you. Most of 'em stay there. A few others go back to the Prime, which is what we call the land of the living. Some like me figure out how to travel through other sanctuaries. When they get bored or tired or just plain curious though, all of them go back to the River. "

Thomas shook his head, completely overwhelmed by what he was learning. Every question he thought to ask immediately opened ten more questions he might want to know first. He felt he might be able to spend an eternity quizzing Jack about the new 'life' he had woken up into when he died. Jack seemed to read his thoughts. "Could he actually do that too here?" Thomas wondered.

"It's a lot to take in, lad. I know, I was new-dead once too. Even now after twenty some odd years, I don't have but a fraction of the answers I wish I was knowing. But, I've been able to learn more than others in this relatively short time due to the job. From everything I've seen of you, I think you'll be a good fit too, but the final decision relies on you. "

"So what would this entail?"

Jack smiled and poked at the fire. "Still be time for that later. You've got more pressing things to come to terms with first."

Thomas looked around. A monkey howled in the background, and the moon held its place in the cloudless sky. He considered how the night sky might look with a few clouds and was pleasantly surprised to see a light haze form. Jack smiled.

"Now you're getting it."

Too many thoughts and questions crowded into Thomas's head for him to be satisfied with his minor achievement. "I just died, for gods' sake!" And yet, there was so much to learn, so much potential to this new world that Thomas found he barely missed his life.

Except Shari. The thought of her suddenly hit him like a freight train. He regretted leaving Shari behind. He didn't want to think about her, for fear he might once again accidentally slip back to see what she was going through. Being there to see her go through this kind of loss without being able to comfort her would be even more heartbreaking than being apart. He loved her too much to helplessly watch her go through that. But he wanted to see her. He wanted to see her smile, and feel her leaning against his body. He could almost smell her shampoo, could even feel her…

"Be careful, laddie."

"Huh?" Thomas found himself stroking the air next to him, as if he were stroking her hair. Had he been?

"You can create anything here." Jack said with a smile that bordered on sadness. "But it's a shell. A living embodiment of your own memories. It can't act on its own and it won't be like having the real thing. Some people are okay with that. They surround themselves with people they knew when they were alive, and revel in the fact that those people do and act exactly as they want them to. But me, well, I died before my wife too. I tried creating her for awhile, still do sometimes when I'm feeling like reveling in the past, but, well… she never feels… complete. And to tell you the truth that just makes missing her all the worse."

Thomas wasn't sure if his words completely made sense, but the sadness attached to them left no doubt that it certainly true for Jack. "*Something to try later*." He thought. They sat in silence for a while, staring at the fire. Thomas fought to keep his mind away from Shari but doing so just brought her to his thoughts more quickly. He decided to keep the conversation going to try and think of something else. "Has she…. Has she died yet?"

"Who?"

"Your wife."

"No. She was a wee bit younger than me, maybe ten years or so. Guess she'd probably be in her fifties now. Wow. I'd be over sixty if I were still alive. Imagine that? Anyway, I checked in on her quite a bit in the early years. It was hard to see her but it helped at the same time, you know? Slowly, well, slowly she seemed to recover some of her happiness. Last time I was there it seemed she might have met someone. I hope she has but I really didn't want to watch either. So I haven't been back. That's been…. oh I don't know…. five years now?"

The two sat again in silence. Thomas looked around the world that had become his "sanctuary". His world. It was comforting, somehow. "*Maybe that was why I woke up to it instead of something like the house Shari and I shared.*" The night, however, wasn't helping his mood. Morning would help.

On queue, dawn broke on the horizon. It brought a smile to Thomas's face. "Have we really been here all night?"

Jack smiled. "No. That was you. Did you intend to?"

Thomas shrugged. "I figured I would feel better in the morning."

Jack smiled. "Time means little here, Thomas me boy, other than what you want it to be. You can have a thousand days in the time one would pass in the Prime. Or you can have a day that never fades to night no matter how many years pass. It's your sanctuary. Do with it as you will. "

"So much to learn. So much to think about it. Maybe doing something would help, but right now...." Right now Thomas had little desire to do anything other than let some of this set in.

Jack seemed to pick up on that.

"I'll give you more information on me job offer next time I see you. For now, take some time to yourself. Get used to your new afterlife."

"Thanks." Thomas stood up and shook Jack's hand. "I think I would like to take some time to think through all of this. It's... it's so much to comprehend."

"Aye. Explore your sanctuary. Practice your manipulation of it. Remember, whatever you create, you can dismiss, so don't let yourself get mauled by your own wild animals. Also, don't touch the River. Even the slightest touch could completely unmake you."

Thomas didn't think he would be getting anywhere near the River for awhile, but he thanked Jack for his advise. As an afterthought he asked "And how will I get a hold of you if I need you?"

"I'll check in on you in a week or two. If you need me before then just concentrate hard on me being here in front of you. I'll hear your call and return as quickly as I can."

Thomas realized he was a little sad to see the man go. "Thank you, Jack. You've made dying a little easier than it probably would have been."

Jack smiled. "Take care."

Jack turned and took a step into nothingness, disappearing completely. Thomas found himself alone on the cliff top; a dead man in a world of his own imagination.

Two

It felt good to Thomas when he realized that geekdom is not something you lose at death. Obviously he had lost many things in his transition. The need to eat, drink, go to the bathroom, and more were gone, but those were to be expected. No body obviously meant no bodily needs. No hormones either, he realized, and he wondered what implications that might have. Curiosity, however, that was something he had plenty of.

He didn't know how long he spent playing with the basics. When the sun rose and set at will, time ceased its meaning. For fun he even did an eclipse and stared straight at it. It was beautiful, and without retinas to sear, there were no repercussions.

He changed the seasons. He changed the temperature. He lost himself in the magic, a wizard in the afterworld. He smiled at the thought. "*I always wanted a wizard's tower. Why shouldn't I have one now?*"

Thomas turned and starred at the center of the plateau that he stood on. He wished for a tower to be there. For a moment, something flickered, but in the end nothing changed.

"*Apparently you have to work a bit harder than just wishing.*" He thought as he considered how to make this actually work.

He closed his eyes and thought about all the towers he'd seen in paintings and pictures. None really fit with what he wanted. "*Maybe I could design this one step at a time?*"

The closest thing he'd ever been to a real wizard's tower was the lighthouse near his aunt's home in Maine. Thomas had visited it a couple of times growing up and he had always marveled at it. He closed his eyes and tried to picture what it looked like. It surprised him how easy the memory was to access.

He opened his eyes to find a tall structure standing before him. It matched his memory of the one from his aunt's house perfectly. The modern look, however, wasn't quite what he was looking for. He thought about it a few minutes and finally the metal veneer shifted to impressively masoned stonework matching the wall around his old elementary school. He added large wooden door for good measure. It occurred to him that he could just teleport to the top if he wanted, but that seemed somehow less fulfilling right now. He gave the door a hard tug. It stuck for a moment, then slowly creaked open. The sound was pitch perfect. The weight of it felt good. It was odd. In a world designed by your imagination, reality seemed all the more important. Torchlight flickered on the other side of the room as he found himself at the bottom of a staircase spiraling up into the distance. He had known it would be there, which, he supposed, was the reason that it was. He took a deep breath out of habit and began the walk up. The steps were a rough dark wood, and looked as if they should creak, so they did. The noise, however, struck him as repetitive, so he decided maybe that should happen less often. Every fourth step now creaked. That seemed somewhat predictable, but he wasn't sure how to get around that. The world responded to his thoughts. That was an incredibly awesome and amazing feeling, yet at the same time Thomas realized there would be no surprise here. There would be no discovery of new things.

That was disappointing, but he supposed he could spend some time just pushing the bounds of his reality to see what he could and couldn't do. That might hold him for a while, but how long did he have here? Eternity? Thomas suddenly understood why someone might want to take a job like Jack was offering, assuming it came with new things to learn and new places to see.

As he circled back around to what he knew to be the side of the tower facing forward, he decided that he should be coming up on a window. He did, and the view amazed him. The forest stretched out towards the horizon like a green blanket. The River twisted along its boundary bringing a smile to Thomas's face. That wasn't part of his memory. That still held some surprises.

 Thomas continued his trudge up the stairs. The complete lack of resistance felt strange. No fatigue, no muscle strain, no issues at all. He hadn't been in bad shape when he was alive, but he had just bounced up who knows how many flights of stairs (“*Okay,*” he thought, “…*fifteen*”) and felt as if he had just walked across the living room. He concentrated for a moment and could almost feel a burning in his chest and heaviness in his feet, but that seemed silly so he stopped it. Some parts of reality were, perhaps, less important than others.

After he had climbed far enough, he came to a door. This one pushed in, and as he stepped through he found himself at the back of a large circular room. The door was flush with the wall. Thomas looked back through the doorway and confirmed briefly that this position was, as he thought, impossible. It was good to note that physics and spatial position were flexible here.

The room stretched a hundred foot in diameter. The front half of the wall consisted entirely of glass, and looked out again over the forest and River. Thomas walked across the room and then through an opening now in the glass to a circular balcony surrounding the tower on its outside. Another beautiful view greeted him there. He added a few large eagles circling lazily in the distance for good measure. He turned back and looked at the tower. The exterior remained solid stone, save for the archway leading inside. From here the circumference of the tower couldn't be more than fifty feet. "*Bigger on the inside*," he smiled, "*maybe I should make a blue police box….*"

He walked back inside and smiled as the stone arch naturally melded back to a glass wall. He decided the floor should be covered in plush white carpet, and so it was. The room as a whole looked beautifully decorated with the furniture he knew would be there. He walked over and sunk into the couch. He had always loved this couch. It was one of the first things that he and Shari had picked out together. "*Shari…*"

He reached over and grabbed their engagement picture from its place on the end table next to the couch. How many times had he stared at this and smiled? The flower gardens had been beautiful and they had done fifty or more classic poses with her in that blue cocktail dress and him in the matching dress shirt and slacks. Yet it was this out-take of her on his back laughing that had been her favorite. It was a completely silly shot, but that had been its charm. The love positively beamed from both of their faces.

The reality of his situation sliced through the magic of his sanctuary like a serrated blade. He threw the photo across the room as hard as he could. It hit the wall and shattered with a satisfying sound. *"Oh Sha*ri*...."* He turned back to the end table and studied the picture, which had again found its way to its natural spot. *"Oh Shari, I'm.... I don't know if I can do this."*

"There there, Baby."

Thomas felt her weight as she sat down next to him on the couch. She settled into his arms as she always did and laid her head on his shoulder. Thomas pulled her tight and took a deep breath of the lavender shampoo that she always used. He could almost forget that none of this was real.

"Will you love me forevers?" she whispered. It was the question she always asked. The reassurance that he wouldn't do what he had just inadvertently done... leave her alone.

"For evers and evers." He had always believed those words to be true, but now somehow it felt like a lie. He still loved her with all his being, but he had left her. This would be the most painful day of her life, more so than when her father had died from cancer. At least she had known that was coming. This... Thomas knew that he had done this to her and could do absolutely nothing to make it right. That knowledge alone hurt more than any physical pain ever could. He pulled the not-quite Shari as close and tight as he could, tears openly flowing now down his face. "Shari, I am so so sorry."

"It's okay, Baby. I think I'll keep you, anyway." She had always been fond of saying that when they were making up from one of their arguments.

He rocked back and forth with her in his arms for a small eternity. It was almost as if she really was there. Here weight and size was perfect in his arms. Her skin felt as soft as ever where it caressed against his. Her lavender shampoo mingled with her natural scents the way it always did when he held her this close. *Almost perfect. Something though....* Something was missing, and for some reason that something seemed amplified now. "Tell me something I don't know about you."

"You know I can't."

"You're not real, are you?"

"No baby. I'm not real."

With that she was gone and Thomas Salazar crumpled into the floor with only his pain and tears for company.

*****

Years could have passed while Thomas lay there sobbing. He didn't know nor did he care, and he would have gladly remained lost in his misery if something extraordinary had not happened. A large soft tongue suddenly started licking the side of his face. Thomas jumped in spite of himself as he looked up to see a large German shepherd standing over him. He realized with a start that it had been the first time he had truly been surprised since he had woken up dead. The dog licked Thomas once more and then looked at him with a natural smile. Thomas suddenly understood that, like everything else in this world of his, he knew this dog very well. "Buster!" Buster had been his constant companion for the first twelve years of his life. His parents had gotten him a few years prior to Thomas's birth, but after that he was Thomas's dog. As an only child, the dog became as much a sibling as a pet. "Buster, you have no idea how much I need you right now."

"He always did know how to cheer you up."

Thomas gasped with the recognition of the new voice. He looked up to see his mother walking across the room. "Mom…" He shook his head. "*Of course… I must have subconsciously created other people to take my mind off Shari…*"

"Hello, son. It's been a long time."

That it had been. It had been five years since his mother Sylvia had died, oddly enough in her own auto accident. He smiled despite himself at the idea that he could now recreate her here. Still, there was something about her that seemed odd. She was far younger than he remembered, and he couldn't recall having ever seen the sixties era mini-dress she wore. The way he recalled her…. She shifted for a moment, and suddenly appeared some thirty years older, her favorite pants suit giving her that familiar look of authority. She seemed surprised for a moment as she looked down at herself. She then shook her head and suddenly returned to the twenty-year-old version of herself.

"Come now Tommy, is that really necessary? I know it's your world, but can't you leave a girl her illusions?"

Thomas's jaw dropped. He stood up and closed the distance between them, slowly walking around her with close inspection. Her re-assuring smile was very familiar, but the rest of her... he remembered seeing a few photos of her from before she had met dad, but nothing of this detail.

"Are you...." Thomas realized that the thing missing from the Not-Shari wasn't missing now. Suddenly he knew without a doubt that this was no creation of his. "MOM!" His smile exploded as he wrapped his arms around her and pulled her close. "Mom, it's really you!"

"Of course it is, Tommy. There, there. It's okay."

They stood there in each other's arms for some time before she finally pulled back and stared at her son.

"Let me have a look at you. Oh, son, it's so good to see you, but I'm so very sorry you're here this soon. "

Thomas tried to respond to her, but couldn't think of anything to say. She squeezed his hand. "I'm sorry I wasn't here sooner. Buster came and told me of your passing. We travelled to the prime in time to see your funeral."

"My... my funeral?"

His mother nodded. "Yes, son. It was closed casket, but it was a very moving service. You should be proud of how many lives you touched. And that girl.... Shelly?"

"Shari."

"Shari. Yes. I'm very sorry you were torn away from her, but I'm very proud you chose so well with her. "

Thomas hugged her again. "I'm glad you approved. That would have meant a lot to her. Gods. I'm so worried about her. I don't know how she's going to make it through this."

Sylvia reached up and moved an errant hair out of Thomas's face, much as she always had when he was younger. "She'll make it. I could tell that one is strong. It's going to be terribly hard, take it from me. When I lost your father I really thought my world died too. It took me a long time to move forward, but I did, and so will she. She's got the same things I had to keep me going. You two built an incredible network of friends who will be there to support her. Take it from me, that's extremely important."

Thomas sighed. He wanted very much to believe that. "Good. Hopefully that will be enough. I know you always told me that having to be strong for me got you through the worst."

"It did. And she'll have to be strong for… well…"

She looked away. Thomas knew that look. It was the same one she had when she would catch herself almost telling him about one of his Christmas presents.

"She'll have to be strong for whom? Mom?"

"Tommy, I'm really really sorry you had to leave when you did."

Thomas knew better than to let up now. "What are you telling me, Mom?"

Sylvia looked away, obviously gathering her thoughts. Then she turned back and began speaking once more in a nervous, much quieter tone. "Your Shari. She told everyone at the funeral that she had something to pull her through this. The night you died, she was waiting for you with a special dinner. She had just found out she was… well… Tommy, she's pregnant."

Thomas collapsed back onto the sofa, which located itself right behind him once more.

"Pregnant? She's… I'm…. I mean I would have been a dad?" Buster nuzzled his nose beneath Thomas's hand. Thomas began stroking him absentmindedly.

Thomas's mother sat down next to him and squeezed his other hand. "She said she's hoping it's a boy. If so she's naming it after you. Though she'll no doubt be equally happy with a girl."

"Shari's pregnant."

Sylvia put her arm around him. Thomas let her pull him in tight, holding him close as she had whenever he had been sad as a child. It was weird with her being so young, but at this point he didn't care. "Congratulations, Tommy. You left her with a piece of you to hold on to. That should mean a lot. It will to her."

"Wow… I um…. Uh…" There was too much going on for Thomas's mind to work. He was still heartbroken, perhaps more so now that he would not be there to hold his baby and see all of the firsts, but there was a baby and somehow that made him proud. Shari would be an incredible mother, and her mother would make certain the child wanted for nothing. Maybe this would cushion the blow of losing him. He would have done anything to make that time easier for her. "I can go back and watch, can't I? See what my baby looks like?"

"Yes, son. I'd wait though. I tried seeing you just after my accident, and you broke down each time. Apparently people close to you can sense you, and if they haven't had time to come to grips with your passing, the reminder of your presence can be a bit much. She's being watched over though. The living weren't the only ones who made an appearance at your funeral. She has several guardians who will be doing what they can to sooth her during this time. "

It was what it was. Thomas couldn't think of any way to change this, and his Mom was now the second person to tell him that going back right now was a bad plan. They had both been at this longer than he had and he had no reason to doubt them. Still… the idea that he would be able to actually see his baby at some points made him feel better. He wouldn't miss everything, even if Shari and the baby didn't know he was there.

"Nice place, by the way."

Thomas recognized that his mother was obviously trying to change the subject. Under the circumstances, he felt inclined to let her.

"Thanks. I used Aunt Martha's lighthouse as a base, then tweaked it from there."

"I'm impressed. I've visited a number of sanctuaries since I've been dead. Not many of them 'tweak' things. They tend to be either a direct copy of the world or an ideal of what they had expected from the afterlife. Your Aunt Martha has actually rebuilt the original lighthouse next to the River if you're ever interested in visiting it. Your cousin Mary, well…" Mom actually chuckled, 'She has a halo and her whole sanctuary looks like cloud tops. Really, I remember that girl as a teenager. A saint she was not. Ah well. She's the one who has to live with an eternity of harp music. "

Thomas sat and listened as his mother caught him up on some of their other long passed relatives. It once again occurred to him just how amazing it was to hear her talking. He'd dreamed of her voice so many times since her passing, but never thought he would actually hear it again. In some ways, death wasn't near so bad as he had worried it might be. The idea that he could go see other sanctuaries excited him. He vaguely remembered Jack making reference to that, but now that he understood his own sanctuary better the idea was more appealing. The ultimate power of creation was very exciting, but Thomas already missed the lack of surprise and discovery, and he'd only been dead a week or so. If this sanctuary were all he had he could see why people would considerer returning to the River for another run at life. As his Mom quietly sat there stroking Buster's fur he realized there was a name missing from her long list of updates.

"Oh and your grandfather Rich… Well you remember the stories of the ranch he grew up on? It's worth a visit if you…"

"What about Dad?"

His Mom's smile immediately flattened. "Your father…" She pursed her lips, obviously thinking of a way to explain something she didn't feel comfortable with, "well, this wasn't really something he cared for. He watched over you for many years, apparently, and when I died he stayed with me for awhile, but… well, you know how he always had strong opinions on what should and should not be, and this place just never really lived up to what he had thought it should. He didn't say so, but I suspect he also remembered a few of his past lives that he really wasn't happy with remembering. A hazard I guess. A few years ago, living time, he said his final goodbyes and returned to the River. He was at peace, son. I don't fault or blame him, and I hope you don't either."

Thomas sighed. Inevitably, not everyone could be waiting here for a reunion. Then again, he hadn't expected to see anyone, so at least he had his Mom. He hadn't seen his Dad since he was seven. It would have been nice to see him again, and truth be told Thomas had grown used to his not being around. He thought back to the discs on the River and the stories Jack told him. Maybe some kid out there had already been born with an uncanny knowledge of how to make winning Pinewood Derby cars. That thought made him smile, despite the sadness of not being able to see his dad once more. "Well, I'm glad you stuck around, Mom."

"Oh, I don't plan on taking that plunge for a while. Even if I did I wouldn't have left before you arrived, you know that. Now, tell me what you've been up to. I checked up on you a few times, but not as often as I would have preferred. How was your life?"

Thomas began filling his mother in on all the highlights of his life since her passing. After awhile, two thoughts occurred to him. The first was that his memory was incredibly vivid. The second, that it's hard to know how much time passes in a world you control, especially when you have no bodily needs to interrupt you. Thomas and his mom sat talking for what could have been days. At some point Buster crawled onto the couch next to him and laid his head in Thomas's lap to better facilitate pettings. Thomas laughed at the idea of Shari's horror to see such a big dog curled up on their couch. She had always been a cat person, and even then preferred the cats not get on this couch for fear of them damaging it. Being the first thing that was truly "theirs" she was very protective of it. Thomas told his Mom all about Shari, as well as his jobs and education and misadventures in the years after (and sometimes prior to) her passing over. He caught her up on what he knew of some of their family friends and relatives that were still alive, and she continued to let him know about people on this side. After a long and very satisfying visit she finally stood.

"Well, son, it's been incredible to see you, but I know you still have a lot to get used to here, so I'm not going to keep you. "

"Thank you, Mom. You've made me feel a lot better. I'm very grateful to be able to see you again, too."

Thomas's young mother hugged him and gave him a very motherly kiss on the cheek, then stepped back and looked him over once more. "Think about me being here when you want to see me again. Really being here, so you don't just create a doppelganger of me instead. It may take a bit but I'll be here as quickly as I can. Maybe next time I'll take you back to my sanctuary. It currently looks like the little place we had in the country just before your father died, only with the Beatles playing in the the living room. I like to remodel it every so often. Maybe next time I'll try your little trick of creating something completely new. "

Thomas shook his head at the idea that his mom had recreated her favorite concert event of her childhood in her living room. "Tell you what, I'll visit you if you promise not to turn me into an eight year old when I get there."

"But you were so cute at that age!" She laughed again. The sound fluttered in his ears like a long forgotten favorite song. "Buster, are you traveling with me?"

"No. I will stay with Thomas now."

Thomas stared, jaw dropped, at the large German shepherd at his side. "Buster? You can talk?"

His mother laughed again. "That's right. I guess we didn't tell you that, did we?"

Buster looked up at me. "Yes." His lips never seemed to move, but his voice sounded clear and deep. "I remember a human life." For a brief moment he shimmered, then stood before me as a tall dark man in some form of tribal garb. He looked like a proud Native American warrior, then the German Sheppard stood once more. "Those memories allow me to communicate. "

"Well," Thomas said, scratching his head. "I guess you and I have some catching up to do, too."

Buster didn't reply, but instead let his tongue roll out to show his happiness. Thomas looked back at Mom. "Thanks for everything, Mom."

"You're welcome, son. Goodbye, Tommy." She closed her eyes, and seemed to concentrate for a moment, then opened her eyes with a hint of surprised. "You've locked down teleporting."

Thomas smiled as he remembered the thoughts he had had while building the stairs. He hadn't realized that the restrictions he put on himself worked on others too. "Umm… Walking seemed more natural."

She smiled once more at him. "You're going to be a strong one." And with that she turned and began descending the staircase.

Three

"Smells not right."

Buster wasn't the most talkative of companions, but his presence comforted Thomas immensely. It was nice to have something around that wasn't completely predictable. Thomas and Buster had been walking through the forest for a day or two now. If not for the fact that he instinctively knew every inch of this world, Thomas would have been thoroughly lost by now.

He'd put in a few deer, some squirrels for Buster to chase, and even a few monkeys for fun who now made the calls Jack had originally added as ambient noise. Thomas found that with some work he could sort of program basic behaviors into them. This made them at least move about on their own, though he had to be careful. He found that any time he thought they should be doing something different than they were they automatically started following his unconscious suggestion. Buster chased them happily, though, as it turns out, he was a surprising perfectionist on some things.

"Sorry, Boy. I have no idea what squirrels are supposed to smell like. It's hard for me to make something when I don't know where to start. "

Buster padded back over to me and began sniffing Thomas closely. "You could. You have many lives in you. Least two dogs." He continued and sniffing, then snorted in disgust. "And one cat."

That made Thomas chuckle. "Sorry boy. I'm sure that must be horrifying for you."

Buster stretched, and almost seemed to shrug. "Cannot be helped. I was a cricket."

"So you can actually tell by scent what past lives someone has?"

"Some. Humans smell alike. Bugs tough too. Most animals easy, though only if I have smelled them before. "

"So if I had, like, a T-rex in my past lives you couldn't tell."

"No. Have not smelled a T-Rex yet. "

"Good to know". *Two dogs and a cat, as well as other humans. And who knows what else? Interesting.* Thomas wondered how exactly he could get access to those memories. Running around with Buster as another dog could prove interesting. Climbing a tree as a cat might be fun too.

Suddenly Buster began a low growl.

"What is it, boy?" Thomas realized that the term of endearment from his childhood seemed kind of odd now, but old habits died hard.

"Someone new here. Not yours."

Thomas followed Buster's gaze and concentrated for a moment. Suddenly a familiar man in a Hawaiian shirt came strolling through the forest.

"Hello lad! How's it going?"

Thomas waved and smiled back at him. "It's okay, Buster. He's a friend."

Buster again snorted contemptuously. "If you say so. Smells like bird."

❋ ❋ ❋ ❋ ❋

Thomas popped the three of them back to the tower, then locked teleportation back down again. He didn't really think there was much danger here. It wasn't like anything could be stolen, and if it was it could easily be replaced, but his Mom and Jack had both shown that others could wander into his realm, and until he could figure out how to sense things as keenly as Buster he saw no reason to let himself get surprised again.

Jack looked around admiringly. "Wow, look at ya. You've been busy while I was gone."

"Thanks. I've been doing what I could to practice."

"You pick up fast. We thought you would, but I got to say you've exceeded my expectations. Bending reality. Not everyone has it in them. "

Thomas shrugged. "So I hear. Seems natural."

"For some it is." Jack laughed, plopping himself down on the sofa and propping his feet up. "Do you like beer?"

Thomas twisted his mouth in involuntarily in disgust. "Uh, no. Not really." That was a well rehearsed understatement. He actually despised beer, but often found that to be a socially unacceptable response. Most people he knew loved beer and were quite certain he could "acquire a taste for it". Why he would drink something that tasted bad long enough to convince his taste buds that it was acceptable was beyond him.

To his credit, Jack didn't push it. "Hmm, what did ye like then?"

"I don't know. I didn't drink a lot. Some wines. Occasional tequila drink. Guess I drank ciders more than anything."

Jack's eyes lit up. "Ooh, haven't had one of those in a while. Tell me lad, what's your favorite?"

"A private brew a friend of mine used to make. Great stuff."

"Why don't you make us some."

The concept caught Thomas off guard. No body would mean no bodily needs, wouldn't it? "What? Why? It's not like you need to drink for any reason, do you?"

"Well, no, but I didna need to drink beer when I was alive either, and that never really stopped me now did it? "

Thomas supposed he couldn't argue that. "Guess you've got a point. Just didn't think about actually eating and drinking here."

"You can do pretty much anything here you could do in life. You just don't have to do the things ya don't want. I make me own beers all the time, but it's the brands I had while living. I don't get to try new stuff unless I'm with someone else. Then it has to be something they liked, because the taste isn't so much how it actually tasted but how they interpreted it as tasting. You don't like beer, so if you made me one, even one of me normal favorites, it'd probably taste abit like sheep piss."

"Fair enough, I guess. Hang on." Thomas walked over to the kitchen area and found he now had a kegarator next to the fridge. He produced a couple of pint glasses from a near by freezer, then filled the frosty pints with some sparkling hard apple cider. He took a test drink, and realized that it most certainly tasted as good as he remembered. He then passed a glass over to Jack.

"Wow. That is tasty. You really thought your friend brewed a good drink."

"He did. Can we actually get drunk off this? I mean the real stuff packed a hell of a punch."

Jack had a seat in a papa san chair near the couch. "Well, yes and no. I mean you can make yourself feel drunk as ya like, that's not really an issue. But in the end you're always in control and the moment you want to be sober you are. You won't ever actually lose control the same way you would when you had an actual body to inhibit."

"So no blackouts but no hangovers either?"

"Aye, I'd say that bout sums it up. At least, not unless you actually want a hangover." Jack looked over at Buster, who remained very wary of the new comer. "You didn't make a very friendly looking dog there, lad."

"Don't mind him. He thinks you smell like a bird."

Jack raised an eyebrow in surprise. "He thinks? Thomas, my boy, did you figure out how to make a Homunculus?"

Before Thomas could ask Jack what he was talking about, Buster raised his head and seemed to almost spit in disgust. "No. I am full soul, birdman."

Jack smiled and looked genuinely amazed. "Interesting."

"It's true." Thomas offered, "Buster was my pet when I was a kid." He then reconsidered the term. "Actually, he was more like my best friend. He came to visit me with my Mom recently. He decided to stick around after she left. "

Jack looked over Buster more intently now. "And I take it you have memory of a human soul?"

"I do. You have memory of a bird soul and…." Buster sniffed the air, "And a goat."

"Wow. A goat you say? That could be useful. Thomas, I can honestly say I've never met anyone quite like your friend here."

Thomas laughed as he reached down to console Buster with a good ear scratch. "I thought you knew everything about this place, Jack."

Jack smiled, and sipped his drink as he walked over towards the glass wall. "Oh aye, I do at that. The problem is, that knowing everything about this place can be summed up in one sentence 'Anything is possible'. When there are no rules, it's hard to not be surprised by some of the things you'll encounter."

"No rules? You've made it sound like there was some form of structure."

"Ah. Well. There are what you would call common practices. Most people fall into certain categories, do certain things, and have certain abilities, but that's probably due more to the limits on human will power and imagination rather than anything else. As far as anyone can tell there really is no limit to what is possible. Think of it in terms of Hindu religion. To them, the 'Supreme God' had three facets, Brahma the creator, Vishnu the Preserver, and Shiva the destroyer. That River," Jack motioned his glass towards the horizon, "is made of all three of those facets, and we in term, are made up of that river. "

"So we're made up of these three facets?"

"Well, not really. At least it doesn't seem like it. Point of fact, most people seem to have only one facet in em. We're just tiny drops of the River, all things considered."

Jack downed the last of his pint, then wandered over to refill it. "From what I can tell, the preservation part of the River seems most common. Which I guess makes sense. Creation and destruction are extremely powerful, but we don't see new things popping into existence on the prime all the time, nor do things disappear in a poof. Preservation stands up to both, keeping things overall stable. It's the dominant influence, though in the end things do get broken down and remade into new. Same thing seems to be the case over here. Most people create what they remember. Even those who create something new do so out of images or stories that were so well known to them they that they may as well be physical memories. You go to the sanctuary of some truly by the bible Christians and you'll likely find the ground looks like clouds, an ornate wall in the distance, and a set of pearl gates marking their entrance. The texture will change, the style of the music may change, but the overall premise is what they had promised to them, so it's what they go with. It's what they know even if they didna see anything like it when they were alive. "

The possibilities made Thomas's mind reel. "So, literally, anything is possible. I mean, I could make us all look like cartoon characters if I wanted."

Jack shrugged. "I guess you probably could. Like I said, the limits seem to be imagination and willpower. You've got a good amount of both, and even more in your own sanctuary, so it's entirely possible you could pull it off, though for now I'm gonna ask that you don't. I'm not entirely sure I feel up to being in a Bugs Bunny episode. "

Thomas smiled, but decided not to try anything that drastic just yet. Instead he sat back and enjoyed his still full glass of perfectly chilled cider. He had to admit, being dead had its privileges. Jack took another swig of his drink, and then continued talking.

"So, let me tell you a wee bit more about what I'm offering you. The up side is that you'll be able to see many different Sanctuaries. You'll be taught things that you may have never learned to do on your own, like travel quickly between Sanctuaries and how to have a better chance at affecting the Sanctuaries of other people. We'll teach you what we know about the Prime, which is what we call the world where the living are at. We'll also do what we can to teach you about recovering memories of past lives and using those memories here. That's the good."

"Sounds like a no-brainer."

Jack plopped himself back in the poppa san. "Aye, well, in the spirit of honesty, I've got to tell you the bad too. We call these

Sanctuaries for a reason. There is very little that can hurt you here. You could tell me no and stay here and rest easy in the knowledge that you can continue your existence for pretty much as long as you want to. There is a tiny chance you could come into contact with what we call a Rogue Soul, but given how far you've come in just a few days, if one ever managed to find you then you could beat it back into the River without a second thought. If you go with me, we're going to be going after these things. I won't lie to ye lad, they're often embodiments of destruction. They're dangerous and you'll be encountering them on neutral territory, or worse territory they've begun to assimilate, putting you at a disadvantage. You could lose your existence and be returned to the River at any time."

"So you're basically a policeman for the dead?"

"Eh. More like a bounty hunter, though we don't really get paid for it."

"And it's that dangerous?"

"Well, I've seen bad things happen more times than I'd care to admit. You'll also be exposed to a lot of new knowledge, which may very well be the most dangerous thing in the universe. You cannot unlearn the things you see, and you are less likely to forget things here. I'll tell you this lad, there's some fucked up sanctuaries out there, and sometimes we're charged with protecting people and things that we find abhorrent. But it's what we do, and part of joining the order is the vow that you will use what you learn to protect those in need, regardless of what you think of them or their sanctuary. "

Thomas thought of all the weird fetishes he had heard of and what it might be like to have to defend someone in the middle of the worst of it. He also thought about what his Mom had said about his Dad. "*He didn't say so, but I suspect he also remembered a few of his past lives that he really wasn't happy with remembering. A hazard I guess.*" Thomas couldn't be certain of how this whole past life thing worked yet, but if he had memories of being a murderer or rapist or some other bizarre and twisted individual, what would that do to the full current him?

He hoped he had no such skeletons in his past life closet, but it bared thinking about. Whatever he uncovered would be stuck there as surely as the memories of Shari, or anything else that had occurred in his life (all of which still seemed strangely more accessible than it had before… another weird quirk of dying?). As for the risk to his wellbeing, that seemed less an issue. Thomas had heard it said that dying is a risk of living. Oddly it appeared that carried over into the afterlife as well. But as interesting as his death had been so far, he could see it quickly giving way to an eternity of boredom. Boredom would be far worse than the River.

Besides, unlike life, Thomas at least now knew where he would go if something happened to him here. Strange that after a lifetime of agnosticism, his death now allowed him an almost perfect faith. When his time here finished, he would return to the River, and from there he would be reborn. Or perhaps, reincarnated was a better term. Regardless, he found it far less scary than the unknown of life.

"I'll do it. Truthfully, of all the risks of being here, being bored probably scares me the most."

Jack smiled and downed his glass again. "We thought you'd say yes but I'm still glad to hear it. You've got a lot of promise. I think you'll be good at this gig. Who knows? Maybe one day you can even be as good as me."

*****

Thomas made it first light when they started out. It seemed like an appropriate time to be leaving. Jack lead the way, and Buster trotted along next to Thomas, tongue hanging out in anticipation of a new journey. Obviously Buster had travelled rather extensively since dying. That might make him as good of a resource to have around as Jack, especially given that Thomas trusted Buster far more than he could possibly trust Jack. Even Buster's new found ability to chat didn't distract from how real and natural he felt. Thomas's formative years were spent almost entirely with this dog at his side. What better companion could he ask for as he learned the ropes of his new life here?

Jack walked over to the edge of the cliff, and stopped, staring intently at a space a few feet above the ground. Thomas realized after a moment that they were in almost the exact same spot they had been when he first met Jack.

"Where are we going?"

"Well, there's a lot of lessons for ye to learn. But I'm thinking the first is how to leave your sanctuary. There are a few different ways, but this is the first most people figure out on their own, so we'll start with it."

"Okay. Makes sense. That still doesn't really answer my question though. Where are we going?"

Jack smiled, obviously spotting whatever he had been looking for. "We're gonna go to the Prime, lad." And with that he stepped forward and vanished.

Thomas looked over at Buster and shrugged. "I guess we follow him then."

Buster seemed to smile back, then leapt into the spot where Jack had last been seen, and in a blink he too disappeared. Thomas took one last look at his sanctuary, then took what would have been a deep breath and walked forward.

*****

Cold chilled his bones. Instinctively Thomas tried to change the temperature to something more comfortable, but with a shock he realized nothing happened. "*It's amazing how quickly you can get spoiled to having your every whim catered to...*" He shuddered and looked up to see Jack smiling, obviously aware of his discomfort.

"Don't worry, you get used to it pretty quickly."

"*Well, at least I made it to the right place.*" Thomas had halfway wondered what would have happened if he had stepped through into a different place than Jack and Buster. Would he have been able to find them? Or his way back? The questions seemed silly now, but it drove home just how ignorant he truly was and how quickly he might really find himself in trouble without guides. The sanctuary had been very comforting, and the thought that he might find himself unable to return to it filled him with a momentary sense of panic. It was like traveling a foreign country where all of the signs were in an unrecognizable language, and only his guide spoke English. Luckily, he reminded himself, his guide was already dead, so losing him would prove trickier than it could be.

Jack and Buster waited patiently while Thomas regained his composure. At least they looked normal. And sounded normal, he realized. While Jack's words had been crystal clear, everything else sounded like he had earplugs in. Thomas shook his head and focused on adjusting himself to these strange new surroundings. After he steadied, Jack glanced around.

"Do you recognize this place?"

Thomas looked around. Aside from the obnoxious chill in the air, the first thing that popped out was how incredibly drab everything looked. They were at the base of a hill, and there were some trees around them, but the only color was a dull drab grey. If he focused, he could make out hints of shades of different colors in the leaves, grass, and bark, like someone had taken a photo and pulled the saturation level down to just above zero. A muted noise caught his attention, and Thomas realized there was a road at the top of the hill. A road with a sharp corner....

The light rain drizzled gently. It hadn't rained in forever, so it was good to see it. Of course, it would have been better if it had waited a few hours. Shari had texted telling him to be sure he wasn't late. He would have been fine, but that last phone call ran longer than normal, and now he was behind. Luckily traffic dispersed, allowing him to make up some lost time and avoid disappointing.... The car suddenly began sliding sideways as he came around the corner. Thomas realized with a surge of adrenalin that the tires no longer seemed in contact with the road. The long drought must have allowed oil to build up on the road and now the rain had turned it slick. He should have known better than to take that turn that fast.... The world slowed to a crawl as he tried to correct the tires, but to no avail. The edge of the road was coming up fast and just beyond it a steep hill into the trees. If it went over.....

"This is where I crashed."

"Aye. More importantly for our purposes, this is where you died. Right there where you're standing, in fact. Thrown from your car as it rolled down the hill there. They're still investigating why your seatbelt released, but at this point I suppose that does little good for you. You slammed into the ground and were killed on impact. "

Thomas looked around and spotted a dark spot in the ground with some scattered glass. If he looked closely, would he find his own life's blood? "Wow. That's so…. Wow."

"Sorry again, lad. I know it's all still a bit tough for you. Take your time. The important thing to note here is that there is always a soft spot between the prime and someone's sanctuary in the place where they died. If ya know that, you can track down most anyone."

"So it's where they died, not where their body remains?"

Jack nodded. "Oh, aye. Graveyards hardly have any portals at all, in fact. Do ya know how few people actually die in graveyards? Hospitals on the other hand…."

Jack shook his head and gestured broadly. "Woo! Mate, if someone dies in the operating room you might spend a month digging through portals trying to find the right one. Even then you may find yourself repeating portals rather than finding new ones. It can be a nightmare. "

Thomas walked over and spotted a scarf tied to a tree, a few nails helping to hold this into place. Jack noticed it too as he saw Thomas walk towards it. "That's an odd thing to be seeing on a tree."

Even with the faded colors, Thomas recognized the design on it quickly. "It was mine. Shari made it for me. Guess this was one of her little memorials to me."

Jack shrugged, looking a little uncomfortable all the sudden. "Always been partial to the cross memorials myself. Guess that's me own upbringing though."

"Yeah. That would definitely not be her style." Thomas reached up to stroke the scarf, to feel the texture of something that Shari had felt since he passed, but instead encountered the shocking realization that he couldn't. His hand passed through it as if it were a projection. Or more likely, he quickly realized, as if he were a projection.

"You're a ghost now, lad. You're on a slightly different wavelength than everything else here. That's why things look and sound so strange. If you come here and practice ye might eventually work your way up to affecting small things in the world around you, but it's insanely difficult. We're talking hours of effort just to push a button on a remote control. Don't even think about actually picking the remote up. "

"Wow. I don't know why but I hadn't really thought about that. We're ghosts. So we can like, walk through walls and stuff now?"

"Aye. Very little in this plane can touch you. Well, very little native to the plane anyway. You can walk through walls, fires, bullets, people, you name it. Feels kind of weird, especially when you walk through a person, but you get used to it. Lot of people come back and start watching other people. It does break up the monotony of existence, but it can be insanely frustrating as well. You'll find without hormones, any teenage voyeur dreams you might have are a lot less fulfilling, and while you can do things like spy on top secret meetings or listen to private conversations, you can't tell anyone it would matter to about it, and often times watching someone make a mistake when you know what's going to happen is an exercise in extreme bloody frustration. I'm told there are those who spend enough time here that they can get small messages across to people. Feelings and such like that. That might just be wishful thinking though, lad, I can't say. I mean, when a soul appoints themselves as a guardian of someone, they care about that person's wellbeing. So of course they'll try their best to steer that person away from harm. If that person does avoid the harm, then it probably feels good to take credit for it whether you really affected the outcome or not."

Thomas thought about what his Mom said about Shari having several guardians watching over her. He hoped they could actually keep her safe. Maybe one day he'd get to meet one and see for himself how much affect they could have on 'the prime'. Clearly, for whatever skills Jack possessed on the other side, this area was not his forte. Thomas shivered again. "Why is it so cold here?"

"Ah, yes. You can fix that, lad. The trick, however, is a wee bit different than you've probably gotten used to. In a sanctuary, you tell your surroundings not to be cold and the world adjusts to your needs. Here, you have to tell yourself not to be cold, and you'll adjust to the world."

The idea seemed kind of strange, but as he thought about it, it really wasn't any weirder than anything else that had happened since he died. Just a more extreme 'mind over matter' effect. Thomas concentrated again, but this time rather than trying to warm up his surroundings he focused on just not being cold. To his surprise, it worked pretty easily. "Wow. Thanks."

"You pick up quickly, lad. That's good. It'll make the rest of this a wee bit simpler. Remember the basics of that lesson. You cannot affect the prime. Well, not without a huge amount of effort anyway. Yourself, however, well you have more power there. You're standing on the ground because you feel you need to be, but in truth…" Jack closed his eyes, and suddenly began drifting upwards. He opened them again once he floated about a foot off the ground. "Gravity has no effect on you. Nor do physics. Your limitations remain your own will and imagination. And while you cannot change what your surroundings are…" Jack suddenly disappeared, then tapped him on the back. Thomas whirled around to find Jack standing behind him. "You can very easily change where you are in your surroundings. "

Thomas had to admit, some aspects of being dead were really cool. He almost felt like a superhero. He could fly and teleport as easily as he could walk. Yet, looking over at the scarf on the tree he realized that he couldn't do something as simple as stroke a piece of fabric. He could walk through walls, visit any location in the blink of an eye, climb mountains or walk through an active volcano without fear, but he couldn't pick up a piece of paper, pet a cat, or stroke his fiancée's cheek. He could sit in on a meeting with world leaders but he would never be able to hold his own child. It was a strange trade off.

"Thomas, you with me, lad?"

"Oh, sorry. Yes." Thomas chastised himself for drifting off.

"Good. Let's try it. First, let's see you get yourself off the ground."

Thomas thought about being lighter than air, about lifting off the ground and floating up. For a moment, nothing happened, then suddenly he saw the world start shrinking away. He realized as he began floating that he hadn't really felt the ground beneath his feet like he would have normally. He suppose the only reason he hadn't sunk was that he didn't think he was supposed to. Otherwise….

"You had it, now you're going the wrong way."

Thomas looked down, surprised to find himself buried up to his knees in the ground. "Sorry." He quickly pulled back up to a foot above the ground. "I guess letting your mind wander can be kind of dangerous when the world responds to your thoughts."

Jack smiled. "You'll get used to it. Focus is a bit more important here. It's difficult to suddenly put yourself in danger, but yes, you will find that a wandering mind often results in a wandering body as well. Very good, by the way. Many people take awhile before they can let go of their notion of how things 'should' work and embrace the way it does. I have to admit, it took me a few hours the first time I got even a couple of inches above the ground." Jack pointed up. "Come on. Let's have a bird's eye look around."

Jack floated up, slowly passing the tree limbs. Thomas looked down at Buster. The dog's feet remained firmly planted to the ground. "Come on, buddy. Let's have a look around."

Buster shook his head. "No. Don't like flying. For birds."

Thomas smiled and shrugged. "Suit yourself. We'll be back for you in a bit." Thomas stuck his arm out, striking his best 'Superman' pose, and zoomed upwards, passing Jack in a blink. The feeling fascinated him, though the exhilaration was less than he had hoped it would be. The view of the world shrinking below was incredible, but he realized with a slight bit of disappointment that he could not feel the change of temperature, nor, breaking through the low lying cloud cover, did the sudden sunlight beaming on his face bring any warmth. The lack of physical stimulation brought an odd detachment from the visceral feel of being high above the clouds, however the ability to drop and rise in the blink of an eye was no less incredible. For fun he did a few loops, then plummeted to the earth like a bullet, stopping himself with another blink next to where Jack had settled in just above the tree line, somewhat parallel with the road a few yards over. "Okay, this is kind of fun."

"Wait till you try it back in a sanctuary, where you actually have wind in your hair and control the view."

"I dunno." Thomas replied, looking around. "Despite the kind of muted look everything has here, there's something to be said for not knowing what you're going to see. Though I guess I sort of know what I would see here. I bet if I went up just a bit I could actually see my house from here."

"Which you probably shouldn't be visiting just yet, so let's get onto your next lesson before you get tempted. Have you ever travelled outside of the U.S.?"

Thomas nodded. "Yeah. My Uncle used to fly my mom and me out to see him wherever he was working at the time. So I've spent a bit of time in some places in Asia, and Shari's Mom once paid for the two of us to go to Australia . Shari and I had talked about going to Europe in a couple of years, but… well… guess that's not happening now."

"No, unfortunately, though you'll be able to visit there if you want." Jack put his hand on Thomas's shoulder. "For now, I want you to picture a place that you have been to over there and found interesting."

Thomas thought about his first trip over seas when he was 10. His uncle had been stationed in Central Java in Indonesia, and he took them to a local temple that had been restored called Borobudur. He told Thomas it was the largest Buddhist pyramid in the world. As Thomas thought about it, he realized that once again he could remember the trip with extreme clarity. Impossible clarity. He had a video of the entire event in his head, and could rewind or play it at will. As he considered it, he realized that his entire life opened in the same way, laid out for study in minutia if he wanted. All of the ups and downs, good and bad, all in the same detail it existed in when he first lived it.

"Got a place in mind?" Jack interrupted.

"Yeah. Why is it I can remember it so clearly?"

Jack smiled. "Your memories of your life are basically imprinted on your soul. It's like that for everyone. While you rely on your brain to remember things when you are alive, you have no actual physical limitations here."

"That's… weird." Thomas replayed seeing Shari for the first time. He remembered seeing her with fresh eyes. She walked past him as just one his many classmates in Freshman English. Oddly he just glanced over her that day. It would be another day, nearly two years later, before they actually spoke to each other. Now that he thought about it, he had never even realized that they had that class in common till now. "Cool… but weird."

"A friend of mine theorizes that our entire reason for existence is collecting memories, but that's a lesson for another day. Do you have the place in pictured?"

"Yes." Thomas replayed the first time he stepped out of the car and saw the monument looming in front of him. The site was staggering in its beauty, magnificence and solitude. The huge stone structure rose up against the jungle in the background, beneath the looming mountains and volcanoes of the horizon.

"Good. Now picture yourself standing there now."

Thomas did as instructed. He matched up his view with what he had seen back then. Suddenly he felt a surge of some kind of odd energy, and he opened his eyes to a moonlit parking lot. Ahead a dark structure loomed beneath the clear night sky.

"Wow. That's kinda cool. It felt different than it does on the other side."

"Aye. And it may take you a bit to remember time changes in the real world, but it's very useful to be able to pop from place to place. It's easier if you travelled there before. Some people can just go anywhere they've heard about, but most people I've encountered have to have visited a place before they can just shift there. "

"Well, we're here after hours, it would seem. Mind if we have a look around?"

Jack looked like he was about to say yes before stopping suddenly and staring at the pyramid in the distance. As Thomas followed his glance, he saw a number of figures in the distance. Their more vibrant color, an orangish red from the looks of it, made them stand out dramatically from the surroundings.

For the first time since Thomas had met him, Jack looked wary. "How long since this place was actually used as a monastery?"

"I dunno. Like 1500 years I think. "

"We should go then. Quickly before they notice us."

"Too late for that." Buster's voice caught both men off guard. Thomas hadn't expected him to be able to follow them, and from the look on Jack's face, he seemed equally surprised. There he sat though, just at Thomas's side, looking off to his right at the largest most brilliantly colored butterfly Thomas had ever seen. "They know we're here, and this one would like us to follow."

Jack looked somewhat visibly nervous. "Let's hope they have kept their Buddhist tendencies into death."

Four

The three followed the butterfly, which fluttered along just in front
of them, leading them slowly towards the pyramid. Thomas had
the strange sensation of following Tinkerbell from the Peter Pan
books he loved as a kid. As they got closer, the bright colored
shapes around the temple took better form, and it soon became
clear there were some twenty monks in orange and red robes
scattered around the various levels of the pyramid. In truth, most
appeared to completely ignore their arrival. Even in the dark, the
pyramid's stone carvings, each, Thomas remembered, having some
hidden Buddhist lesson, came into view. Each of the monks were
intently studying their own lessons, likely the same thing they had
done during their lives here, whenever that might have been.
"Could these people really be close to 2000 years old?" Thomas
thought such a thing odd, but he couldn't dismiss the possibility.
As they approached closer, Thomas noticed that one monk did not
study the pyramid's reliefs. He stood instead in front of the bottom
level, intently watching the trio's approach. As they came closer he
reached out his hand. The Butterfly fluttered up and landed gently
in his palm, fluttered its wings for a moment, then seemed to melt
into the monk's palm and disappear. The man then bowed.

"Welcome travelers. I am Ardru. Prior to that I was Shan Wei, and
before that Jawaka Sidhu. We do not see western ghosts travel
these lands often. What brings you here, young ones?"

Jack bowed, visibly nervous. His reaction caught Thomas off
guard.. Ardru's introduction had been very cordial, and his
brothers had not so much as made notice of our existence. Jack,
however, looked like he had wandered into a mafia owned
restaurant and confronted the local Don. At least his voice seemed
more certain than his body language implied.

"Good to meet you, Master Ardru. I'm Jack Macintyre, and this lad
is my protégé, Thomas Salazar. I am instructing Thomas on how to
travel here on the prime, and, well, this is where he chose to come.
We did not mean to disturb you and your brethren."

"It is no disturbance at all, young Jack. And you…. Thomas? Why did you opt for this destination?"

Thomas fumbled, not certain by Jack's reaction if he should be open in his answer or not. "I uh… I was here as a kid. It just seemed like an interesting place"

Ardru looked Thomas over carefully. Uncomfortably carefully. It seemed Ardru was actually looking through him for a moment. "Yes, you were. But your name was not Thomas then."

"I'm pretty sure it was."

Ardru reached across and put his hand on the side of Thomas's forehead. Buster began a very low and menacing growl, but Ardru merely smiled at him. "Do not worry." To Thomas's surprise, Buster silenced. Ardrue closed his eyes, and then suddenly the world flashed.

*****

It felt as if he had studied this carving his entire life. The relief was very intricately carved, and the plaster that is hard as diamond made it shine in the morning sun. In the center, a Buddha sat in peaceful contemplation. To his right four figures stared at him with rapt attention, a fifth completely disinterested. To his left the opposite played out, with four figures showing no interest and a fifth staring dutifully. Deep meaning hid itself here. A lesson wanted to be learned. But as of yet, it had not revealed itself. He remained on the bottom level, and barely started at that. Looking up at the giant Buddha statues near the top of the pyramid, he realized Nirvana would be for more difficult to acquire than expected. He closed his eyes and took in the deep, perfumed scent of the jungle. At least he had that. He still missed the palace, but the crowds of people took its toll. Here the gift of peace offered itself in wondrous splendor.

"Deep in contemplation, Young Irwan. That is good." The brothers always moved so quietly. And it seemed they took great joy in scaring their newer members. But Irwan tried to remain as calm as he had been shown to do and keep his reverence towards his teachers.

"Thank you, Brother. I am trying."

"And what have we learned from this relief?"

He knew Irwan would not know, but pupils were expected to try anyway. Brother Deepak was fond of saying that failure often taught more than success. Irwan thought for a moment, then offered his best guess: "That suffering is inevitable, and only by accepting that can we learn to appreciate life."

Brother Deepak smiled. "A noble lesson indeed. But not the one this relief would teach you. Continue."

*****

Thomas looked up. The brilliant white plaster that had covered the pyramid when he was there last was gone, leaving a dull brown that nearly made the entire pyramid disappear against the night sky. Even in the dark however, he could still see the spot where he had stood staring at the relief.

"No." He thought in a moment of confused clarity. *"Not me. Irwan. Eighth child of the Sultan and student of the Brothers of Borobudur. But... that...."* He shook his head, realizing what must have happened. "So um... that's what a past life feels like, huh?"

Ardru nodded. Jack and Buster both looked at him with a hint of confusion and more than a little bit of worry, but Thomas waved them off. "I'm fine. I just... wow... Ardru helped me relive a day in a long ago life. It was... odd. Peaceful, interesting, but... odd. "

Jack seemed to relax slightly. "Yeah, well, that can be a wee bit odd. I remember remembering me own first past life experience. A street urchin I was, in London back in 1842. It was interesting too, but I wouldna call it peaceful."

Ardru stepped back, smiling. "There is much in your pasts that could be useful in your future." His eyes focused on Thomas. "Your friends are afraid, and they have reason to be. Learn from your past, but do not repeat it."

Thomas realized, slightly surprised, that during that last comment, the monk's lips never actually moved. *"Well. That's not dire or cryptic sounding at all."*

"Umm… okay. What do you mean?"

Ardru bowed, and began speaking aloud once more, "Your path is yours to walk. I have illuminated what I can of it at this point."

Jack put his hand on Thomas's shoulder. "Okay then. Mr. Ardru it has been very… informative. But we have an engagement to keep."

Ardru smiled. "Yes of course. Even the dead do not have forever. Good luck." And with that Ardru turned and vanished. Thomas looked up and realized that the other monks around the temple were gone as well. The three were alone with the ancient stone monument.

"Well," said Jack, visibly relieved. "Bit more creepy than I intended for your first day of training. Let's get ourselves out of here." With the last syllable the world dissolved.

Five

The sun hung low on the horizon. The rolling hills, while still dull in color, were quite beautiful.

Thomas looked around, but didn't recognize anything of the area. "Where are we?"

"Italy. Luckily, our Mr. Ardru let us go."

Buster raised his hackles and let out a low growl. "I did not like him."

While the monk had definitely seemed odd, Thomas didn't get the same sense from Ardru that his companions obviously had. "I don't see what the big deal is."

Jack looked at him with a raised eye, then adopted what Thomas quickly realized was a lecture tone. "Listen lad, there's a hand full of things that can make you truly dangerous. Will Power, Raw Ability, and Knowledge come to mind. In truth, Knowledge probably trumps much of the other two. Most people don't make it more than a few hundred years dead before they return to the River. This guy's been around close to two thousand at least and remembers two lives before that. That's A LOT of time to learn things, and a lot of will power to stick around. That alone makes him dangerous."

"A few hundred years? Really? I would have expected there to be a lot of older people around."

"Most people stick to their own sanctuaries, and there's only so much you can do there. Those that venture out often find themselves back in the River against their will. Others still get bored as everyone they know re-assimilates, or they just get excited about what a new life might bring. It's very rare for someone to stick around half a millennium. Hells, most people don't have past lives back more than five hundred years, unless it's a quick glimpse of someone with a potent personality."

"Really?"

"Aye. They get diluted. Grow smaller and smaller and so they get tougher to access. I'm sure everyone of us has a few Neanderthals in our make up, but good luck accessing the five seconds or so of memory locked in there. Usually if you remember any length at all, it's likely no older than the 1500s. What about yours you just had?"

"I used a different calendar there, but…" Thomas thought about it, suddenly grateful for his class in world history studies that included how different world calendars synced up. "I think it would be around 452 ad or so. "

Jack stared at him for a moment, somewhat incredulous. "Hmm. Guess you have some older souls in you. Maybe Mr. Monk has some trick for helping bring them out?"

"I dunno." Thomas shrugged. "But I remember it pretty well now. It's really kind of… disconcerting. I can barely tell the difference between my memories of Thomas and those of Irwan."

"That's pretty normal. Wait until you get your first non-human memories. Those will really mess you up for a bit. But it usually doesn't take long to get used to having them, and they're very useful to draw off of. "

"Okay, so… Question. Aside from having two thousand years to get used to being dead, what could be dangerous about Ardru, or anyone else in this plane for that matter?"

"He could dissipate you." Said Buster, matter-of-factly.

Jack nodded in agreement. "Understand lad, you can still be hurt. But when you are you don't lose blood so much as energy. It takes a wee bit more to do it, but it can certainly be done. I have no doubt he could do it in style, but that's really not even the easiest way. Here. Teleport somewhere. Anywhere you would like."

Thomas thought about it for a moment, then settled on the place in the country that he and his family had lived at when he was still a kid. He had always enjoyed running around the woods there, and hadn't seen it in years. It would be interesting to see if it remained there. Thomas closed his eyes, and brought it up in his mind clearly. He tried as before to picture himself standing in front of the house. His mind went calm and as before he felt a surge of something strange, but unlike before it seemed to have stopped almost as quickly as it started. He opened his eyes to find he still stood atop the rolling hills of Italy. "Okay. I'll bite. Why didn't it work?"

"It's hard to affect the world around you here. Not impossible, but really hard. Affecting other souls, however, is a lot easier. If you're good, you can lock them down pretty quickly to keep them from escaping you. Unless they know what is happening, it's pretty much impossible to escape. If both sides know what they're doing, it's a matter of who's stronger and better practiced."

"And he's probably very well practiced."

"Aye. I tried to get us out of there right away. I couldn't. Normally when you sense yourself being locked down it's like having a rope around you. Sense the knot and untie it and you can go where you want. With this guy it was like a web. I didn't even sense anything that could be undone till he wanted us to leave. "

Thomas nodded, suddenly realizing just how much danger they might have been in. "Okay, that is just a little scary."

"Oh, aye. And here's the other thing he could do."

Before Thomas realized what was happening, Jack reached across and gave him a shove. He fell backwards… and kept falling. A blur of colors surrounded him and suddenly Thomas found himself plummeting along side a brilliantly colored cliff. He looked below to see water of the exotic color he immediately recognized as The River. *"Oh crap."*

In a frantic bid to keep from literally becoming one with the infinite, Thomas flipped his body around and reached into the wall. His fingers dug in like he was reaching into soft mud. To his somewhat surprise he came to a jarring stop. His second surprise was that it actually hurt, though not in the muscle ripping fashion he had expected it to. He looked up to see Jack standing at the top of the cliff, laughing uncontrollably.

Jack managed to get out "Okay, lad. Come back up." Before disappearing from view over the edge.

Thomas closed his eyes and pictured himself standing at Jack's side. He knew instantly that he now was. He opened his eyes again to find Jack nearly doubled over in laughter. Thomas shook his head. "You're an ass, you know that?"

"Oh, aye lad." If he had had breath, Jack wouldn't be able to catch it. "But you should have seen the look on your face. Oi that was fun."

Thomas glared at him then back over the edge at the River below. "How did you know I would save myself?"

"Actually, I didn't think you would, mate. I mean, you could have tried to just will yourself to stop falling, or turned yourself into a bird if ye suddenly remembered having been one, but I really figured you'd get wet. Wasn't too concerned though, since that's not the real River." He waved his hand and the River turned to blue, suddenly looking like regular water. "This is a training sanctuary we use to show new trainees like yourself the ropes. The real river is off in the distance that way. If we were this close to the real one we wouldn't be able to hear each other this well."

Thomas felt that he should have noticed that, but in his panic he went into instinct mode. Now that he thought about it he suppose that panic could be just as dangerous here as when he still drew breath. It was an obnoxious lesson, but one Thomas wouldn't be forgetting any time soon.

"So, you can force me back into a sanctuary?"

Jack wiped his eyes out of instinct, and managed to bring himself back to just a smile and a slight giggle. "Yeah. Sorry, lad. But that's a fun way to teach. And effective. The point is, unless you know how to protect yourself, someone can get you into the River pretty easily. That happens and you're gone."

"Okay. So how do I stop it?"

Buster came padding up next to me. "Ground yourself and don't fight things stronger than you."

Jack shrugged. "Well, that's a bit over simplified, but aye, what he said. You know how you can set your body so that you're prepared for someone running towards you? You're essentially doing the same thing, except instead of just bracing yourself against stepping backwards, you're bracing yourself against shifting planes as well. And instead of using your muscles, which you no longer really have now do ya, you're using your will."

"Oookay." Thomas felt lost at that explanation, but he didn't really want to admit it. "I guess that makes sense. Sort of."

"Let's give it a try. Plant your feet."

Thomas did so.

"Now. I want you to picture yourself as an immovable object. Something that cannot be shifted."

Thomas thought for a moment, then pictured himself as a towering oak tree. He remembered as a kid how impregnable those seemed to be. He and his friends could play on them, climb them, bounce off them, swing from them or hit them with sticks or whatever else, and the tree never seemed to notice. He would be the tree. Nothing would faze him. He put his roots down, deep into the ground. He would not be moved. Thomas opened his eyes to see Jack staring at him incredulously once more.

"Okay. Yeah. That is impressive. Impractical, but impressive. For the record, when I said 'plant your feet' I didna mean literally. I've never seen anyone do that "

Thomas looked down to find, partially to his own amazement, that from the waste down he had become a tree. He was quite literally rooted to the ground. All he could do was shrug. "You said immovable."

"Aye, I did at that, didn't I. Let's forget for a moment that you probably shouldn't be capable of shape changing half your body into a tree, and concentrate on the fact that this technique is something you'll need to be able to do on a regular bases. You need to learn to always keep your guard up, because surprises can come out of nowhere. That…."he gestured to Thomas's lower half, "doesn't seem like something you'll want to keep up."

Thomas switched gears, trying to picture himself in his normal form, but still keeping the tree's natural foundation. This time he felt his body shifting back into place. It was actually a really cool feeling when he noticed it. He looked down and saw that his legs once again looked normal, however he could still feel himself penetrating deep within the ground. He tested taking a small step forward. His feet lifted without issue, then locked into place with every down step like magnetic boots on a steel floor. "Okay. Try and push me."

Jack looked at him for a moment, then with as little notice as possible nailed him square in the chest with both hands. It felt to Thomas like two sledgehammers had hit him, but he was the immovable oak, and Jack rebounded off.

Jack looked genuinely surprised. "Good job. I'll say it again, you learn fast."

"Thanks. It's really not as…"

That was the extent of what Thomas got out of his mouth before he realized he was on his back looking up at the sky. Buster was sitting on his chest, tongue rolling out.

"Still need practice." The dog said with a head tilt.

"Ouch." Thomas attempted, to no avail, to push the dog off of his chest. "Down boy."

Buster leapt off and sat himself down at Thomas's side. "You did not stay up. But you stayed where you were. Better to be able to do both, but if you have to choose one you chose correctly."

Thomas sat up. To his surprise, he actually felt tired for the first time since dying. He was also oddly sore, but it was difficult to pinpoint where the pain was coming from. "I feel like I've done a two-hour work out. With a black belt hitting me."

Jack smiled. "Welcome to death's version of being out of shape."

"Ugh. I have to exercise here, too?" Thomas shook his head in disgust.

"Aye. Well, if you want to do much outside your sanctuary you do. Just like when you're alive, the things you do draw energy. The afterlife works a wee bit different than actual life though in that while you're in your sanctuary you can replenish that energy pretty rapidly. It's one of the reasons a soul is so much stronger when they're on their own turf. Outside your sanctuary you replenish at a much slower rate. So the more you do the more you draw from your stores. How much energy you store naturally has a bit to do with your willpower and a lot to do with how much you've pushed yourself. It's a lot like your cardio system in your real body. You push your limits, and your limits grow. You stay within them, and your limits will stay the same or shrink."

Thomas plopped down on the edge of the cliff and reached over to scratch Buster's ears. Buster responded by tilting his head to give a better angle.

"So Exercise. Do I need to eat right and get plenty of rest too?"

Jack smiled and created himself a lounge chair, then set it down next to Thomas. "Personally, I recommend eating all of the things you love that are bad for you in life. As for rest, well, that's multiple choice. You can just not do anything, and you'll slowly feel better. You can pop back to your sanctuary and you'll feel better almost immediately. Or you can meditate, and you'll be somewhere in between. "

"You've talked about meditating before. Something about helping you to remember your past lives?"

Jack nodded, producing a beer from somewhere. "It's how I've uncovered the few I know." He cracked his drink open and took a swig, then set back, apparently admiring the view from the cliff side. "Obviously doesn't always result in new memories, but it's a good way to get your energy back without making the trip back to your own place. Here, I'll show you. Close your eyes."

"Do I need to assume a lotus position first?" Thomas asked, only half joking.

"No. This isn't yoga. It's just relaxing. "

Thomas laid back on the ground with his lower legs still dangling off the edge of the cliff. He closed his eyes and tried to relax his body as he would have when he still had a real one.

"Okay, Thomas. I want you first to feel the energy around you. You should sense a pulsing feeling. Concentrate on that."

Thomas felt around but could not feel anything but the ground beneath his back. Jack seemed to pick up on this.

"Relax. There is no wind. There is no sun. There is no earth. There is only the energy. "

Thomas let go, and after a moment, he sensed it. Energy truly flowed all around him, meandering like fog while simultaneously pulsing like a heartbeat. "I've got it."

"Good. Now open yourself up to it. Let it flow into your body."

Thomas tried to picture himself as a water pitcher, and he let the energy begin flowing into his body. The sheer capacity he felt in comparison to the flow surprised him. It was a barely turned on water spout being used to fill a rain barrel. "This might take awhile".

"Yes. Outside your sanctuary, it's not a quick process, but much faster than just letting it happen naturally. Now, while we're waiting, I want you to try something. Think back to your earliest memory."

"I'm three. I'm trying to climb onto Buster's back so he can give me a ride."

"Interesting. Now. Think. What can you remember from before that?"

As Thomas concentrated, more memories filed into place. "I'm just learning to walk. It's hard, but everyone's encouraging me, and they seem to make it easy, so I keep trying."

"Before that?"

Thomas thought again. Slowly, more memories opened. "I'm cold. The world is so strange. The big ones have left me alone. I don't like it. It's not safe away from them. I cry out. I've done that before and it summoned them. Maybe it will work again."

"Good. And before that?"

Six

"The meat was getting tired. It lost site of me. It thinks I'm gone, but that's wishful thinking. It's bleeding. It will never lose me now. I stalk quietly through the underbrush, circling around. It is reduced to limping. It may still have a sprint left in it though, and there's no use in risking more energy, or one of its kicks, if I don't have to. Patience. Patience is always the key. It's limping towards me now. It looks over its shoulder, trying to see if I'm coming up behind. I see it sniff the air, but I'm down wind. It will not smell me. But I smell it. It smells delicious. I have not eaten in two days, but this will be a meal worth savoring. It's almost here. I stretch my claws and my mouth opens wide in anticipation. I can almost taste it. Just a few more steps and..."

*****

"So. Tommy. I'm... I'm sorry I haven't visited you."

Thomas blinked his eyes in confusion. The dull muted grey surroundings to him almost immediately he was back in the Prime, though the lack of color could have been as much from the light drizzle that appeared to permeate the world around him as much as anything else. It should have been cold and wet. It wasn't. Further inspection told him that he was in a graveyard.

"I meant to... it's just... just..."

Shari was kneeling in front of him, staring at a tombstone on a still somewhat fresh grave. Horror and anguish ripped through him, soaking through his entire being just as the rain that fell through him should have. He didn't have to look to know it was his grave. Nor did he have to look to see that her tears were starting to flow. The overwhelming sadness ripped his heart from his chest.

"Dammit Tommy! Why? I can't do this without you! I should have been planning a wedding not your... your..."

She broke down, rocking herself into a near fetal position. The pouring rain drenched her long chestnut hair as it covered her face. Her arms wrapped tightly around her knees and for a moment her sobs were the only audible sound aside from the increasingly hard falling rain. It was too much. Thomas reached forward to put his arms around her, to hold her and comfort her, but there was nothing there. He was watching a hologram. He could see and hear everything but he could do absolutely nothing. Helplessness blistered his soul. He was worthless. "Shari. I'm sorry. I'm so so sorry."

"Tommy. God I miss you. You know, sometimes it still feels like you're right here with me? Stupid isn't it? I mean, I actually forget and turn to tell you something and then… then it hits me all over again. You'd think if I could remember anything it would be that you were dead but no." She slumped further into the mud, curling up against the unforgiving tombstone. "I guess…. I guess I just keep hoping it's all a bad dream. I'll wake up any time now and you'll be lying next to me. And I'll tell you about this horrible dream and you'll laugh at me for being silly and tell me you'll always be there like you always did."

Thomas wanted nothing more in that moment than to be able to touch her. To wipe the tears from her cheeks and see her smile. The futility ripped him apart. He fell to his knees next to her, trying desperately to touch her, hold her, give her any kind of comfort. Instead he was greeted by unforgiving emptiness. It was too much to bear.

"God dammit, Tommy! You said you would be there!" Her screams were hoarse and painful, punctuated by sobs that visibly wracked her entire body. "You promised! Why did you leave me? Why?"

Buster trotted up to Thomas's side. "This not a good place to be."

Thomas reached down and wrapped his arms around his dog. The relief of something solid overwhelmed him almost as much as the scene in front of him. It did very little to lesson the pain of not being able to comfort Shari, though. If anything, it made it worse. "I..." His voice was barely audible in the pouring rain, "I don't really know how I even got here."

"She called you and you answered. Now, keep hold of me."

Thomas held Buster close and looked up once more to see Shari rocking herself quietly. Then she was gone.

Seven

Jack knelt down and patted him gently on the shoulder. "Welcome back, laddie."

Thomas wiped the tears from his face. With some relief he realized he felt a lot better here. He also confirmed he was back in the training sanctuary. "Thanks, Jack."

"Wasn't sure what happened. One moment you were morphing into a large cat, then you were gone. Luckily your wonder pet here seems to be able to track you across planes."

"Yeah. Thanks Buster." Thomas stood back up, feeling emotionally drained but far more refreshed. He really needed a distraction. Something that would make him feel less helpless. "I think I've had enough meditation for awhile. What's say we practice some more?"

*****

Thomas's first non-human memories turned out to be that of some kind of saber toothed cat. Jack just shook his head when Thomas tried out his transformation.

"I tell you no one remembers lives older than five hundred years and you just insist on proving me wrong don't you?"

Thomas tried shrugging his massive shoulders. "Maybe it's a side affect of whatever Ardru did." It was weird to talk with six inch blades sticking out of his mouth, but somehow he managed to do so instinctive, as if he'd always had this body. He now stood close to Buster's height, but his back legs were a bit shorter and his chest a lot wider. He felt amazingly agile, jumping from left to right without much of a thought.

"Probably. Still it's a bit weird, but I suppose it's useful. You'll be like the bloody Spanish inquisition now, nobody will suspect you."

There was that. They spent a great deal of time (it could have been hours or days, Thomas couldn't say) with him getting used to his new body. The senses were sharper than he would have ever dreamed experiencing. He could see well with little to no light. He could hear things far beyond what he would have been able to as human.

But by far the most incredible aspect was the sense of smell. He could now easily distinguish things by their scent. The problem was that without human memories to balance them out, his recognition of things skewed dramatically. Jack, flying high above, was easily identified as "Flying Meat". He could also pick out other scents surrounding him, including "two-legged meat". As he adjusted to his senses and the memories associated with them, he was surprised at just how many other things were identified by their relationship to food. One of the few exceptions was Buster, who registered as 'nuisance'. Thomas had to fight down a severe level of distrust that came with that scent. He realized that as a saber toothed cat, he frequently had to fight to protect his kills from wolf packs. While Buster's scent wasn't an exact match for his larger forefathers, it smelled close enough. Luckily his human memories were still dominant, and Thomas buried the feelings of distrust and disdain deep down and enjoyed the moment.

Buster and Thomas galloped at full throttled for hours. Jack obviously couldn't keep up with his natural flying skills, and was forced to teleported frequently to keep pace. Thomas couldn't believe the pure exhilaration he felt. "This is absolutely amazing".

Buster's tongue was rolled out in agreement. "Yes. Wind in your face is good. Scents still wrong but that is expected."

Thomas smiled, which no doubt looked less friendly to anyone who might have looked on than he intended. "I still don't know what a squirrel is supposed to smell like, but I can agree with you that the scents are off. I remember what grass and trees are supposed to smell like. This is close but still not on. It all smells... I don't know..."

"Like its creators."

Thomas thought about it as he took in more of the surrounding scents. "You're right. It does all have an underlying scent of two legged me... err.. of human."

"Most sanctuaries do. Unless they know scents enough to mask it."

Thomas took in more of the surrounding air. He could actually pick out something matching Jack's scent, but it seemed there were others as well. He slammed his paws into the ground, sliding to a stop. Buster shot past him a few more feet, then slid his hind legs around, spinning into an almost perfect seating position.

"Why stop?"

"I've got a question for Jack."

After a few minutes, a rather large pigeon swooped down onto the ground in front of them. Thomas briefly considered which flying meat it would taste the most like, before shaking such thoughts out of his head and morphing back to his 'real' body. By the time he did Jack stood in front of them in his own natural form.

"Bout bloody time you two decided to take a break."

"Whose sanctuary is this?"

Jack smiled. "Aye, good question that. It actually belongs to several of us."

Thomas sniffed again, but oddly couldn't smell the same range he had before. He felt blinded. He shook the thought from his head. He still felt more comfortable in this form, despite the benefits of the other one. Heavy fatigue had also settled itself back into his bones once more; little wonder given just how much running he had done. "So this isn't your original sanctuary, is it?"

"No. You can sort of 'split off' a small piece of your sanctuary into a completely different place. That's what happened here. Another soul I once worked with created this one. Now, the second thing you would probably want to be knowing is that with any sanctuary, you can let someone else bind themselves to it. That essentially makes it theirs too. "

That explained why he smelled so many different souls attached to this place. "So can they only do it with permission?"

Jack shook his head. "No lad. If you've got time and strength, you can basically bully yourself into someone's sanctuary. Doesn't happen often but it does happen."

"*That's where we come in.*" Thomas thought to himself, then asked "How do you get rid of them?"

"We'll get to that. For now, rest up. And do it in this form. While it might not feel like it, being shape changed drains your energy more quickly. At the very least it will keep you from regaining what you've lost."

"Fine. But if it's all the same to you I still don't feel like meditating. If we're going to rest, let's do this the old fashion way."

Jack shrugged. "If that's the way ye prefer it." He waved his hand. The sun set and a fire put crackled into being front of them, a spit of deer meat twirling slowly above it.

Eight

Thomas stood with Jack and Buster at the base of a mountain. The peak disappeared into the dense cloud cover that congregated around it, leaving the surrounding sky clear and blue. Jack smiled as he explained his handiwork, and with it Thomas's first test.

"Welcome to Mount Jack. At 6,200 meters it's a wee bit taller than Mount McKinley. Your job is simple. When the hourglass I give you runs out of sand, you'll start your climb. I want you to get to the top quickly by any means necessary."

"Sounds simple enough."

"Aye, well. I'll we watching you like Zeus from atop Olympus."

"So I can expect a few lightning bolts?"

"No spoiling the surprises. Now, are you ready?"

Thomas took a look around. He felt refreshed, and this was, after all, what he had left his sanctuary for. "Ready as I'm going to be I guess."

"Good." Jack handed me an hourglass quickly losing sands. "When that runs out, you can begin." With that, he and Buster disappeared.

Thomas watched the sands speed from the top to bottom of the glass. Once Jack vanished from site it didn't take long. Within a minute the last grains emptied out, signaling the start of his training. He looked up at the top weighing his options. Obviously the easiest way would be the same path they took.

Thomas closed his eyes and concentrated, picturing himself next to Jack. As he expected, the wave of energy surrounded him for a moment, then stopped and dissipated. When he opened his eyes he found himself right where he had been. "Of course it couldn't be that easy."

Thomas shrugged and leapt forward so that when he shape changed into his more sure-footed cat form he would be on all fours. To his surprise, he hit the ground in a face plant, still in human form. "Damn. Guess he can lock down shape shifting too."

Thomas pushed himself back to his feet, dusted himself off, and shrugged. *"Not going to make it just standing around here."* He thought, and began walking the path ahead of him.

*****

"So this is the wondrous Thomas Salazar you seem so excited about."

Brother Coughlin had addressed the bird on his shoulder, but the bird didn't reply. He knew it wouldn't, but it felt good sometimes to talk to someone else.

"The bindings on him are rather sloppy. He should be able to break them with ease based on what you've said. Interesting that he doesn't."

Brother Coughlin watched as the young boy slowly made his way up the mountain path. *"A young boy… but definitely an old soul."* Perhaps, the Brother thought, the oldest he had actually encountered. How strange that he would appear now.

"It must be a sign that we're on the right track. The creator has sent us this boon, that we may complete his work." Brother Coughlin looked at the bird on his shoulder, who looked somewhat blankly ahead. "I suspect you might disagree if I let you. Sad. Your vision is amazing. I'm really surprised you cannot see the truth in this. Perhaps one day you will."

Brother Coughlin watched awhile longer. The child took the most painfully tedious path, however. There was much to be done. He had been working at this near a century now, and the fruits of his labor now began to flower. Still, he could not rush things. Unification remained a delicate process. The creator had not wanted just anyone to be able to do it. Substantial power was required to open the gates of Heaven and Hell, and if it fell to the hands of someone too weak to wield it… well... Brother Coughlin would see that that did not happen.

"I suppose I should introduce myself." He turned to the bird perched at his shoulder and smiled. "You may return to your other business. It's best he not see you anyway."

With a quick wave, Coughlin dismissed the bird, teleporting it away. He then turned his attentions back to the boy.

*****

Thomas had been making decent progress at a steady pace for a few hours, but now the path grew steeper and rockier, while his footing turned treacherous. He had to remind himself a few times that a fall would not be fatal when his path took him along narrow ledges overlooking steep drop offs that even this low on the mountain's base looked like they would have been deadly back in life. The view was spectacular. Thomas had never really done much in the way of mountain climbing when he was alive, but he could see where it held appeal. *Then again I never stayed in the shape required to keep up the pace I'm managing now.*

He came up to another ledge, even narrower than the ones he'd encountered previously. Looking over the edge, the ground fell away for at least a thousand feet. "That just leaves around nineteen thousand to go…"

Thomas looked up, and sure enough, the mountain continued disappearing into the cloud cover above. "This is going to take forever."

"You're a hard soul to find when you're by yourself."

The startling sound of another voice almost caused Thomas to jump off of the ledge. He spun around to see a man in his mid fifties standing behind me. Thomas didn't recognize him. The man stood tall. Thomas judged him to be about six foot two or more. He had mostly grey hair mixed with what had probably been a dark brown natural color. He wore a suit of black with a high collar. He looked almost as if it were a late nineteenth or early twentieth century preacher, though without the white collar marking his station. Thomas felt like the man was appraising him, but there was little indication as to how well Thomas had faired in that appraisal.

"I'm sorry, I thought I was going to be alone in this test. Guess I should learn to expect the unexpected."

The man smiled. "Yes. Yes you should. However, I'm not with your…" he glanced up to the top of the mountain, pausing for a moment before finishing "…friends. I merely wanted to meet you and deliver a message. Forgive my poor manners. I am the late Brother Parkes Coughlin."

"Umm. Okay. Well, I'm Thomas Salazar, then."

"It is such a pleasure to finally meet you, Thomas. I've looked forward to making your acquaintance for some time, now."

Thomas couldn't help but feel once again that he knew entirely too little about this world. Everyone he met seemed to know something he didn't, and he grew less comfortable with that by the meeting. "Thanks. Umm. Why?"

Brother Coughlin smiled. Thomas got the sense that while it contained some genuine warmth, something else hid within it as well. "Your father has told me much about you."

That caught Thomas off guard. "You mean, before he returned to the River?"

The preacher shook his head with another smile. "Oh, no, dear boy. Your father has not yet returned to the Creator. In fact, I have sent him to watch over your loved ones back on Earth. It was a task that he was only too happy to accept."

"Whoa. What? My dad is still around?" Thomas forced himself back along the path; afraid his now spinning head might now take him over the narrow ledge. "I mean, I can talk to him?"

"Of course you can, dear boy. He's a bit nervous about meeting you. He really wasn't certain you would even want to; hence he's not contacted you himself. But I have always felt that it was important for a child to know his father."

Thomas pushed his back against the cliff's wall. If he had had a body he now felt it probably would have collapsed. "My dad's still here. Wow. I mean.. but.. why did Mom say…."

"Ah, yes, I suspect I know the answer to that. Understand, your father had every intent on returning to his Maker. He would have to, had I not had a chance encounter with him first." Brother Coughlin shook his head, looking down sadly. "He had many demons within him, young Thomas. Many indeed. I thank the Maker that he had us cross paths. You see, Thomas, we all have a gift. Mine, well, mine is banishing the demons within." He clasped a hand on Thomas's shoulder. "Your father is much happier now. He has been assisting me with my work ever since that day."

His father lived.

Thomas wasn't certain whether he should dare allow himself to believe this man, but he couldn't help but do so anyway. He had thought everyone he knew to be gone when he first found his mom, so it was easy to keep that acceptance tampered down. But deep down he knew he had been very disappointed that he had not been able to speak with his father once more. Now…"When can I see him?"

"Soon I'm sure. That is up to you and your… friends up there. If you'd like I can have him seek you out next time you return to your sanctuary."

"*My father is ALIVE!*" Thomas could barely contain his excitement. He wanted to head off immediately to his sanctuary. But he knew he would be unable to do so until he completed his test, and besides, this Brother Coughlin would need time to let his father know he absolutely wanted to see him. "That would be great, thank you!"

Brother Coughlin bowed. "Then it is settled. And truly, it has been a pleasure, young Thomas."

"Thank you." Thomas was extremely excited. Something, however, caught his notice. Something in Brother Coughlin's demeanor. He realized the way the man kept referring to Buster and Jack was very odd. "Question though. Why did you feel you needed to meet me alone?"

Brother Coughlin sighed. It was a strange site for someone who didn't actually need to breathe. "Young Thomas, you still have much to learn." He looked back up towards the top of the mountain when he spoke again. "Remember, death is like life. Everyone has their own agenda." The man bowed once more. "I must go. Many things demand my attention. I will leave you with this last piece of advice for your current test. There are two ways to achieve a goal that your opponent does not wish you to achieve. You can be better at doing than they are at stopping, or you can take a route that they cannot foresee, and therefore have not tried to stop." Brother Coughlin smiled again, this time with genuine mirth. "Given your own gifts, I would suggest the latter. Perhaps you can achieve what Bellerophon could not?"

And with that Brother Coughlin was gone. Thomas found it odd that the man could teleport here. Thomas tried himself once more, to see if perhaps they had stopped locking it down, but to no avail. Either Brother Coughlin was stronger than Jack's ability to lock things down, or he was working with Jack as part of this test (something Thomas couldn't dismiss as a possibility, though it seemed unlikely). Of course given his advice, it was also possible he used a different technique than Jack had locked down. For now Thomas didn't know which and it seemed unlikely he was going to figure it out on his own just yet.

The Bellerophon reference intrigued him. Thomas recognized it from somewhere. He started digging through his memories, trying to figure out where he might have heard that. It was weird. It wasn't quite like Googling something, but more like digging through an old card catalog for a specific book. It was slow but methodical and dependable. Within a few moments, he found the memory.

When he was eight, he loved reading a classical mythology book from his dad's library. One of them told the story of the Greek hero Bellerophon. He had slain the Chimera with the help of the winged horse Pegasus, then got cocky and tried to…. "Of course."

Thomas closed his eyes. Like the tower of his sanctuary, he started with something he knew well, and then modified it. He pictured a horse in his mind. His Uncle Billy had owned several when Thomas had been a kid, so he easily remembered how they felt and looked. He pictured his favorite, a grey mare he had called Shadow. He made it lighter and more graceful, then added a set of expansive wings to it. When he opened his eyes, the Pegasus was drinking from a small pool of water in front of him. Thomas smiled. "This will be much faster."

He reached down and picked up a golden bridle from his feet and wandered forward to saddle up.

Nine

Heather walked out onto the plateau of Leo's sanctuary dressed in her black leather outfit and spiked heel boots. One of the advantages of being dead was that practicality in footwear was a thing of the past (not having to take care of her long red hair was another bonus). No one else would have been able to appear at the top of this plateau. Being able to tune into other people's links to their sanctuary had its perks, including getting around teleportation lock downs. It was also the ability that ensured Jack and his crew quickly brought her into their group soon after she died. It made her very good at the job, though it would have also made her very dangerous if she'd decided to do what she now chose to stop.

She could see the small Italian in his renaissance era clothing bent over his koi pool, starring intently into its abyss. He probably knew she was there, though he may have tuned her out. As excitable as the little man was most of the time, he had an amazing knack of blocking out all of his surroundings when he was focused on a task. She decided to walk quietly up behind him to see which was going to be the case this time.

"I really wish you wouldn't circumvent my lockdown." Leo called back without turning from his pool. "She is there for a reason."

Heather smiled. She knew it bothered him when he wasn't in complete control of his own sanctuary. She also knew he could deal with it. "You don't really expect me to climb that cliff in these shoes do you?"

As usual when Leo became annoyed at something, he quickly changed the subject. "The pool, Heather, what do you see in her?"

His unwillingness to actually have any kind of confrontation was the main reason Heather refused to give into his request not to teleport within his sanctuary. She loved Leo and his almost constant cheeriness, but sometimes she felt he was too much of a pushover. She supposed that she secretly hoped by pushing his buttons she would get him to stand up for himself, though in truth she doubted that would happen. It obviously wouldn't happen with her today so she dismissed it and walked up next to him.

The pool was, as she usually saw it without his assistance, a pool. "I see your koi are over fed. That orange and black one there would die of heart failure if it wasn't a figment of your imagination.

Leo shook his head emphatically. "No no no. Do not look at the pool, Heather. Look through her."

Heather pursed her lips and stared more intently. She knew what she was supposed to be doing, and she knew with concentration she could at least do some of it, but it still didn't come as easily as Leo seemed to expect it should of her. After a few excruciating minutes of concentrating, the koi began to fade, replaced by something else. "I see... a garden... no it's... a town? Looks torn up... no, it's a garden again."

Leo nodded with gusto and pride. "Yes, yes. You do good, Heather! You will get it just yet, you wait you see!"

Heather shook her head, clearing the fuzziness that often accompanied the pool's visions. "And take your job? Wouldn't dream of it, Leo. I'll stick to the front lines for now. Speaking of which, is that our next job?"

Leo shook his head. "No Heather. This job? She is beneath you."

"I'm good with an easy assignment every now and then. That last one with the twins? Do you know how hard it was to figure out which one was actually the invader?"

Leo smiled. "Yours skills, they would be wasted here. Better for a new recruit to take this one. For you and Jacob, I have another job."

Heather shrugged. "Far be it from me to take a gimme job from the newbies. Where are my boys anyway?"

"There." Leo pointed behind her.

Heather turned to see Jacob spring over the edge of the plateau and begin his stroll towards her. A few seconds later the quiet giant Huang slowly and methodically climbed over the edge as well.

Jacob called out to her as he approached. "S'up, Red? You all rested and ready?"

As he moved closer, she noticed he was slightly more insubstantial than he should have been; an indication that the last job was just as difficult as the last few before had been. "Better than you, from the looks of it. You sure you don't need to sit this one out?"

Jacob popped his chest with fake indignation. "I can wait my turn. This ain't nothing my boy Leo here can't take care of, right? Sides, that last weasel says he ain't stalking the pretty girls no more. My man Huang and I played bad cop and bad cop on his ass. Convinced him he was better off playing in his own neighborhood than invading someone else's turf."

Huang for his part merely stood quietly, as always. Heather chuckled, knowing the story she was likely to hear would be at least partially embellished. It took her forever to get Jacob to actually talk comfortably around her. Now it seemed he was rarely quiet with her. She was never quite certain if he truly enjoyed joking with her or just felt some weird need to impress her. She really didn't care either. Both Jacob and Huang were great partners to have, and she was proud to work with both, but Jacob always reminded her of her older brother, which brought her a bit closer to him than the silent and stoic giant Huang. "I'm sure you two did great. Now it's my turn up to bat."

Leo reached across and laid a hand on Jacob. The small Italian flinched visibly for a moment as he transferred some of his energy into the tall bald black man, but when he finished Jacob looked good as new. Heather could have done the same, but since they were in Leo's sanctuary, he would recover far quicker. When he finished he turned back towards the pool, which suddenly took on the look of sand. "This place, it is your next job."

Heather pursed her lips. "I'm betting that's not a tropical beach tour, is it?"

Leo shook his head.

"Too bad." Jacob joked with a wry smile. "Red here could have rocked a bikini."

Heather raised an eyebrow at him. "In your dreams, eight ball." Before he could comment back she stepped forward into the pool and plunged in. She knew Jacob would be right behind her, and it amused her to catch him off guard and make him chase after her.

Sure enough, within about thirty second of touching down in the blistering desert-scape, Jacob popped up behind her. "Always in a hurry, eh Red?"

Heather shrugged and smiled. "Can't get back to my time off till I finish my missions right?" She looked around at her surroundings. Harsh sunlight blasted a sugar sand landscape with rolling dunes floating off in all directions. To their right, a large black cloud hung over the horizon with what looked like a sand tornado twisting from its base. She didn't even need to read the sanctuary's markers to know that was where they were needed. "That way."

Jacob shook his head. "Fraid you were going to say that. Let's go introduce ourselves."

Ten

Thomas had never felt such exhilaration in his life. Or his death, he realized.

The wind rushed against his face. The air cooled and the ground and mountain shrank beneath him. Shadow the Pegasus responded to his thoughts: diving, swooping, then lazily beating its powerful wings against the air, carrying both winged horse and rider inexorably upwards.

Within ten minutes they had climbed higher than Thomas would otherwise have done in the next two days on his own. They were already entering into the cloud cover that encircled the mountain's crown. Sunlight faded, but Thomas spurred his mount to a faster ascent. Within minutes they broke through to a golden realm of puffy clouds glittering in the brilliant sunlight. In the distance, shining like the promised Olympus itself, a golden temple sat upon the mountain's crown. There was no doubt that this was their destination.

Shadow touched down gently on the cobblestones that made up the temple's floor. Buster trotted up and nuzzled his head under Thomas's hand as soon as he dismounted. Jack stood there clapping. "Bravo, laddie. I thought for certain you were going to walk all the way up and we'd be here a bloody week." He shook his head, walking around the Pegasus with an obvious sense of awe. "Didn't expect you to create a bloody flying horse."

"Weren't you watching?"

"Oh aye. You made it right boring the first few hours, let me tell ya. Then you stopped to apparently consider for a wee bit. Looked like ye were bleeding talking to yourself, then ye created the Pegasus." Jack shook his head. "Straight outta mythology it looks. Good job. Tried figuring out a way to stop you, but short of a lightning storm I wasn't sure would work I couldn't think of anything."

Thomas felt that was odd. It seemed like Jack actually did not see the Brother. "So, you saw me talking to… myself?"

"Aye." Jack's face darkened. "Why? Did you see something?"

"I wasn't alone, Jack. Someone else was down there. I thought he might be part of your test."

Jack raised an eyebrow. "Nay lad. There weren't nobody there. Shouldn't have been, anyway."

Buster looked up. His face grew darker as well. "No strange scents."

Thomas wished that he had had access to his saber tooth senses. "Maybe you were too far away."

"No. Can smell the entire sanctuary. No new scents."

"So what, he had no scent? Or he was here the entire time?"

If a dog could shrug, Thomas felt Buster would have. "Do not know."

"Could have been any number of things." Jack himself shrugged. Then his face grew darker and slightly confused. "None of which I really like though. I should have been able to sense anyone here aside from us, and I haven't. Hells, apparently I was looking right at him when you were talking to him and didn't see him. Whoever he is, he's insanely good, mate."

"Or he knows a trick we don't."

"Aye. Tis always a possibility, that. You're learning well."

There was that. Thomas just wondered who he was learning from. Jack waved his arms and a couple of overstuffed arm chairs appeared overlooking the now clear valley below them. They were completely out of place in the temple, but looked comfortable nonetheless. The sun sunk just below the horizon, giving enough light to see the world below. The valley morphed into a sea of green. A few large birds of prey circled lazily on the currents of air, as other lesser mountains broke up the horizon. Jack plopped down in his recliner, then reached over and tossed Thomas a beer he had produced from somewhere. Thomas politely declined, tossing it back.

"No thanks. I never really liked beer, remember?"

"Aye, but I did." Jack smiled and once again tossed the beer to Thomas. "Remember, here that's the more important thing."

Thomas shrugged and took a seat and a drink. To his surprise, the beer tasted clean and refreshing. "Wow. If beer had tasted like that when I was alive I would have drunken a lot more of it too."

"Tis amazingly tasty. One of my favorite summer brews. Now, tell me more about this fellow you saw."

Thomas filled Jack and Buster in on the conversation he had had with Brother Parkes Coughlin. He thought about leaving out the man's obvious distrust of his 'friends', but in the end decided he had to trust someone here, and so far Jack and Buster had not given him any indication that they had anything less than his best interests in mind. Buster perked up when Jack mentioned what he had heard about his father.

"Your father still lives?"

"Yeah. Amazing, isn't it? I mean, I don't know whether I completely trust him or not, but god, can you imagine being able to see Dad again?" Thomas sank into the thought, thinking happily of what it would be like to talk with his father after all these years.

"If true, your mother must know this."

"You're right. I'm sure she would definitely want to, though I don't know why he wouldn't have gone and found her himself by now."

Jack shrugged. "Who knows? This fellow you met had one thing correct. Souls are no less complex than living people are. They all have their own reasons for doing what they do."

Buster stood up and stretched. "I wish to investigate. If your father lives, I will let your mother know."

"Buster, you're a free Soul. You don't need my permission to do anything. Truthfully, I'm kind of curious if this guy's telling the truth myself."

Buster nodded. "Then I will return to let you know after I tell her."

Jack looked over to him. "I've opened shifting back up. Do you remember where the soft spot to the prime is?

Buster nodded his large head. "Yes. I will find you when I finish. Be safe."

With that he vanished.

Jack shook his head. "Damn. Wish we'd had a dog like that in our family. Now. How rested are ye feeling?"

Eleven

Buster raced along the path between worlds. He could easily have passed straight into the prime, but he was hesitant to do so. The fact that Thomas had been visited literally beneath his nose disturbed him. To also find out this visitor had played on Thomas's feeling for his family concerned him more. Buster hoped to be wrong, but he didn't dare take a chance. This soul had to have some power to be that stealthy. Given his interest in Thomas, and that he had been able to gain entrance to the Training sanctuary undetected, Buster suspected this was the soul that had disturbed The Great Spirit.

"Watch your charge." The Spirit had told him. *"The balance is tilting, and if we are not careful, the old ways could return. Or worse."*

Buster felt bad for leaving Thomas alone, but he had to know if Roger Salazar really did still exist, and if so what level his former master existed on. He had not been lying when he said that Sylvia would want and deserve to know. But the information might also shed light on whether this mysterious stranger really was a benefactor or something else.

The something else was the reason Buster now took the long way to the Prime. Obviously the Brother Coughlin knew how to disguise his scent. If he could escape detection within Jack Macintyre's Training sanctuary, it was probable that he could do the same on the Prime. If he knew where the Training sanctuary's soft spot existed, he would expect those leaving it to come through that point. So Buster would come through elsewhere.

Buster chose a spot close to the Salazar's family farm to break back into the Prime. The wild, near overwhelming colors and scents of the Great Path immediately gave way to the more subdued Prime. His early travels between the two had been overwhelmingly disconcerting. Now he barely broke stride.

He had taken note of the scent of Thomas's love Shari when he had witnessed Thomas's memorial. Without pausing he began sifting through the Prime's many scents until he picked up on the one unique to her. If this stranger had told Thomas the truth, then Roger Salazar would be close to her. The living were much easier to track on the Prime than the dead were, but if Roger Salazar still smelled as he once did then Buster would have no trouble locating him once he was closer.

It did not take long to lock onto Shari's scent. Buster headed straight for it. The advantage, he'd learned, of the prime was that there was no need to run around obstacles. Trees, cars, houses, people, they all offered the resistance of fog. With a scent to follow he could make a beeline without slowing pace.

After about half an hour Buster found himself running through a city plaza. The scent grew stronger, but also shifted upwards in direction. Thomas's Love must be in a building. He slowed down at a very tall one and took note of the scent's direction. *"This is it."*

He judged his target was likely three or four floors up. He took stock of his options. He could teleport directly next to her at this distance, but if she were being watched he would be seen. Something subtler was called for. He could 'fly' up, but dogs didn't fly. Even in death. Buster settled on the stairs. He rushed through the wall, and through the throng of people. He made note of the visitors. It was obviously a public building. Judging by the dress of the people he passed, he suspected it to be some kind of human veterinarian place. It didn't take long to locate the stairs, which not surprisingly were completely empty (he'd noted over the years that humans had a tendency to be lazy these days). Buster rushed up the flights of stairs, stopping at each door to check the scent and confirm if it was still above him or not. When he reached the fourth floor, the scent's direction changed noticeably. *"This is it."*

Now the dangerous part. Hiding in a forest was not much of an issue. Hiding in a building was trickier. If he rushed in, he would easily be spotted by any other souls about. Buster took a moment to suppress his scent. He doubted anyone here would be able to pick him out by it, but better not to take any chances. He then hunkered down as best he could and slowly pushed himself through the first wall. An empty room with a strange bed and an assortment of machines greeted him. Buster scanned to confirm there were no souls about, then rushed across to the next wall and slowly poked his head through it.

"Oh yes. You've got an active little one there!"

Shari laid on one of the strange beds with her stomach exposed. A vet looking human rubbed something across it while looking up at a tv. Shari giggled, with tears visible on her face as she watched a grainy image on the screen.

"Oh My God, He's Beautiful!"

"It's still too early to confirm it is a 'He', but yes. You do appear to have a beautiful healthy baby from the looks of it."

"She'll be happy with either, no doubt." This voice was different. Buster kept mostly in the wall, and slowly moved himself around the room. A middle aged human soul with looks that bore a strong resemblance to Thomas's Shari slowly came into view. Buster suspected this was her father. Next to him stood a small brown skin man that Buster knew well.

Roger Salazar.

"Of course she will. I remember when Thomas was born. We were convinced he was going to be a girl, but when he came out... well I knew he could not have been any more perfect. "

The two souls continued talking of parenting days past as Shari and the vet continued discussing what must have been some kind of view of Thomas's child. Buster ignored all of them, focusing on remaining hidden while examining his former master. The scent was true. It seemed to have changed slightly, but that could have been just the time that had passed since Buster had last seen him. *"Maybe it truly is him?"* That would prove a huge relief all around.

One more test remained. Buster continued slowly circling the room. He pulled himself back into the wall as the two souls moved closer to the screen, apparently seeking better views themselves. This was it. Buster watched as Roger Salazar moved around the bed to get a better view. He turned the corner and....

Buster felt his heart drop. A shining silver cord attached to the back of Roger Salazar's right shoulder. It drifted lazily out for a few feet before fading into the planes.

"*So that's it then.*" Buster had hoped not to see it, but he had suspected he would. Shari's father clasped the man that had been Roger Salazar on the back, just above the silver cord. He wouldn't be able to see it. Only those with one of their own could spot them on anyone else.

Buster withdrew and considered what to do next. He would obviously need to report this, and Sylvia would still want to know. With luck the man that had been Roger Salazar would still be mostly Roger Salazar. He considered how much to tell her and Thomas. Knowing could possibly put them all in danger, and that was the last thing he wanted to see happen. Better to remain vague. That would give him time to learn more.

Buster took one last look at his former master, then turned and rushed back to the Great Path Between the Worlds.

Twelve

"I think we have a good intro job. You ready, lad?"

Thomas looked up from his place by the fire. Jack seemed to relish pushing him to the brink of exhaustion, and this session had been no different. Thomas found it easier and easier to create things from nothing. He had even managed to create a crossbow despite having never had contact with a real one in his life, though he suspected the fact that he had held a gun and a normal bow might have helped out there. He was also far more comfortable shape shifting than he had been before. Still, there was much to learn and every step he mastered matched up to a laundry list of things he struggled with.

Jack could still lock him down without a thought, and Thomas still couldn't even see the chains much less free himself from them. Jack had tried to explain how to see them, but it felt like being told how to see what card someone held up in a house a town away. Oddly, though Jack could prevent him from teleporting and shape shifting, he could not prevent him from creating things. He could slow the process down, but the more unusual the item or creature Thomas created, the less likely Jack could to stop it. Thomas had to smile when he frustrated Jack, but doing so only ensured Jack would hit him with something else he hadn't seen before.

So it had been for the entire time since Buster had left, which to Thomas felt like probably around two weeks. It was impossible to tell with any certainty, however, with Jack controlling the passage of time within the sanctuary. Each 'day' they would kick up with a series of warm up tests devised by Jack to test Thomas's imagination. They would then move into mock combat that seemed to be growing increasingly more realistic by the fight. Finally they would finish with some form of endurance test meant to push Thomas's boundaries to the breaking point before Jack called it an evening, allowing Thomas to recharge before starting all over again. The routine was nothing if not predictable.

Till now, at least, when Jack looked off into the darkness as if he were listening to someone, then turned back and asked his question. The change caught Thomas more off guard than most of Jack's surprises.

"Err.. A job? You mean like a real fight with a real rogue soul?"

"Seems to be."

"How do you know?"

Jack smiled. "I am linked to this sanctuary with several others of the order. Aside from allowing me to regenerate energy more quickly here it allows us to know where the others are and contact each other. "

"And they just did?"

"Aye. Leo, one of me mates in the order, wants us to come see him. He's got a knack for finding sanctuaries that have been invaded, so a call from him usually means a job."

"I'm still pretty beat. When do we need to go?"

"Sooner is better, lad. One thing you'll learn is the longer a rogue soul has in a sanctuary, the tougher they are to get out. If you can get them before they attach themselves it's not bad but if they link… well you're in for the fight of your death."

Thomas stretched and stood. "Fine. But I'm not even close to full strength."

Jack shrugged. "Let's do this first then." Jack reached over and grabbed Thomas's shoulder.

Thomas felt a familiar but more powerful than normal surge of energy. The world exploded and suddenly he stood on the cliff top next to his tower. "Wow. It really is good to be home." He looked over and saw Jack grimacing. "You okay?"

Jack waved him off. "Fine. Fine lad. Takes a wee bit more energy to pull off a jump like that, and I wasn't at full power meself, but I've got more than enough in the tank to get us to Leo's and he can recharge me there pretty quickly. "

Thomas had a better understanding now of what he meant. Where he had felt energy flowing into him like a water faucet before, it now felt like someone had taken the cap off of a fire hydrant. Within a few minutes he felt more awake and alive than he had since, he quickly realized, he had left. "Damn. I take that back It feels amazingly good to be home."

Jack nodded. "Now you have a better understanding of why most folks stick to their own sanctuary. Even if they do figure out how to leave, you're never quite the same as you are when you're here. That's also why it's important we get this job taken care of quickly before our adversary links to whatever sanctuary they've invaded. You don't want them feeling like you do right now when you try and deal with them."

Thomas nodded. "Could be bad. I feel way more powerful here than I did before. I'm ready. Let's do this."

"Alright lad. One more stop." Jack reached out and grabbed Thomas's arm. The world broke apart once again, and suddenly Thomas found himself next to Jack at the base of a giant cliff. The River roared obnoxiously loud. So much so Thomas jumped back against the cliff's face in spite of himself.

"Only way in!" Jack screamed over the cacophony of life. "We'll have to fly up from here!"

Jack turned himself into his now seemingly normal pigeon form. Thomas shrugged and looked to his side where a Pegasus now stood. He pulled himself up onto its back and nudged it upwards. *"Probably good that Buster hasn't made it back yet..."*

As the two climbed, it surprised Thomas to notice a large number of massive birds perched among the rock ledges in pretty much every direction he looked. Birds of prey all, the sheer number of them keeping an eye on him disturbed him greatly. He assumed this Leo person must have put them there as some kind of security, and he now suspected that if he had shown up without Jack, his flight would have been far more eventful. As it was, the birds merely observed as he passed their nests by. After about twenty minutes of steady climbing, the peak came into view.

The two came over the edge onto a large plateau. While a few hundred feet across, this appeared to be the extent of the habitable terrain. Everything else within sight in the sanctuary was open air. Jack morphed back to human shape as he touched down softly. Thomas slowed Shadow the Pegasus to a halt as it too touched down on the cobblestones that seemed to cover the top of the plateau.

Thomas looked around and admired the view. A small cottage stood in the center of the Plateau. It was simple, with a thatch roof and wooden walls. A large rocky pool stood visible in the front of the house, circled almost completely by a group of gnarly trees. The remaining bit of the plateau was open, and covered in old warn cobblestones. The only signs of life Thomas noticed as Shadow slowly cantered up was a large amount of koi in the pool and a lone owl in the one of the gnarled trees across the pond. As the two men approached the owl swooped down across the water, rising up on the same side of the pool Thomas and Jack were on then morphing into a man that Thomas assumed was 'Leo'.

"Jack! You look good. And this… this must be the Mr. Salazar."

Leo was a small man, even to Thomas. He wore a plain set of robes, with a hat that looked as if it belonged in an Italian Renaissance painting. He spoke with a thick Italian accent that left no doubt to his heritage. Thomas swung down from his mount and extended his hand, which was met with an almost over zealous shake. "Umm… nice to meet you, Mr. Leo."

"No Mister! Only Leo. And It is my pleasure to be meeting you! And your mount! She is a beauty! Jack you were not lying about this boy's talents. Not that you would, would you?" Leo grinned as if he were telling a joke. "Mr. Salazar. Can I call you Thomas?"

"Err. Yeah. Of course."

"Thomas! You simply must make a Harpy for me some a time. I have always wanted one, but did not think it possible until you arrived on that magnificent stallion!"

Thomas shrugged. "I guess I could try and do that for you."

"Beautiful! Now come this a way. I'm sure you are anxious to get to work, and I have no doubts that your target's target would prefer you arrive sooner rather than the later."

Leo seemed a bundle of energy. Thomas found himself a little overwhelmed at the man's excitability, but he dutifully fell into line as Leo turned back towards the pool. He dismissed the Pegasus, which disappeared as if it had never been. Leo and Jack continued to exchange small pleasantries. Thomas was a bit surprised that he could understand them as well as he could. "Your English is very good, Mr. Leo."

Leo looked over at him and smiled. "As is a your Italian, Thomas."

Jack could obviously see the confusion on Thomas's face and spoke up with a smile. "Thomas, laddie, we don't really all speak the same language here. Don't need to. It's more that we project what it is we want to say, and the people around us pick it up. To you it sounds like we all speak English. Everyone hears what you say in their native tongue. To Leo here it's all Italian. It's what we know, and so it's what we hear. Really we're just getting the meaning that each of us projects."

"That's…. odd…."

"Aye. I suppose it is. But it keeps things simpler. Very little misunderstandings here in the afterlife. If someone says something that's vague it's because they want it to be, or they're unsure themselves. Either way, not much is lost in translation."

Leo stopped at the edge of the pool and stared into it. "Here we go."

Jack wandered up next to him and looked as well. Thomas shrugged and followed suit. He was surprised as the water began to ripple oddly, then alter in color. Jack obviously expected this to happen.

"So what are we dealing with, Leo?"

"Just what you asked me to look for, Jack. She is your run of a mill Anarchist soul. Found her way out of her own sanctuary and wandered into a poor soul's world that doesn't know how to handle himself. This…" He motioned to the pool, which now seemed to be a window into a dingy looking town "This was a beautiful garden a few days ago. Now… Not so much."

Thomas watched as the window, like a camera, scrolled its way through dirty streets, past broken windows. It looked like a small town that had been ground zero for a major riot. Trash filled the roads, doors were kicked in, cars torched. Jack studied it all intently.

"Was a garden?"

"Yes. Change was rapid. And not very kind."

Jack whistled. "Bloody hell. She's strong or he's weak. Not sure which."

"I would go with both. Safer to assume the worst."

"Aye. Thomas, lad. Ya ready?"

Thomas looked at the scene playing out beneath his view then back at the two men at his side, then back down at the street. He had known this would be coming soon, but somehow, thinking back on all of the warnings Jack had given him on what could go wrong, now that it was here he found himself far more nervous than he expected. But, there was no getting around it. He could back out now and return to his sanctuary, ever the safer and no doubt far more bored and embarrassed, or he could trust that Jack wouldn't be throwing him into something he wasn't ready for and take the plunge. With a deep breath, he gave his assent. "Yeah. Ready as I'm likely to be."

Jack smiled. "Good lad. Let's make our entrance grand then, right?" He took a step into the pool, and then fell through the 'window' on the water, landing in the street they happened to be viewing. Thomas was very surprised, which likely showed on his face as he looked back over at Leo.

The short Italian just smiled at him. "You better be going if you plan to be."

Thomas shrugged. He took what would have been a deep breath, then stepped forward.

*****

There was a brief cold sensation, almost as if he really had passed through water, then Thomas found himself kneeling on a black top road. Jack reached down and offered a hand, which Thomas readily accepted as he stood up to take stock of where he landed.

There was no sign of the window back to Leo's pool. The world around him appeared dull in color but not in content. The scene matched exactly what he had seen through the pool, except that it was more real now that he stood in the middle of it. An acrid smoke burned his nose, causing the entire area to smell of sulfur, rot, and gasoline.

"Ug." Thomas twisted up his nose. "Glad I didn't come in here in cat form."

Jack held up a hand, asking his silence. He strained as if listening for something. Thomas closed his eyes and listened as well. To his left, in the distance, he could hear a faint sound that could be a woman's voice, but it was too far to make out much more than that. Apparently Jack heard it as well. With a quick and quiet "Let's go" he began jogging that direct.

After two blocks of post-apocalyptic destruction, the voice started becoming clearer. "Come on, kitty boy. Let's play some more." The voice sounded somewhat young, with the hint of frustration. Jack and Thomas continued their jog towards the sound. They rounded the corner of what looked to have till recently been a convenience or small grocery store, before Thomas ran head long into the voice's owner.

"Well hello there, big boy." The woman looked to be in her mid twenties. Half her hair was black, the other an unnatural shade of red. It looked like it had been cut completely randomly, then covered in styling gel and allowed to set at whatever angle it landed when she woke up that morning. She wore an ensemble of black leather pants and a matching vest, and combat boots. What skin that wasn't covered by leather was instead covered by either tattoos or piercings. "You come to play with me too?"

Jack nodded. "Aye, lass. We're here to play with ya."

The woman backed away and then slowly began to circle both men, obviously sizing them up. "Hmm… you two aren't like kitty boy, are you?" She smiled, which made her look more like a predator. "You won't go hiding at the first little sign of head trauma, will ya?"

Jack smiled. "Let's fine out, shall we?" With that, he took a swing at the girl, obviously trying to catch her off guard. She must have been ready for it, as she dodged with ease.

"Old man, you're slow."

As Jack spun to compensate for missing the punch, he met with a combat boot to the rib cage. With an audible "ugh' he flew backwards a few feet, but remained standing.

This earned him a raised eyebrow from the woman. "You may be more fun that you look."

Jack turned and looked at Thomas. "Feel free to jump in anytime you like, laddie."

Thomas shook himself from the sidelines and rushed ahead, turning into cat form as he did. The sulfur smell hit his more sensitive nose like a nauseating stink bomb, but the increased speed and flexibility compensated. The shock of his new look also caught the woman complete off guard. She dodged as if expecting another punch, but instead found herself stepping straight into a razor like claw that slashed her vest open at the side with bit deep into flesh. If she had had blood, it would have been pouring out, but Thomas suspected she had taken a good hit to her energy.

"Holy fuck, cat boy. That hurt!"

Before she could say or do anything else, Jack slammed the blade of a cricket bat he pulled from nowhere into the back of her spine. She hit the ground with an audible thud. Thomas, acting on instinct as much as anything else, saw an opening and took it. He leapt onto the woman's back as she started to push herself back up, flattening her down again. In one smooth motion he clamped down with his saber-toothed fangs, ripping the back of her neck out. He had claimed much food with that move. If she were alive, it would have killed her. It must have still done some serious damage, because the woman's demeanor changed and she raised her hands up.

"Fine! I give! I give! You bastards cheat."

Jack rested his new bat on his shoulder. "Aye, well, if you were playing by the rules we wouldn't have been here to begin with. Then again, neither would you."

Thomas leapt off the woman, allowing her to turn over and sit up as he morphed back into human form. The acrid smoke was much more bearable now.

"My place is BORING." The woman wined. "I know where everybody's at and what they're going to do. They fall down when I tell them to, and come out of hiding when I tell them to. No fun."

Jack shrugged. "There's a billion plus souls out there. Some of them are into your type of… er… fun. You concentrate and find one of them and we're all happy. Catch you taking over someone else's sanctuary without their say so again, though and it's the River for you. That means you'll cease to be. No more fun to be had."

The woman spit. "You guys suck." And with that she was gone.

As soon as the woman disappeared, the buildings began to dissipate as if they had been made of gas the entire time. Within a few moments, the dull browns and grays of the hollowed out city were replaced by brilliant greens and blues of a flower garden. Off to his left, a small orange stripped tabby cat cautiously made his way through the grass towards them.

Jack let his bat disappear, then tried to present himself in a less threatening manner. "It's okay, mate. We're just here to shoo off your trouble. We've got no intentions of causing you more."

The cat continued to move cautiously, but morphed into a man as it moved. The new man looked to Thomas like an accountant. He stood just a little shorter than Thomas, wearing a solid light blue button up shirt, dark slacks, and red suspenders with a thin black tie. He was also barefoot. It seemed an odd attire to be wandering about a garden in, but the man moved with the familiarity Thomas would expect of someone in his own element. He stopped about twenty foot from where Thomas and Jack stood. He finally spoke with a nervous reedy voice:

"Um… Thank you. She… she came out of nowhere. Everything started changing. I… I wasn't sure how to get rid of her or what to do."

"Happens, laddie. Though not often. In all likelihood you'll never see another soul like her but…" Jack tossed the man an item that looked to be a card with a compass of some sort printed on it. "If ye want to learn how to better defend your sanctuary go to the prime and follow the arrow there till it disappears. Man named Willy'll be there who can teach you a few basic tricks. He's not as mean as he puts on, and his price is reasonable, trust me. Probably all you will need to keep people like her out."

The man nervously examined the card that had landed at his feet. He picked it up with a small partial smile. "Thank you. I…. I might do that."

"Good luck to ye then. Thomas, shall we?"

Before Thomas could respond Jack turned and started walking the opposite direction. Thomas quickly fell in line and followed, looking back just once at the sanctuary's owner, who stared intently at the card. The man then slipped it into his pocket before morphing back into kitty form and pounced off into the flowers.

Thirteen

"You better hurry, Red. I can't keep this up!"

Heather didn't need the reminder to know what the stakes were. When she first joined the Order, most of their jobs were fairly easy with two people. Lately every job had seemed a fight for their existence. This one was no exception. The sand tornado was brutal, and it had, of all things, a self styled female Djinn in the center. The rogue soul had been tormenting the local inhabitant, a twenty-ish guy of Arab look and dress, who was flying wildly about the storm when they arrived. Heather had managed to get him down while Jacob fought directly against the Djinn herself, but so far Heather had not been able to get through to the near catatonic owner.

While it appeared the Djinn had not yet established a connection to the sanctuary itself, there was an obvious link established between the Persian boy and his invader, and the female intruder was using it to gain energy far above what she would have had on her own. This put Jacob at a severe disadvantage in the fight despite his experience. If Heather was unable to sever that link then Jacob would be done for and the Djinn would turn its attention on her.

Heather closed her eyes, placed a hand on the guy's forehead, and read what information she could. His name was... Pezhman... Pezhman Anoush. "Odd name, but okay. Let's go, Pez. I need you to wake up and help me." She continued focusing. After a few moments she found the link to the Djinn. The rogue soul was drawing a large amount of energy from him. "No wonder Jacob is struggling."

Something about the link was very odd though. It seemed like the energy was being *pushed* rather than *pulled*, but that made no sense. Heather chalked it up to the weirdness of the sanctuary and focused on the link itself. She pushed the chaos of her surroundings away, and focused on the makeup of the sanctuary rather than the actual appearance of it. When she felt she had a good read of it, she turned back to the link and focused on making its substance match that of the sanctuary. If the Djinn had any clue what she was doing it would have been able to stop her quickly, but luckily it was either too focused on its assault on Jacob or, more likely, just too inexperienced to realize what was going on. Heather smiled as she felt the makeup of the link shift subtly to harmonize with the surrounding sanctuary.

She opened her eyes and saw the link now existed within the surrounding reality, a pulsing blue cord not too different from the one that linked her and Jacob to the training sanctuary. Since it now existed in the local reality...

In one smooth motion Heather produced a rapier and slashed through the cord, severing the connection of the Rogue Spirit from her victim. "NOW JACOB!"

Jacob, who had been in a barely controlled spin about the top of the sand tornado, wasted no time in pushing himself off of the windy walls towards the Djinn that was currently in the center of the destructive storm. With practiced precision he flipped forward, bringing the weight of his momentum down through the tip of his baseball bat through the shoulder of the female rogue spirit. The blow, along with the shock of the cut cord was obviously too much for the woman. The entire storm system quickly dissipated as the Djinn tumbled towards the ground, morphing as she did into a young Arab teenage girl.

The girl hit the ground with a hard thud about fifteen feet from where Heather stood over the sanctuary owner. Jacob, without the wind to sustain him in the air, began his own tumble, but he had already positioned himself to land feet first on the back of the rogue soul, no doubt hoping to keep her from a quick recovery. Heather knew the move was unlikely to dissipate her, but Jacob would ensure it did as much damage as possible.

"NO! DON'T HURT HER!" It was the first sound Heather had heard the boy Pez make since their arrival, and it caught her completely off guard. The boy sat upright and extended his hand, creating a shell around the girl on the ground that sent Jacob tumbling into the sand.

Heather quickly put her hand on his shoulder. "Pezhman! We're the good guys. That girl was attacking you. We're here to help you."

The boy shook his head vehemently, his eyes and face reddening as tears began to flow. "No. I deserve it. I deserve it and worse."

As Heather and Jacob watched, the sugary sand desert gave way to a packed dirt ground village in a scrub desert. Their perspective shifted to the inside of one of the small huts, a single room dwelling with little more than a hand woven blanket as a floor. In the center of the floor were two children, who were staring at a sheet of paper. Heather recognized the seven year old boy quickly enough as Pez. She suspected now that the little girl next to him must be the rogue soul they had been facing. Pezhman quickly confirmed those suspicions.

"I taught Ghodsi to read as I was learning myself. I knew it was forbidden, but she wanted to know so bad and I could not see the harm in it. I wish now I would have been more firm with her, but how could I have known?"

The scene shifted and now the two children were older, probably 10 and nine. Both were huddled inside a rocky cavern reading a ragged looking book together that appeared to be on the verge of completely falling apart.

"We had few things to read, so we reread the one book we could find over and over." Pezhman's spirit continued. "It was 1001 Arabian Nights. It belonged to a villager who died several years earlier. I took it from his house and no one ever missed it."

The older Pezhman next to Heather continued with a sad reflective voice. "The only other book I knew of in town was the Qur'an, and I was only allowed to see it when I was in Elder Nimah's home for my studies. He would never have approved of me showing that to Ghodsi."

The two children giggled as they turned the pages together, completely immersed in their tales. The scene shifted again, this time to a much improved home. It was only a few rooms in size and had only a wooden floor, but compared to the other huts it seemed lavish. Heather watched as a young teenager girl tiptoed in, opened a drawer, and pulled out a much more cared for book.

Pez continued narrating the events. "By the time we were coming into age, Ghodsi could quote our book from memory. It was no longer enough. She talked me into telling her where Elder Nimah kept his Qur'an, and while they were out with the goats she would sneak in and read it. One day it went all wrong."

Heather watched as a man with a long beard walked into the room. As he and Ghodsi saw each other the young girls slammed the book closed in horror, but it was obviously too late. The man, this Elder Nimah, Heather realized, stomped over and backhanded her into the floor. Oddly, there was no sound, which made the entire scene more horrifying. The little girl screamed as the elder yelled back at her, pointing at the book. When she nodded in response to some question he had, he picked up a strip of leather and began whipping her while she continued to scream in anguish and pain. It was all Heather could do not to attack the phantasm of the elder to make him stop, but she knew this was all just a vision of the past.

Pezhman continued, but his voice was now choked with tears. "'A woman of education is an abomination,' the elder said. 'She has the knowledge but not the wisdom to use that knowledge, and she will only bring downfall to those around her.'"

The scene shifted again to a fire, with several people, all men Heather noted, argued over what Heather knew to be the fate of the girl. The fourteen-year-old version of Pez looked on from the side with almost the same anguished expression that his slightly older self had.

The older version continued, "Some argued to have her killed, or that her eyes be taken so she may never again read, or even that her hands be taken for holding a sacred book. In the end it was decided she would be offered a different fate. There was a goat herder who traded with the villages at times, a nomad of ill temper. She would be offered to him during his next stop as a wife in exchange for provisions he often had on him from other villages."

The boy's tears continued flowing freely. "I was horrified. I had always thought Ghodsi and I would one day be wed, but now I knew with certainty that was never to be. Because of my misdeeds, because I had not the strength to say no to her when she was young, she would now be wed to someone who would treat her no better than his animals and she would never again be able to read a book, for her husband would surely forbid it under punishment too severe to endure."

Heather tightened her hand with each word of the boy's story, feeling more and more like she had attacked the wrong soul. She knew that by right the boy's sanctuary was his own, but his ignorance and sexism infuriated her in a way she would have thought impossible since her own death. She held her tongue however as the boy continued his tale.

"Ghodsi knew what was in store for her when she was told of her punishment. On the day the old herder showed up, she ran away. Part of me was angry at her for not taking me with her. I guess that was part of what made me give in to Elder Nimah."

Heather watched as the bearded elder came into the tent where young Pez sat. He sat down next to the boy and began speaking to him in a way that looked very calm and fatherly. It was an odd juxtaposition to what she had seen go on between the elder and Ghodsi.

"The elder told me that Ghodsi had sinned against God, and that God would be furious with both her and me. He told me that she would be damned to eternal torment if she were left on her own. He knew that I cared for her, but as a righteous man I had a duty to God above all others. If I did not want to see both of our souls doomed to suffering, then I must tell him where to find her."

Heather looked over at the rogue soul version of Ghodsi, who had now stood and was staring at Pezhman. Most of her now looked for all the world just like the little girl who had been caught reading a book. The main difference was her eyes, which burned with a fury of fiery coal. Jacob stood about ten foot behind her and flexed the baseball bat that he always used as a weapon, but Heather caught his eye and shook her head. As furious as the girl looked, she hadn't made a move yet to attack, and Heather still wasn't entirely certain she would want to stop her if she did. Jacob lowered his bat as the boy continued talking.

"I... I really thought I was doing the right thing. I thought I was doing God's work and that as a result both Ghodsi and I might be saved. I was wrong. I told them where she would be hiding at. There really was only one likely place where we both knew to be safe. The elder lead the party to get her himself, along with a couple of other adults and the herder she was to marry."

Heather watched as the scene Pez described unfolded in front of them; with a gruff and dirty looking man of around fifty lead a donkey behind the Elder Nimah and two of the other men who had decided that this little girl should be given like a piece of meat to man four times her age because she had the audacity to educate herself. Heather didn't know what Jacob would do if the girl attacked Pez again, but she was pretty certain she wouldn't be able to help him this time. That thought was amplified when she saw what unfolded next.

The men came out of the desert towards the village once more. Behind the old herder was again the donkey, but this time an old twisted rope trailed behind the donkey dragging the young girl through the rocky sandy ground by her hands. Her clothes were torn to the point of indecency, and every bit of her exposed flesh was covered in blood or bruises. A crowd gathered round as the horrible display wound its way into the center of the village. The girl's rope was cut and she was dragged by her arms and tossed bodily into the center of the village near the fire pit. She struggled just enough to show she was still alive, but barely moved beyond that.

Elder Nimah pointed at the girl and began speaking. The scene still had no sound, but this time Pezhman spoke the Elder's words in perfect match to the man's lip movements.

"This girl has sinned against God. She has been unrepentant in that sin and she has now compounded her crimes by bringing shame to this village. Her soul is a taint upon this righteous group and there is but one-way to free her and us. She must face this cleansing punishment that her soul will be saved in death and her deeds not bring further shame upon all of us!"

As the final word left he elder's lips, the herder that was to be
Ghodsi's husband picked up a rock the size of his fist and through
it like a baseball, pelting the young girl in the ribs. The girl cried
out in agony and tightened as much as she could into a ball. Elder
Nimah threw the second rock, which again found its mark. Others
in the village joined in, and soon a storm of rocks hailed down as
the increasingly bloodied form crumpled on the ground. Following
a stern look from the elder, even Pezhman joined in, though
Heather noted the boy's projectiles all fell wide. After a few
agonizing minutes, the body stopped all movement, and soon after
the rocks ceased to fall. The body was all but buried at this point,
with only an arm and a foot showing through the cairn.

The scene faded, and Pezhman looked up at her, his eyes red with
tears despite the fact that he no longer possessed a body to create
them. "After that, I was numb. I no longer questioned what the
elder told me to do, for I saw the damage that such things did.
When, a few years later, he sent me with some of the other men in
our village to join in the fight against infidels, I gladly went. When
they asked for someone to go on a mission for God that would
surely be suicide, I volunteered for the glory. I had nothing to live
for anyway, and the sooner I joined God's glory, the sooner I could
be free of what I had done. When I died and woke up here, I
thought I had achieved all that the Elder had promised."

He dropped once more to his knees, and raised a quivering finger
towards the soul of Ghodsi. "Then she showed up, and I knew
without a doubt that what I had done had been a lie. It was not
righteous at all. Ours had been the sin, and Ghodsi had been the
victim. She has a duty to punish me for what I have done."

"No."

It was the first word that Heather had heard the girl Ghodsi
actually say, and it was stated with a force that surprised her. The
girl's spirit walked forward. Jacob made a move to stop her, but
Heather again shook him off, stepping to the side.

Pez couldn't maintain eye contact with the girl as she closed in,
dropping his head down in prostration before her. "I have wronged
you, Ghodsi. You were the most important person in my life. You

were the only source of happiness I ever knew and I betrayed you. You must punish me."

"No." The word was slightly softer this time. Ghodsi reached down and placed a hand under Pezhman's chin and lifted his face up. Heather noted that the look of anger still gleamed in her eyes, but it had soften, and was now joined by something else... pity? The girl spoke quietly but firmly. "I will never forgive you, Pezhman. But I see now that no punishment I could come up with would be greater than what you will do to yourself. Worse, my punishing you seems to give you redemption. I won't do that either."

Pezhman shuddered, almost to the point of sobbing. "You can't go! I need you, Ghodsi! I'm sorry! I'm so so sorry."

Ghodsi let go of his chin and stepped back. "I know." Her body then shifted as her skin paled and her lower half took on the form of a whirlwind, returning to the Djinn form she wore when they had first arrived. "But others aren't."

With that, she was gone.

Pezhman collapsed, sobbing uncontrollably. "What do I do? What do I do?"

Heather looked at the spot where Ghodsi had disappeared from, then over at Jacob who was visibly uncomfortable around the emotional spirit of Pez and motioning as if he were more than ready to leave.

Heather kneeled down next to the sobbing soul and spoke quietly into his ear. "You've got two choices kid. You either learn to accept the pain of what you've done..." She reached down and turned his head so that his eye line was directly facing The River, the source and eventual destination of all life, "...or you go there and end it all. No more pain, no more memories. Your choice." She stood up and started to turn away from him. "Hope you make a better choice than you did before."

Heather moved to leave, but not before noticing the boy quiet down, sit up and stare at the River. She grabbed Jacob and teleported the two of them back tot the sanctuary's entrance.

Jacob looked back towards where the boy was. "You think he'll go back into the River?"

Heather shrugged. "Kinda hoping so."

Jacob shook his head with a slight smile. "Remind me never to get on your bad side. You can be cold!"

Heather felt no remorse for wishing the boy a speedy unmaking. "He deserves it and more for what that girl went through."

Jacob nodded. "That may be, but she still doesn't need to be taking over Sanctuaries. Too much chance she'll keep going from there. Speaking of which, should we go after her?"

Heather shook her head. "No. Our job was to get her out of this sanctuary. We did. I say that's a job well done."

"Yeah, but you know that girl's gonna go all evil elemental on some of those other people when they die, if they haven't already."

"Probably. Let's hope Roberto and John get that job. I don't think I could stop her after seeing what they did to her."

Jacob shrugged. "Yeah well, we'll see. Right now I say we get out of here before Mr. Cries-a-lot gets the balls to off himself and this whole place comes crumbling down."

Heather smiled as she stepped into the portal leading out of the Pezhman's sanctuary. "Good idea. Hopefully Leo's got a better mission lined up than this one. I want to find a good old fashion asshole rogue soul I can beat some sense into. That would be very cathartic right now."

Jacob again shook his head. "I really don't want to get on your bad side."

Fourteen

Thomas and Jack walked noiselessly through the garden. Thomas still felt a sense of elation at having survived his first encounter with a truly dangerous soul. It wasn't quite an adrenalin rush, but it felt very similar. He replayed the encounter in his head, very pleased with his part in it. Finally, Jack broke the silence.

"You did good there, lad. Damn girl kicked like a mule." He rubbed his side for emphasis. "I had to fight the urge to laugh at her though when you changed into that damned cat shape of yours though. She was NOT expecting that, I can tell you for certain."

"Think she'll behave now?"

"Who knows?" Jack shrugged. "She'll at least think twice before invading someone else's sanctuary, so that's a win. I think this might have been her first assault. She had strength but not much experience. Since we busted her with such apparent ease, she'll hopefully be too scared of us to try again. Regardless, Leo will keep an eye on her now and then. If she tries this again hopefully we'll know quickly and be there."

"So we don't toss them all back into the River, do we?"

Jack smiled. "Nay lad. Not if we can help it. Sometimes there's no other choice, but if there is… well, think of it as the death penalty when you were alive. Cops didn't use it on everyone caught breaking and entering. "

Thomas supposed that made sense. All in all, he had to admit this wasn't quite what he expected from a "rogue soul". He had expected more…. Alien. Evil. But this… this had been a punk kid. This seemed like someone he might have encountered when he was alive, though thinking back to what he could have done when he was alive he was suddenly glad he hadn't.

Jack stopped ahead of him. "Do you see it?"

Thomas looked around the garden. So far the entire place resembled the same green grass and blue flowers they'd seen since the wreckage of the city had disappeared. "I suppose you're not talking about flowers?"

"No lad." Jack shook his head. "Concentrate and look."

Thomas did as he was told. He scanned around. All directions looked identical. Even the sanctuary's owner had long since disappeared from view, leaving no marker to tell one way from another. Thomas wasn't entirely certain what he was supposed to be looking for. Each direction looked completely identical to every other direction. Like the same flowers had been replicated over and over. Ahead, behind, left, and right… all the same… Thomas stopped. To his right there actually was something different. A slight shimmer, almost invisible. Now that he saw it though, it definitely stood out against the surrounding landscape. "There." He pointed.

Jack smiled. "Aye. There's hope for you yet. Maybe." And with that he walked into the shimmer and disappeared from view.

"*So that's what a soft spot looks like…*" Thomas thought. Then he followed Jack back to the prime.

*****

Thomas stepped back into the dull world of the prime and found himself on a five by ten foot balcony in the middle of a large city. He didn't immediately recognize any of the surrounding buildings, so he couldn't be certain which city he was in. He did, however, see a number of flowerpots set neatly around the balcony. Each held a withered stalk that Thomas suspected once grew as a green plant with blue flowers. "Guess we found the inspiration for his sanctuary."

Jack nodded. "Aye. Usually like that. People hold onto the familiar. Whatever gave them peace in life is still what gives them the most joy in death."

Thomas supposed that made sense. "Any idea where we are?"

Jack shook his head as he looked around. "New York? Brisbane? Someplace with tall buildings. Spose we could site see and find out, but personally I think you should do a wee bit more training.

That wasn't bad but that's the low end of what we're likely to encounter. I'd rather you be a bit more prepared."

"Fair enough. Where to?"

Jack reached out and grabbed his shoulder. "Remember, doesn't really matter if you know where you are, only that you know where you're going. See if you can get us back to the hills that lead to the Training sanctuary. "

Thomas closed his eyes, pictured the view from the hills of Italy firmly in his mind, and then felt the surge of energy that told him he had done it correctly. He opened his eyes and noticed something he had missed before: a slightly off color shimmer. "And there's our doorway."

Jack smiled once more. "Aye. Very good. Now if we can just figure out how to get you to sense a bloody lockdown."

Fifteen

"Buster, are you absolutely certain of this?"

It had taken some time to track Sylvia down. She had often been characterized as both adventurous and social when she was alive, and this had not changed at all in death. If anything the two had expanded. She rarely remained in her own sanctuary, and while the Great Spirit had seen to it that he could keep track of Thomas, that connection had not expanded to Thomas's family members.

Thus Buster had been forced to start in her sanctuary and track her scent across four other realms before he finally found her on her Father's ranch watching wild stallions race across a field.

"Yes, Sylvia. There is no doubt to me that Roger Salazar is alive. I have seen him myself and smelled him myself. He may be changed, that I do not know, but it is him."

Sylvia hopped down from the fence, obviously trying to let this information soak in. "That's… it's just odd. Why would he not come tell me if he changed his mind? For that matter, why did he change his mind? Roger was never anything if not stubborn as a mule. When he had his mind set on something he did it, come hell or high water. He had that look when he told me his decision."

"I do not know for certain. I have reason to believe that someone interfered with his plans. Perhaps they helped him. Perhaps they just stopped him. I cannot tell you if this was the cause or if there were other reasons."

Sylvia considered for a moment, and then seemed to reach some internal decision that gave her some measure of peace from the look on her face. "Well, thank you for letting me know, Buster. I appreciate it."

"Are you going to seek Roger Salazar out?"

Sylvia shook her head. "No. I have said goodbye to him twice now. I'm not certain how well I could handle a third time. If he seeks me out I will see him, but if not… I have very fond memories of our time together. That will suffice for now."

Buster wasn't certain he understood. But then again despite his memories of a human life, there was still a great many things he did not understand about them anymore. If Sylvia chose not to seek out her life mate then it made his life easier. Potentially it kept her out of danger as well, which he viewed as a positive. Sylvia had always been kind to him. He felt very protective of her, but there were larger things at play, and his duties had been made very clear. "Very well, Sylvia. I must go."

"Thank you again, Buster. Really. I do appreciate it, and I always enjoy your company."

"I enjoy yours as well."

"Are you going back to Thomas?"

"Soon. I have other things I would check first. Then I will return to his side. I have left him with the human Jack Macintyre. He seems to have Thomas's best interest in mind."

Sylvia shook her head. "I still don't really understand why you think he should put himself in harm's way like that, but I'll trust you that it's the right thing for him."

"It is for the best, Sylvia. His cannot be the peaceful afterlife you have enjoyed. He must learn to take care of himself. Until he does, I will look after him."

"I know. Thank you for that as well, Buster."

"You are welcome. Goodbye Sylvia." And with that the German shepherd turned and trotted back to the Great Path.

Sixteen

"You would have been hit. And it would have hurt, let me tell ya."

Thomas looked down at the light on his chest. "You've got a flashlight beam."

Jack shrugged. "I can't do lasers. But some people can. And it hurts like the dickens, I can tell you that for certain."

Thomas smiled. "I'll keep that in mind. How exactly do you suggest I avoid flashli… er… lasers then."

"Shiny objects? I dunno. Last time we just took the guy down before he could hit us again. But we might not be so lucky next time. I'm rather hoping you can come up with an idea before it happens again."

Thomas shrugged. "I'll think about it." Thomas had made the mistake of asking Jack to show him some of the things he may get attacked by. So far he had been hit by guns, knives, swords, arrows, shuriken, a torch, a baseball bat, spiked gloves, rotten food, an ice ball, a chainsaw, a grenade, and now a flashlight beam. He'd faired very well against some, and not well at all against others. The chainsaw had been the worst, especially given the unexpected deftness with which Jack could wield it. It had been a crucial reminder that weight and size limits don't have to apply. The ice ball had also been particularly painful. Far more so that he had expected. Each new item had also reinforced one more lesson that Jack continued to tell him: expect anything. "It's hard to prepare for everything, isn't it?"

"Impossible. You prepare for what ye can. Sharp, blunt, energy, teleportation, projectile, explosive. But the details, aye well, there's too much, too many bloody variables. And you also need to be aware of things you might not consider a weapon. Think about the real world. Police shoot bean bags at rioters with dangerous results. Hells, with enough force, a piece of straw can pierce a tree. Here, force is completely dependent on the enemy's will and experience. For example…" In one smooth motion Jack produced and threw a large red ball. Having played one too many games of dodge ball in gym class, Thomas instinctively caught it.

It was like taking a cannonball to the stomach.

Thomas flew backwards, landing on his back. He hit the ground with the same force of falling off of a horse, but barely managed to keep hold on to the ball anyway. After confirming that he was, in fact, still in existence, if not very low on energy and in a great deal of pain, he raised the ball in meek victory. "Caught it."

Jack smiled. "Aye, lad. That you did. Not necessarily the best plan. Here, throw it back.'

Thomas took a deep breath. He tried to remind himself that this was training, and the more realistic it was, the more likely he was to survive a real fight, but Jack was enjoying this just a little too much. "Here you go." Thomas pictured his arm releasing with the force of a catapult. He was pleasantly surprised when he felt the ball leave his hand with what felt to be a brutal amount of force. It sped towards Jack in the blink of an eye, who acted as if he were going to catch it, then at the last second waved his hand instead. The ball blinked out of existence. "Nice try laddie. Remember what I told you when we first met. You can get rid of anything you create. Don't ever let yourself get taken down by your own creation."

That was it. Thomas decided he was tired of playing the part of the fool, and Jack's seeming inability to stop the more unusual things Thomas created gave him an idea of how to do it. Thomas pictured his favorite kung fu movie in his mind. He swung his arms around, slamming the base of his palms together and pushed out as he stepped forward with a loud "Hy-YAA". A flare of heat ignited from his outstretched hands, rocketing a fireball into Jack's chest. It hit the very surprised Scotsman square in the chest, tossing him backwards into the dirt. Thomas looked down at his hands, and over at Jack, who frantically patted out the fire on his Hawaiian shirt.

"I uh… I really didn't expect that to work."

Jack sat up, his shirt strangely showing no signs that it had a moment ago been engulfed in flames. Thomas expected him to kick the fight into full gear now, and prepared himself for an onslaught of flaming ice chainsaws that exploded. Instead, he was met with a hearty laugh. "Ah, laddie. That was good. Remember, when all else fails, the best defense is a good offense. If ye take them out, they can't hurt you. Now, help me up."

Thomas walked over and extended Jack his hand. Jack took it, but rather than pull himself up he rolled backwards, putting a foot in Thomas's stomach and flipped him. Thomas suddenly found himself flying over a cliff that a moment ago didn't exist. This time he kept himself from panicking, and instead froze himself in mid air.

Jack smiled down in approval. "Great stop. Almost makes up for you dropping your guard! Remember though, this isn't your world, so it's not your rules." Jack slammed his hand down and suddenly Thomas felt gravity take hold and once again he found himself plummeting to the ground. He fought down panic again and instead focused on his fall back safety net. The Pegasus swept beneath him, and, with slightly less pain than he would have had when he lived, Thomas landed in the saddle and swept up back to the cliff's edge, touching down next to Jack."

"Ya know, one of these days you're going to face someone who knows how to stop that blasted beast from coming into existence."

"Let's hope they can't also stop me from flying on my own then."

"Aye. Let's hope." Jack cocked his ear as if hearing something. He skewed his face then shook his head. "I gotta go for awhile, Thomas. Duty calls."

"Another job?"

"Aye."

"Where we going this time?"

Jack shook his head. "Not we, me. I'll handle this one on me own." Jack smiled, trying from the look of it to be more nonchalant than he succeeded at. "You've done enough for now. Take a break. Anyway, didn't ye wanna try and see your father?"

Thomas had wanted to take a break from training, and Jack was right that he was curious about seeing his dad after all this time, but something bothered him about Jack not wanting him to go. Did he feel he wasn't ready? Was this job that much more dangerous than the last? He could tell from the look on Jack's face that he really didn't want him following. He thought briefly of trying to trail him anyway. Unsure that he could actually pull it off, he finally decided not to push it. "Alright. Yeah. I guess you know how to find me?"

"Aye. I'll summon you back here when I finish. You'll know, trust me. Get back here as quickly as you can then, but in the mean time have fun and stay out of the River."

"Yeah. You too, Jack."

Jack smiled and vanished, leaving Thomas alone for one of the few times since his death.

Seventeen

Jack touched down on the cobblestone where Leo waited patiently. "This better be amazingly important, mate. I was starting to make real progress with Thomas."

Leo shook his head emphatically, almost adding his entire body into the motion. "Jack, would I bother you if this were not important? No. I would not. Yet here you are so there must be a reason. That reason is terrible. It's John and Roberto, Jack. We have lost them."

"What do ye mean, lost?"

"You know what I mean! Can you sense them? No, you cannot. They went on a job and they did not return. Lost. No Contact. You think I would call you if they went on vacation? No. They are gone, Jack."

Jack closed his eyes and tried to contact his old protégé, Roberto. Nothing. Jack sighed. "BLOODY HELLS. Do we even know if they joined the River this time?"

Leo shrugged. "I do not know, Jack. I suspect that is the case, but like the others I cannot say."

"You didn't witness it this time either, did you?"

"No. I healed them and sent them in, but the window, she closed as soon as they passed over. I tried to warn them, but I do not know if they understood. Just as before, I was unable to reopen the window. I am sorry, Jack, but you needed to know and I did not see the need to scare the new recruit, especially after his stellar performance during the last fight. Better that he keep his spirits high."

"Yeah well, maybe he bloody well should be scared. I am."

"Jack! That will not be helping us."

Jack shook his head, plopping back into a recliner that appeared behind him. "I'm sorry Leo, but that's ridiculous. We lost a member once every few years before. We've lost ten in the past year. That's what, 60% of our members?"

"62.5% my friend. You, me, Charlotte, Jacob, Heather, and Huang. That is what all left unless Thomas and Cho pass their initiations."

"Bloody hells, I'm beginning to wonder if that's a good idea. At least till we know what we're bloody dealing with. Are we getting sloppy, Leo? I don't feel like we've lost our edge. We always go in pairs. We scout the situation ahead of time. We train. As best we can tell we're following the same bloody guidelines the bloody Order's been following for five hundred bloody years and as far as I know we've never lost numbers like this in this bloody short a time!"

Leo stomped his foot angrily. A large group of birds took to the skies from the edges of the cliff. "What would you have us do, Jack? Quit? The rocks, Jack, maybe we go hide under them and let souls do as they would like?"

The unusual site of Leo getting upset caught Jack off guard. He knew that high emotions didn't help, but the frustration was unbearable. "We need to bloody well know who's hunting us and how to stop them. It's gotta be a concerted effort. Maybe a group of rogue souls laying in ambush? I mean, it's rare to lose a team, Leo. Five teams? All after loss of contact? No. That's as unnatural as it can get, even here."

Leo took a deep breath and sat down on an old stool that suddenly appeared next to him. "I agree. But again, Jack. What do you want to do about it? Obviously the safety protocols we put into place after Dominique and Marco did not work. What else should we try?"

Jack thought it over. They had often gone on single missions before, but Jack had ordered that stopped after the last disappearance. He'd also had Leo try harder to keep tabs on teams in danger zones. Neither looked to have made a difference. So it was time to step things up again. "We switch to threes. We've got to. We cover less territory but at this point we're already down so many members that's almost laughable. Jacob, Heather and Huang take as many jobs as they can. Let Charlotte continue training Cho. Alternate them out for two of the other members to give people a rest when needed. I'll continue training Thomas. You can use us as alternates too."

Leo leaned forward, speaking soft and somberly. "That's one team, Jack. We're letting a lot of rogue souls become established. Some we may have to write off as permanent sacrifices. Are you okay with that?"

Jack smiled, but there was no mirth in it. Only sadness. "No mate. I'm not even close to okay with that. But I'm not seeing a better option, are you? I assume Charlotte's pushing Cho as much as she dares. I know I'm bloody well pushing Thomas faster than I would like. That boy's got power, Leo. He caught me off guard and nearly fried me. If I hadn't been in the training sanctuary he could have dissipated me. But like all Changers, he still can't even bloody see a lockdown, much less break it. It could be the ultimate glass jaw for him."

Leo shrugged. "He's an aspect of Change, Jack. They react differently than aspects of Stability, you know that. What's easy for you will not be the same for him, and visa versa."

"Aye, Leo. I know. There's a reason we haven't recruited one the entire time I've been here. But…"

Leo finished his sentence. "But he's powerful and we're a desperate."

A weak amount of mirth returned to Jack's smile. "Yeah. Something like that. Let's hope his astounding imagination is enough to make up for his total lack of defense."

Leo stared at him for a few moments before finally shrugging. "Very well, Jack. Do you want to tell the others or would you like a me to do it?"

"I'll go check on Charlotte and Cho before I go back to get Thomas. I'll leave it to you to inform the other three."

Leo nodded. "Thanks, Jack. I will call you if we need your team to a join in a raid."

"Good. I'll try and get Thomas ready for initiation as soon as possible. With any luck we'll find another couple of recruits as soon as he's ready. In the mean time, be careful. If we are being hunted there's no guarantee they'll stick to waiting on us. They could actually come after us."

"Do not worry about it, Jack. I do not plan to leave my plateau anytime soon, and if anybody makes it past my pets, I'll be long gone before they can get to me. I am a watcher and a finder, my friend. I will continue to leave the fighting to you."

*****

Thomas looked around the dull and drab hills of the Prime. The cold hit him once more, but this time he knew to immediately adjust how he felt it. Within moments it felt comfortable once again. Thomas glanced about, taking in the details, trying to determine exactly what he was looking at. The weather looked like it might be summer, or perhaps fall. He doubted it remained spring.

He'd been gone longer than that, hadn't he? It definitely didn't look yet like winter. How long had it been since he had died? Three months? Four? Or had it actually only been one or two here in the 'real world'? It was tough to say without finding a calendar or newspaper somewhere. Without sleep, and with night coming whenever Jack deemed it necessary rather than a standard cycle, it was amazingly difficult to keep track of how much time passed here where it still held meaning.

He wondered if he should see Shari or not. The urge to do so was almost overwhelming. He wanted to know how the baby was doing and how she had held up. More than anything else he just wanted to see her face and hear her voice. But the last meeting with her had been excruciatingly painful and the burning memory of it gave him pause. He had had much to keep him occupied since then. Perhaps that and the time that had passed would make a meeting much less painful. If she had moved on, even a little bit, that would probably help to.

"Or, perhaps it will be worse."

He thought about what it would feel like if she had met someone. What if she had tried to drown her sorrows in the arms of another man? He couldn't blame her, after all, he couldn't be there for her. Life was, as they say, for the living. She should move on. *"Just not too soon..."*.

Thomas shook his head. He was hopeless, he knew. He would be disappointed either way. Maybe it was best he not see her yet. Still, his father was supposed to be watching over her. So if he were going to track him down, starting with Shari would be the most logical first step. If he happened to see her during that time then surely....

"Ahh. Thomas. I thought perhaps you would come this way."

Thomas turned to see a tall familiar figure approaching. "Brother Coughlin. Were you waiting for me here?"

The Brother smiled a very disarming and innocent smile. Thomas wasn't entirely certain yet whether to trust it. "Yes and no. I have many things that call for my attention, but I left a marker here to let me know if you passed. I was curious how you had faired since our last meeting."

"Fine, thank you. And thank you for your tip from mythology. It was extremely helpful."

Brother Coughlin turned and began walking, making it clear that Thomas should follow along. He did. "So you did it, did you? You created a Pegasus?"

"Yes. And it's been a big help many times since. "

"Good. I'm surprised to see you here alone. On leave from the Society?"

"The Society?"

Brother Coughlin tilted his head curiously at Thomas. "Yes. The Society of the Shield. The order your friend Jack is attempting to get you into? Or, at least, I assume he's still trying to get you into."

"Oh." Thomas considered. "*We have a name? I guess that makes sense.*" He tried not to let his surprise register. "Yes. The Society of the Shield. I'm taking a small break from training. Jack had some business to attend to."

Brother Coughlin let loose another smile. "You do not know much of the group you are looking to spend your afterlife with, do you?"

Thomas realized that he hadn't really given it much thought. He'd been extremely focused on how to survive his new job; there hadn't been much time for discussion of the group's history. Or, he realized, much of anything about them aside from what they did. "I know the important parts, I guess. I know they do good work. They help people."

"I suppose. They mean well anyway."

Thomas considered. Obviously Brother Coughlin seemed to know more than was letting on. It was clear that he distrusted Jack and his comrades. It wasn't yet clear if Thomas should believe a word he had to say. Then again, aside from being the first dead person Thomas had met, he supposed he had no real reason to trust Jack. To his knowledge Jack had never lied to him, but at the same time, had he told him the whole truth? Thomas shook his head. There remained still so much that he didn't know. "*How is it that death is so much more complicated than life?*"

More information had to be better than too little. It seemed obvious Brother Coughlin wanted to give him some of that information. What could it hurt to collect it then make decisions from there? "So um. You don't seem to have a very high opinion of them, do you?"

"Is it that obvious?" Brother Coughlin grinned again. "Don't get me wrong, young Thomas. It is like I said, they mean well. But they are a violent organization with an obsessive view of their own rules. They do not care what is right or wrong. Anyone who breaks their rules is guilty and must be punished. It does not matter what they have already endured or their reason for breaking the rules to begin with."

Thomas thought back to his encounter with the punk female. There seemed little justification for what she had done, and the soul she was after certainly didn't seem to deserve what he was getting. No, that was a good mission. "I'm not sure if you and I are talking about the same group."

"Oh, I believe we are. I've watched them the better part of a hundred years now. You have seen them only a few months. As I said, they mean well. No doubt they often do well, but just as often they have denied justice to those who sought it the only way available to them."

"What do you mean?"

"There is no court system here. And thanks to groups like your Order, no higher authority left to appeal to. So let us say you were murdered in life. The murderer escaped justice while alive and eventually died unrepentant to find himself in a world where he can still do or be anything he wants without punishment. Would it be so outrageous that you or your fellow victims might seek retribution? Might wish to right the wrongs done to you when you were weak here in a world where the tables could be turned and your righteousness makes you strong?"

There was certainly logic to Brother Coughlin's argument. "I guess. I mean, I don't suppose I'd thought about it."

Brother Coughlin's smile was gone, replaced with a look of distinct sadness. "It happens more often than you might realize, Thomas. When it does, your friends deem the former victim a 'rogue soul' and attack it. They defend the guilty, and the righteous often find themselves returned to the River, their thirst for justice unsatisfied…"

Thomas suddenly thought back to what Jack had told him when he had first mentioned what he did. "I won't lie to you, there's some fucked up sanctuaries out there, and some times we're charged with protecting people and things that we find abhorrent." Still, there must be a reason… unless, as Brother Coughlin had said, that reason was just "these are the rules". Thomas had seen more than his fair share of that in life, where rules were made by one group and another had been left to enforce them. Who made the rules up for his society? Who was even in their society outside of Jack and Leo? Thomas had been so busy with training, that it had never even occurred to him to ask.

"Listen, my son. I'm not here to turn you against your friends. I just hate to see someone used for their abilities without their knowing it. You are special, there's no doubt about it, and many people apparently know it. Your Order friends and your guardian's master just happen to be the two looking to take advantage of it. If their goals work for you, then do as you will, but do not let yourself be forced into something simply because you do not know the facts."

Thomas really didn't know what he wanted to do at this point. He realized suddenly that he hadn't been since he died. Everything had been about Shari up until he had passed over. Strangely now that he thought about it, everything he had done had been about trying to stay distracted from Shari since he had died. He hadn't really considered what he wanted from his afterlife aside from getting passed this mourning period so that he could see her again.

Suddenly something in what Brother Coughlin had said registered as strange. "Wait, what was that about my guardian's master?"

"The dog you have protecting you. Such guardians are rare. His master must have a keen interest in you."

"You mean, who, my dad?"

A look of brief confusion passed over Brother Coughlin's face. "You don't know, do you? I'm sorry, Thomas, I would have thought your friends would be more forthcoming than they have apparently been. No, it is not your father. He has a great love for you and your safety, but not anywhere near the power to create that beast. But it is not my place to disclose the secrets of others. If they have not told to you I'm sure there is probably a reason. Now, I must be going. It was good to see you, son. I am glad you are doing well. Are you heading to your sanctuary?"

"Buster? Working for someone else?" There had to be some mistake. "Huh? Oh. Sorry. Yes. Probably. I was thinking of seeing if I could find my dad."

"Wonderful. I'll tell you what. If you're heading home I'll have him meet you there. My journey will be taking me past where I expect he is."

Thomas tried to mask his confusion. "That would be great. Thank you, Brother Coughlin."

If Coughlin noticed, he didn't let on. Instead he smiled broadly and kindly while stating: "Do not mention it, my son. Good fortune to you."

And with that Brother Coughlin turned and began walking away, fading from sight within moments. Out of habit, Thomas once again took a deep breath. He had thought he was finally getting a grip on his life post death. Now he realized he had more questions than ever. First and foremost being, just whom should he really trust?

Eighteen

Jack followed his link back to training sanctuary, and then reached out to find the ones leading to John and Roberto. *"Nothing."* He sighed. He knew that would have been the result. Leo wouldn't have been wrong about something like this. But he had to try. Stranger things had been known to happen. Instead Jack reached out and searched for the link spinning off toward Charlotte. He found it quickly enough and traced it out. As he had suspected, it lead straight to her sanctuary. She'd long preferred doing her training there instead of the Order's training sanctuary. She was a very formidable opponent anywhere, but the extra control and power that came with being in her home sanctuary gave her an edge she could not resist when she pushed someone else's limits.

Jack followed the link, and within moments found himself in blistering sunlight, surrounded by scraggly mesquite bushes and trees. His nose was immediately assaulted by a scent that combined the surrounding mesquite with a tinge of sulfur. How Charlotte could ever consider this a "sanctuary" was beyond him. He supposed that, at the very least, it made it less appealing to any rogue souls that might accidentally stumble across it.

Jack again reached out to the link and followed it. The sun bore down miserably, and within moments he began sweating profusely. He tried to cool himself down, but it didn't work. Not that he had figured it would, but it was more habit than anything else these days. He could try lowering the ambient temperature, and might or might not succeed in the resulting battle of wills with Charlotte that would inevitably occur, but the waste of energy would do little aside from making her laugh when he did actually find her. So he merely did his best to put the heat out of his mind and followed the link. If she hadn't changed things up much, she wouldn't be more than a half an hour hike in anyway. He'd dealt with the miserable surroundings for that long before, he would do it again.

The sweat completely drenched Jack within a few kilometers. He stopped and pulled a canteen from his belt that appeared there full of cold water. He took a large swig, then closed his eyes and poured some of the remaining contents onto his head. It was amazingly refreshing. He shook his hair and opened his eyes to see a blur of motion knock the canteen from his hand. The blur spun around again and Jack realized a split second before a foot would have connected with his jaw that he needed to drop. He hit the ground with a practiced move, rolling back, using his arms and mind to push himself further backwards. Nothing stopped him and he came up standing about ten foot away, cricket bat in hand.

A small Asian man in dusty grey martial arts clothes bowed before him. "Forgive me, teacher. Master Charlotte instructed me to test my speed against you."

Jack smiled, dropped his bat, which disappeared before it hit the ground, and stood straight once more. "Hello Cho. Aye, that sounds like our Charlotte. Guess you shouldn't have hit the canteen first. You might have gotten me."

"She advised I must hit both to pass her test."

"Ah. Aye. That would sound like her as we…" Jack's sentence was interrupted by a hundred pounds of cowgirl landing on his back. Jack barely kept his footing as a small pair of arms locked around his neck and a small pair of blue jeaned legs locked boots around his waste.

"Jack! Sweetheart! How the hell are ya?" Charlotte pulled herself over his shoulder and planted a kiss on his cheek.

As so often happened around Charlotte, Jack was glad that he no longer had a physical body to throw out of whack. "Charlotte, lass, I swear it's more dangerous to be your friend than it could possibly to be to be your enemy."

Charlotte somehow managed to swing herself around his body without ever letting go, so that she was now wrapped around him from the front. She looked into his eyes with a mock pout on her face. "Jackie, sweetheart, you know that's just not true. I'm much meaner to people I don't like."

That Jack had to agree with, as scary as the thought was. Charlotte liked to refer to herself as a firecracker. That seemed to Jack to be as apt a description as he could imagine. She was a small loud bundle of energy guaranteed to get the attention of anyone around her. Jack nodded to her student. "So how is Cho here doing?"

Charlotte dropped back down to her own feet, giving Jack a good foot over her. "Cho, how the hell are you?"

"Learning, Masters. But I still have much to learn."

Jack chuckled. "Cho, I hate to break it to you, but there will always be much to learn. The trick is to figure out how to stay out of the River while you do so."

"Master Charlotte has been very good at instructing me in those lessons."

Charlotte smiled. "And as long as you keep producing that rice wine stuff I'll keep teaching ya! Speaking of teaching, where's the Thomas kid? Figured first time you stepped in here, you'd introduce us."

Jack chuckled again. "I don't know if the lad's ready for you, Charlotte. But whether he is or not, I gave him a bit of a reprieve."

"You always were a soft teacher."

"You bitched loud enough when I was training you. Sides, wasn't really my decision. Leo wanted to talk to me alone. Think I'd like to do the same with you. Sorry Cho, but can you go… err… practice a wee bit?"

"Absolutely, masters." Cho bowed, then turned and left quickly.

"Really wish you'd drill that whole 'Master' thing out of him."

Charlotte laughed loudly. "Tried that. Says 'a teacher should be treated with respect'. The fact that I was born twenty years after him and died twenty years before him doesn't seem to deter him either. But hey, who am I to argue?"

"Given that you seem to like it, I'd wager it's one of the few things you don't actually argue with."

"Oh Jack, you always did know how to flatter a girl."

Jack blinked and realized they were now standing in what looked like a saloon from an American Wild West movie. A colorful assortment of characters livened the place up while simultaneously fitting in perfectly. From the unbathed ruffians playing poker to the overly enthusiastic piano player, each played their part in holding up the movie-like setting. "This is your idea of private?"

Charlotte snapped her fingers over the bar as she took a seat. "Bartender, two of your best rot guts. Relax jack. They're all automatons. Not even a homunculus among them. It's just like being alone, except less boring. "

"Charlotte, wherever you are at, boring will be a word you will never hear used."

"Again with the flattery." Charlotte downed the shot glass set in front of her, then shot the second one as well. "Ahh, that's good. Sorry, I guess I should have asked. Do you want something?"

Jack shook his head. "Got a good beer?"

"Does a bear shit in the woods?"

"Pretty sure it goes wherever it wants, but that's not an appetizing thought. On second thought give me one of those."

"Bartender, just give us the bottle. Oh, and I guess give my buddy here a glass." It only took a few moments before the bartender obediently obliged. Charlotte filled up the glass and slid it over in front of Jack, then took a large swig off the bottle. "So what's this you wanted to talk about?"

Jack took a deep breath and a long swig, then spoke. "It's John and Roberto. We've… we've lost connection with them."

Charlotte stared at him for a moment, as if trying to comprehend what he'd just said. "DAMN IT!" She spun and hurled the bottle at the mirrored wall behind the bar. Both bottle and wall shattered into hundreds of pieces. For a moment the entire room went silent, then as if on queue, went back to its regular routine. "BARTENDER! Another god damned bottle! Who is doing this Jack? It's too much to be coincidence."

"I don't know, Charlotte, but Leo and I both agree with you."

Charlotte gripped her newly acquired bottle so tightly that Jack expected it to shatter. "I'm going to find them, Jack. I'm going to find them and beat the holy living crap out of them. I'm going to rip them apart limb by limb, beat them mercilessly with their own arms then have them watch as I throw each arm and leg in the River."

Jack nodded, knowing better than to interrupt her rant. When he was certain she had finished he reassured her. "Charlotte, while I would pay to see that, whomever or whatever is behind this has taken down most of our membership and so far no one's escaped to tell the tale. We need to keep our heads about us, lass."

"Oh, my head is fully attached. Now when I find them…"

Jack risked breaking in. He knew he had to calm her down before she actually left to go hunting on her own. "You'll be ready for them, I know. We're going out in threes from here out though. Heather, Huang and Jacob will be doing jobs straight through for now, and I want you and Cho prepared to step in and assist as soon as possible."

"He's ready."

"Don't rush him just so you can get back into the fight, Charlotte. Getting him tossed in the River won't bring Dominique or any other team members back."

Charlotte sighed, turned the bottle up and downed half of it, then threw it into the mirror, which had only just been repaired, shattering both again. With a huff she spoke again in a very low, determined voice. "Fine. He's almost ready. I'd planned on inducting him within the month. I'll make sure he's ready before I do."

"Good. I'll go as quick as I dare with Thomas. If need be we'll join together. I think he can handle himself in most situations, so long as he doesn't get locked down."

"That's right, he's a changer, isn't he. You think he'll actually be able to work?"

"I think so. He's strong, Charlotte. He's done things I didn't think could be done."

"Yet he still can't see a lock, can he?"

Jack shook his head. "No. It's a glass jaw."

"And one that will get exploited unless his partners can keep him loose. I'll trust you that he's worth the extra risk."

"He better be. We're running out of other options. Can I get me one of those bottles?"

Nineteen

Thomas found his way back to the clearing where he had been killed. That thought still seamed unreal, even after all he had seen. He looked over at the sweater Shari had tied around the tree as a memorial. It was still there, but much more worse for the wear. The elements had not been kind to it. Thomas sighed. Soon it would give way and fall. It was amazing how fleeting your life could be. A blink of an eye and it passes. A split second and it's gone. Only memories remaining, and even those fading with each passing moment. If not for his child, would there have even been any record at all that he had existed 20 years from now?

Thomas turned and spied the now familiar looking blur that marked a portal. This one, however, he really had no need to spot. This one he felt strongly enough that he could have found it blind. He crossed over into the bright sunlight and brilliant color of his sanctuary. While he still didn't believe he could stay here for long periods without getting bored out of his mind, it always felt amazingly good to return. Like it or not, this was definitely home.

"You look good, son."

Thomas spun away from the tower he was about to step into. Standing at the edge of the cliff, stood a Hispanic man about his height and only slightly older. It had never really occurred to him just how young his father had been when he had died. "DAD!"

Thomas rushed forward. His dad met him halfway and both gave the other a strong embrace. "My son, it is so great to see you." Thomas's father pulled back to arm's length. "Let me look at you. You lucked out; you kept your mother's looks. Must be how you managed to land that amazing fiancée of yours."

"So you really have been keeping an eye on Shari?"

"I have. She is doing well, son. At least as well as she could be in these circumstances. She's strong, like your mother. You really did choose well with her. I am sorry you did not get to spend more time with her."

Thomas smiled sadly. "Thank you, Dad. It means a lot to me to know you like her."

Roger Salazar looked around, taking stock of his surroundings. "And this place? I am glad to see your sanctuary is from one of my favorite places."

Thomas put his arm around his dad and walked out to look over the cliff. "This was the most amazing vacation spot when I was a kid. We always had so much fun here during the summers. I guess subconsciously I couldn't think of any better place to wake up to when I died. Now I can't think of anything I'd rather it be."

"You did very well." Roger cocked his head slightly to the side. "Except for the monkeys. I do not recall those being at our camp site."

"No," Thomas smiled. "Those are… recent additions."

Roger turned and admired the tower behind them. "That seems like it may not have been there either. I do not believe we would have spent so much time setting up our tents if it had."

Thomas smiled proudly. "That's my home here. Based somewhat loosely on Aunt Martha's light house."

"Very loosely I would say."

"Care to see the inside?"

"Absolutely." Roger put his arm around his son's shoulders as they walked back to the tower door. Thomas could hardly contain himself. "I'm talking to my DAD!"

*****

Thomas had been eleven when his father had passed away. He had tried to be the man of the house from that point forward, to be strong for his mother. He'd put up walls telling himself that he had dealt well with his father's passing. He realized now, setting across from him once more, that that had been a total lie. He'd walled up his sorrow, along with most of his other happier memories of his father, choosing instead to try and not feel anything at all rather than try and actually work through his real feelings. It had been strangely easy to forget just how much the man had meant to him when he was alive, and how much it had really hurt when he was gone.

 Thomas sat for what was probably several hours just catching up. It might have actually been days, he wasn't entirely certain, nor did it matter to him. He had his dad back. That was the important thing.

"Honestly son, I can not even tell you now what it was I remembered. It must have been horrible though. It was enough that even the presence of your mother could not lift the gloom. I really thought I would be lost in the darkness. So I decided to end it. Better to cease to be than become something I feared. I would have done it too, had I not encountered someone else just before I returned to the River."

"Brother Coughlin?" Thomas offered.

"Yes. He has an amazing gift, Thomas. He…. he helped me when I was certain no one could help me. He took the memories from me. I was more content than I had been since… well probably since our last camping trip. "

"Why didn't you go back to Mom?"

Roger Salazar looked down, a sad expression drifting over his face. "I do not know, son. It is just…. It just did not seem the right thing to do. I had left her. I could not bring myself to return and force myself back into her life once more."

"So what are you going to do now?"

Thomas's father smiled, some of the sadness dissipating. "I will continue to do what I can for you. I will watch over your fiancée and your child. I remember what it was like to be in your situation, my son. It took a full year before I could comfortably spend more than a few moments around you and your mother without all of us bursting into tears. Even then it never became easy. You will struggle to be there for her. I will be there for you."

Thomas reached out and put his hand on his father's hand. It still felt amazingly unreal that he could be having this conversation. "Thanks, dad."

"It is what I can do. I was not able to do much for you in life. I can at least try and be some service now. Besides, George, Shari's father, and I get along very well. He too is watching over them. It gives me someone interesting to talk to. Shari and the baby are both doing very well, by the way. She thinks it will be a boy, but I do not think so. George and I both feel you are going to have a bouncing baby girl on your hands."

"A girl." It still didn't feel real that Shari was having a baby. His baby. His baby girl? "Wow. I...."

His father reached over and squeezed his hand. "It is okay, son. It will take some time. I was there for every day of your mother's pregnancy, and even then it did not feel real until you were actually born. Trust me when I say that you can love your child from here, and still be there, even if they do not know it. I probably made more of your school events than I would have if I had still been with you."

That made Thomas smile. And perhaps blush a bit at what his father might have seen. "Were you at the horrible school play where I botched all or my lines?"

Roger smiled. "Yes son. You did not do as bad as you thought you had."

"Oh, I'm pretty sure I did. But thank you. I always felt you were probably there, watching over me. It's good to know it was real."

"And you will be there for your child. Maybe not as much as you would like, and no doubt not in the way that she and Shari would prefer, but you will be there. And just as you knew I was there, she will know, deep down, that you are there for her."

Thomas didn't know whether to laugh or cry. He did both. The smile was genuine, and so were the tears, when he stood up and hugged his father once more. "Thanks again, Dad."

"You are welcome, son. Now, I must go. Be careful. I will try and check back in with you to let you know how your family is doing."

"I feel better knowing you're watching over them."

Roger Salazar smiled, then turned without another word and walked down the stairs.

Twenty

Thomas was racing through the trees in cat form when Jack arrived. The scent was a dead give away that something had changed. Buster had been right, there was a strange tinge of flying food in Jack, even when he was in human form. "Buster…"

He had meant to ask his father what he knew of Buster, and whether it was possible that he was being controlled by something more powerful. He didn't like that idea at all, but he couldn't rule it out now. Brother Coughlin had told him many things, and so far, none of it seemed a lie. He was also responsible for saving his father. For that alone he owed the man the benefit of the doubt. But if that were true… *"This is ridiculous. Every answer I get creates twenty more questions."* Thomas shook his massive head. The only thing he could think to do was continue to gather answers anyway. He saw one of the four-legged foods that he had placed in the sanctuary. He considered giving it a chase, losing himself in the hunt.

"No." He shook his large fanged head. Now was not the time. Jack would have some answers. At the very least he could confirm some of what Brother Coughlin had said. That alone might be enough to help him know better who to trust.

He turned and began following the scent trail that emanated from Jack. He considered what to tell Jack, and how. Last time he had been completely forthcoming about his meeting with Brother Coughlin. Now he wasn't so sure that was the best idea. If Jack was using him, keeping information from him, it might be good to do the same. The less they knew he knew, the more chance they might accidentally say something that would confirm or dismiss his suspicions. He hated feeling like he might not be able to trust Jack or Buster, but he felt it was better to be safe than sorry.

Thomas leapt up the rough path leading back to his Tower. He probably should move the entrance further out. That way it would be more secure, like Leo's. He wasn't entirely sure how to do that. He supposed he could add it to the list of questions he would need to ask Jack. He noticed an odd tugging sensation. It felt strangely like something was being pulled from him. He wasn't sure what it was, but it didn't trust letting it go either, so he focused his mind on it and gave a mental yank back on it. The sensation stopped, so he continued.

He came slowly over the top of the cliff's edge, fighting back the need to crouch and slink. It was odd; the more he was in this body, the more difficult it became to fight its natural instincts.

"Nice kitty. Care for some bourbon?" Jack was sitting in his lounge chair again, this time at the edge of the cliff overlooking the valley. "It burns like the dickens, but the woman who makes it swears it's the nectar of the gods, so you'll love the taste."

Thomas smiled as he transformed back to human form. He still wanted to know more about what was going on, but he had to admit to himself that it was a lot more difficult to be suspicious of Jack when you were in his presence. "I suppose I can try some."

"Good. Pull up a chair. Tried to get us a bloody sunset, but you seem to have gotten a little better control since I was here last."

"So that's what that was. Good. I would hope your lessons were paying off." Thomas pulled up a canvas lawn chair and a glass. He handed the glass to Jack as he sat down, and as Jack filled it, Thomas lowered the sun until bright pink and purple colors painted the skyline above a barely visible but brilliantly orange orb of light. He then took the glass from a Jack, who followed by raising his own.

"A toast. To friends found and friends lost."

Thomas wondered briefly if Jack knew he'd talked to his dad, but decided the toast was probably directed elsewhere. "Friends found and friends lost then. And hopefully found again."

"Aye. One can hope."

Thomas took a sip off the glass. It burned the back of his throat like molten lead, but as Jack had promised it finished off with an amazing flavor. "You know, I could probably spend an entire afterlife traveling from sanctuary to sanctuary sampling people's food and drinks."

"Aye." Said Jack with a smile. "I know that indeed. In fact, I've pretty much done that very thing much of my death."

They sat in silence for some time. Unnatural silence for Jack. Thomas was unsure whether to broach the subject of the silence first, or ask him questions about what Brother Coughlin had said. After the silence continued unabated, Thomas decided on the latter, since he'd spent more time trying to formulate how to ask that than anything else. "Jack. Who do we actually work for?"

"Everybody. Or nobody. Guess it depends on your view."

"Not a very helpful answer."

"Sorry lad. Just no really quick or easy answer that."

"Does our little group have a name?"

"Aye. Officially we're the Society of the Shield. I say that it's the official name cause very few blokes use it anymore. Somewhere along the way, maybe even when it was founded, somebody decided groups like ours needed a name. Twas all the rage once I understand."

"Why do we do what we do?"

Jack shrugged. "Needs done."

"What happens if it doesn't?"

Jack cocked his head towards Thomas. "Bad things lad. Very bad things. Why all the questions all the sudden? You've been pretty quiet by the campfires of late."

Thomas shrugged. "Guess I had some time to think since leaving. Realized I knew the what, some of the where, and some of the how, but not much of the who or why."

Jack smiled, but there was a touch of sadness to the smile that Thomas wasn't entirely certain of the source. "Fair enough I suppose. Listen, there's a whole rich history in the job you're doing. I don't even know all of it. Leo knows more than me and he probably doesn't know half of it himself. But there's darkness out there. And it seems to be growing. There's more and more jobs popping up and fewer of us to deal with them than there once was.

So I've had to concentrate on teaching you how to stay out of the River. I figure odds are you're more likely to get someone trying to take your head off than you are demanding to talk your ears off about our past. So that's where I've put me focus."

Thomas considered. It seemed a fair answer. He still had many questions, but the idea that Jack was trying to arbitrarily use him appeared less likely. Jack seemed to at least believe he genuinely needed him, and that the job they were doing really needed done. "I guess that's fair."

Jack laughed a laugh that was unexpectedly loud. "Fair. Aye. Not a lot of that these days, is there? You know, I thought when I died…. I really thought at the time that was the end of my goodbyes. Either the Good book was right and I was headed to a place of endless happiness, or it was complete rubbish and I would just cease to be. Either way I was prepared. But this… After all this time I am still not prepared for this. But I believe it needs doing, lad, and if what I've been told is true, or even partly true, then we're needed. Maybe now more than ever."

Something about Jack's tone raised a number of flags with Thomas. It was normally completely happy-go-lucky, but now it was almost… scared? "What's going on, Jack?"

Jack stared off at the sunset, sipping his bourbon slowly. "I don't know, laddie. Look, Leo doesn't feel you should know this, but I think you've a right to. Especially if you're having second thoughts. Now's the time to get out if you think you don't have the stomach for what we do."

"What am I not supposed to know?"

"We think we're being hunted."

"Hunted?"

Jack nodded his head, still staring out at the setting sun with a distant look in his eyes. "Aye, lad. We had 16 members a year ago. We have six now. At first we thought it was a run of bad luck, but bad luck only goes so far. "

Thomas leaned back, thinking on the severity of what Jack was telling him and what it might mean for his own future. "Ten people in one year? How many of you do you usually lose?"

Jack shook his head. "Accidents happen. It's a dangerous job, this. But even so, we might lose a member every couple of years or so."

Thomas downed the last of his bourbon, and then decided to replace it with a frosted mug of cider instead. He downed half of that while he thought seriously about what Jack had just said. Ten of the 16 souls doing the job he now trained for were dead in the last year. Or re-dead. Whatever you called it here. "So were they, what, thrown back into the River? De-rezzed or whatever you call it?"

"De-rezzed? You mean dissipated?"

"Yeah. That."

Jack shrugged. "I dunno lad. In every loss, there's been a common thread. Once we lose the link to them, we lose the link to the sanctuary they're in as a whole."

"So you haven't seen any bodies or anything, they're just… gone."

"Likely wouldn't be a body to see, but you have the gist of it right. We haven't been able to confirm they've been killed, no. We haven't even been able to go in and face whatever did it. They go on a job just like we did. Except the window Leo views things through shuts, and pretty quickly there after their connection to the Training sanctuary is severed. Without either, it's pretty much impossible to relocate the sanctuary. I mean, it'd be damned unlikely Leo could find the one we were in the other day. There's billions of sanctuaries out there, and we only knew where that one was cause Leo read signs of trouble there. Without those signs, he's not likely to stumble across it again. And unless we back track to where we came out in the prime, we'd be unlikely to know our way back either. Even then there'd be some luck involved in that a soft spot can be hardened, and if it is we're bloody unlikely to be able to find and break through it."

Thomas considered. He had known the job offer was dangerous. This didn't really change much of his feelings about it. Still, he wanted to know that he was doing it for the right reasons, and with what Brother Coughlin had told him, he still wasn't positive on that front. He changed the sunset to sunrise, since this conversation didn't seem like it needed more darkness, then continued. "So… what really happens if we didn't do what we did? I mean, I know like that guy we helped would have suffered, and that alone is probably a good reason, but is that it? Is that the very bad things you were talking about?"

"No lad." Jack shook his head. "I mean, that's bad and all, but truth be told some of those bastards we defend deserve it and worse. But we do what we do because we're told if we don't, far worse things show up from it."

"What kind of worse?"

It wasn't Jack that answered. "The old ones return."

Jack and Thomas both looked over their shoulder to see Buster plodding up to their chairs.

"Your doggie's right. Legends say that you can combine enough souls together, you get something more. If we let rogue souls take in other souls for too long, they may become unstoppable. I dunno that it's true, but I've seen enough to trust it could be."

Buster sat down on his haunches and nodded. "It is not legend. It is real. The stories that now exist of ancient gods and mythical monsters have a basis in reality. Back then Sanctuaries were conquered as countries on the Prime. When enough conquests had been done, the conquerors could use that power to manifest avatars in the Prime. They could affect things there as well as here. Wars were fought. Souls were taken, ravaged. Destroyed. Some gained enough power to continue reincarnating themselves. They were strong enough that if they found themselves in the River they could stay together until they were reborn. They would slowly get their old memories back in their new bodies. Their war would continue, often as gods among mortals."

Thomas shook his head. This was… hard to believe at best. "So if that's true, how did it stop? I mean, if you've really got a group of immortals duking it out, shouldn't they still be doing so?"

Jack shrugged. "Legends say they were sorta betrayed by one of their own. He tricked them and trapped them into what we now call the 'Glacier of Gods and Monsters'. Then threw himself in after it when all was done. "

Buster again agreed. "Jack Macintyre speaks truly. The Final One sacrificed itself with the other immortals. That was a few thousand cycles ago. There has been a few since then who have attempted to gain such power themselves. None have grown in power enough to become truly immortal. The last truly powerful one was created close to seven hundred years ago. It was after him that the groups like the Society of the Shield were created. "

Thomas had watched Jack's expression. It had moved from surprise into distrust and back to surprise, the more Buster spoke. Combined with what Brother Coughlin had told him, he too grew very wary of Buster's sudden insights. "I'm guessing what he's telling you is true, Jack?"

"Aye, laddie. I think so. Except it's in far more detail than I suspect even Leo knows. How do you know this, dog?"

Buster seemed to consider for a moment. "I am an aspect of another who knows."

Jack leapt from his chair, producing his bat from somewhere. "You're a bloody homunculus? I knew it!"

Buster seemed unflustered at Jack's sudden movement. "I am not a homunculus. I am a lesser soul. And there is no need for that, Jack Macintyre. I was assigned to be Thomas's guardian. It is a job I do willingly. So long as you are no threat to him, I will be no threat to you."

Thomas wasn't entirely certain this was good or bad news. "Okay, first off, what's a homunculus, and what's the difference between it and a 'lesser soul' or whatever it was you said you were?"

Jack answered, still not dropping his bat but not taking any further steps towards Buster either. "A homunculus is a memory given its own shape. You could, for example, separate that cat of yours out into its own body. You wouldn't be able to change into it while it was separated, and it would have its own mind based on what it had of its original memories and what your orders were. It'd still pretty much do what you told it to. Not many people can pull that off."

"So, the butterfly that lead us to Ardru?"

"Likely a homunculus. Yeah. A lesser soul, that's sorta different in that it was a complete soul that was bound to someone else. Least that's what history says. Haven't come across one in my death time. That's sorta the thing we're trying to stop from ever happening."

"My soul was given to The Great Spirit long before your order began to oppose such things, Jack Macintyre."

Thomas felt a pang of disappointment as those words sunk in. "So you were never actually my dog, were you?"

The dog cocked his head at him. "Yes, I was. I still am."

Jack lowered his bat. "Okay, if your goal was to confuse the hell out of everyone, you've succeeded admirably."

Buster turned his gaze back and forth between the two men. When he spoke, it was slow and deliberate, as if explaining something to a child. It was even odder than normal coming from Buster's mouth. "I was Running Wolf. I was a mighty brave. I died protecting my people in battle from the fire haired ones. When I passed over, I met the Great Spirit who told me a great war raged on. He asked if I would lend my spirit to his cause. It was an honor to do so. I remember little of what happened after that, until the Great Spirit pulled me forth once more. He told me he had a new charge. I was to go back into the world of the living. He would hold my spirit together. He would push me to be born as a loyal hound. I would soon after find my charge. When I did I was to guard him with my life. I did so. When my body could no longer do its job, I passed back over where the Great Spirit charged me with waiting for your crossing, so that I may continue my charge."

"By the River!" Jack looked as astounded as Thomas felt. "So you're like, a bloody half a millennium old then?"

"I do not know exactly. We did not count time as you do when I was in my first life. So far as I can tell over seven hundred cycle of seasons have passed since I first walked in two legged form."

Jack waved his hand, causing his lounge chair to spin around behind him. He plopped down in it, trading his bat for a mug of beer. He turned to look at Thomas. "I repeat my earlier praise. One hell of a pet you got there."

Thomas still wasn't certain he had a grasp on everything going on. "Why me? In like, 700 years, why did he have you watch me?"

Buster collapsed into a more comfortable looking position. "I do not know. The Great Spirit instructed it to be. So it was."

"Can I meet this… this Great Spirit?"

Buster shook his large head. "No. He has said that now is not the time. He does not believe a meeting would yet do anything for you."

Thomas turned to Jack. "Do you believe the story?"

Jack took a long drink, then looked intently at Buster. "Lad, I don't know what to tell you. I can say something weird's been going on for awhile now, and it seems like you are at least tied to it. I can say the things he says are, in theory, possible, though I've never actually met anyone who can hold another's soul together once they get into the River. But then again I've seen too much weirdness to say it couldn't happen. I guess the question is, can you think of any reason not to believe him?"

Thomas shook his head. Everything seemed to match up with what Brother Coughlin had told him. Was that good or bad? He didn't like the idea that some powerful and old spirit had taken enough of an interest in him to assign him a personal guardian. Looking back at the times Buster had kept him out of trouble as a kid, and the help he had been since Thomas had died a few months back, he supposed he should be glad that this Great Spirit had done so. Whatever the reason, it seemed Buster really was Buster. For that at least he felt grateful.

He reached over and scratched the dog's ears. Buster tilted his head eagerly to make it easier to reach.

"Thanks buddy."

Rather than respond, Buster slid over and put his head on Thomas's lap.

The three sat in quietness for a while, watching the sun very slowly rise over the horizon. It was fully visible above the trees before Jack finally spoke. "Well. That answers a few questions and raises a hell of a lot more of em. But still doesn't change one thing."

"What's that?" Thomas asked.

"You still need practice. Probably now more than ever. Let's go."

Twenty-one

Buster lifted his head up from beside the campfire and sniffed the air. "Someone new."

They had been back in the training sanctuary a few days now. Thomas felt Jack pushing him even harder and faster than before. Thomas welcomed the challenge. He couldn't help but feel completely underprepared for anything justifying the level of attention his death seemed to have drawn. As miserable as the training was, and Jack made certain it was miserable, Thomas did his best to endure and prepare for the next round. He had been about to ask Jack to start again when Buster spoke.

Jack looked away as if concentrating for a minute, then smiled.

"Don't worry. They're friends. Of a sort, anyway."

Thomas watched as two figures wandered into the campfire light. The first was an Asian man, about Thomas's height, dressed in some kind of Bruce Lee style outfit. Next to him walked a tiny brunette woman who looked to be ready for a shoot out in the OK Corral. She wore a bright western shirt, a grey cowboy hat and a belt marked by two objects: a giant belt buckle and a low-slung pistol. She broke the silence first.

"I thought y'all would be training, not telling ghost stories and roasting s'mores."

All of this was said with a broad smile that was quickly returned by Jack as he stood up to give the woman a hug. "How can the lad survive if he can't fix a decent s'more?"

"Hello again, sweetie." The woman said with a laugh. "I sensed you were back here. Figured it would do the boys some good to do a little training against each other."

Jack shrugged as he nodded a greeting to the Asian man. "Probably not a bad idea. We were just about to start another round anyway. Thomas? This is Charlotte. She's another member of the order. That over there is Cho. He's an initiate, like yourself."

Cho bowed deeply towards Thomas. "It is a pleasure to meet you, sir."

Thomas wasn't exactly sure how to respond, so he nervously bowed back. "Uh... thanks. You too." He turned to extend a hand to Charlotte, who walked towards him. She ignored it and reached up to hug his neck.

"Hugs are for strangers, sugar. I don't like being a stranger with someone who's going to be trying to keep my pretty little ass out of the River."

Thomas again found himself unsure exactly how to respond, so he awkwardly hugged her back. "Uh. Nice to meet you."

She stepped back and winked at him. "Well of course it is. Now. You full strength? Cause I want to see what you're capable of, and I don't want any excuses when Cho wipes the floor with you."

Thomas shrugged. "Yeah, I suppose I am. As much as I ever feel outside of my sanctuary anyway."

"Good. Cho, being an initiate like you, doesn't have a link to this plane either, so y'all will be on equal footing there. Jack? What kind of setting should we do for these boys? I know we definitely need some daylight."

With a snap of her fingers, the sun rose high in the sky. Thomas also noticed the ambient temperature quickly jumped from around seventy to around ninety.

Jack smiled and shrugged himself. "I dunno. Do we want a test of skill or a straight up sparring match?"

Charlotte appraised both Thomas and Cho. "I've always found a good old fashion beat the crap out of each other sparring match to be a good place to start. You boys okay with that?"

Cho bowed once more. "What ever you believe to be best, Master Charlotte."

Thomas shrugged. He would probably have been sparring against Jack anyway. It would be good to try his skills against someone new. "Sure. I'm game."

"Great!" Charlotte clapped her hands twice. Suddenly they were in a deep rocky canyon, about as long as a football field and about twenty foot wide. "This seems like a good arena."

"Aye." Jack agreed. "Now for the rules. You two will go when this hourglass…" He waved his hand and a ten-foot hourglass appeared between Thomas and Cho, "runs out of sand. From there, it's a no holds barred, do as you will battle between the two of you until we call for stop. When we do, you stop immediately and without hesitation, understood?"

Jack and Cho quickly agreed. "Good. We'll watch from up there." He pointed to a ledge at the upper edge of the canyon, and then turned to the German shepherd watching with interest from the side. "Buster, why don't you join us? We'll stop the fight before either suffers serious damage to anything other than their pride, so you don't have to worry about your charge."

Buster didn't respond, but instead suddenly blinked out and appeared up on the designated ledge. Jack shrugged. "Good. Guess he agrees. Any questions from you two lads?"

"No, Master Jack." Cho bowed once more.

Thomas shook his head. "I can't think of anything."

Charlotte clapped again. "Awesome! Boys, fight as if your life depends on it. Because soon it will. Cho? Kick his has, honey. No offense, Thomas, but I like to see my students do better than Jack's."

With that, Jack and Charlotte both blinked up to the ledge themselves and the hourglass suddenly started losing sand at a rapid pace. Thomas suspected there was less than a minute's worth of time in there. He looked across at his opponent, who was standing about twenty yards from him. Thomas felt a few butterflies flurry in his stomach. More so when he observed that his opponent, Cho, seemed completely calm.

As the sands passed the halfway point in running out, Cho adopted what appeared to be some sort of fighting stance. Thomas wondered what he should lead off with. Should he change right away? Pull out some sort of weapon like Jack? Maybe he should….

The last grains of sand fell through the center of the hourglass and it snapped out of existence. In less than a blink of an eye Thomas's opponent was on him, moving with super human speed and agility. Thomas saw a punch coming and slid to the right, only to meet up with a sidekick that suddenly appeared there. With a severe amount of pain, Thomas tried dodging to the other side but another kick waited there to pinball him back.

Thomas knew he wouldn't last long against such an onslaught. Cho spun his body into a kick that looked like it was meant to take Thomas's legs out. Thomas pictured himself as a tree, like he had when he first learned to anchor himself. Instantly he solidified from the chest down. Cho's leg met his now solid trunk of a lower body with what would have been bone-shattering force. With an audible crack Cho rebounded off, spinning backwards and stopping ten foot away from Thomas with a hint of approval in his eyes.

Thomas turned back to gain mobility as he saw Cho start to move towards him again. Knowing he didn't have any time, Thomas brought the base of his palms together and pushed forward. He produced a ball of fire as he simultaneously hit Cho in the chest. The resulting explosion sent Thomas stumbling backwards and sent Cho flying a good twenty foot the opposite direction. Cho hit the ground in a roll, and in one fluid motion came up standing. A blur of hand pats put out the flames on his clothes as he smiled and launched himself forward again.

Thomas realized he did not possess anywhere near the speed Cho did in human form. He might stand a better chance in cat form. He made a move to change, but instead met with a now familiar wall. Apparently Cho, like Jack, could lock his shape shifting down. He knew he only had another second to react so he tried to blink on the other side of Cho, but apparently that too was locked down. Cho leapt at the last moment and planted both feet in Thomas's chest. Thomas found himself sprawling through the air, then face planting in the dirt a good ten-foot from where he had been. He looked up to see Cho coming at him again. In a move of desperation he through up a brick wall between Cho and himself, and was surprised it worked. Cho hit the wall with an loud thud, and Thomas then gave it a mental push, allowing the bricks to collapse onto of Cho in a large pile.

*****

"You're boy's pretty damned good, Jack."

"He does tend to make things interesting."

Charlotte smiled as she watched the two battle it out. She winced when Cho hit a brick wall at full force that a moment ago had not existed, but smiled in spite of herself when it collapsed on top of him. "We should have him spar against everybody. He'd be great at teaching us how to deal with the unpredictable. I don't think I've ever seen a half transformation like that tree thing, and I'm kinda surprised he could do it with Cho locking him down."

"No fault of Cho's, I'm sure. It's damned hard to lock something down when you don't understand how it's done. That boy can do some things none of us have thought about."

The two watched as Cho came out of the bricks with enough force to send them flying in all directions. Thomas dismissed the ones heading towards him with a motion, which caused Jack to smile. "Least he remembered that. Few weeks ago he would have gotten himself nailed with his own bricks."

The two combatants continued their back and forth. Thomas gave well, but Charlotte could see several locks on him keeping him from shape changing and teleporting, as well as limiting some of his creation ability. She had little doubt given his obvious ability that he could probably have snapped at least one if not all of the locks if he could see them, but he didn't even try. It confirmed what Jack had told her. Thomas obviously couldn't see or sense them, only their effects. Cho, for his part, had no such restrictions on his abilities. He was fighting at full strength while Thomas had a hand tied behind his back. It was obvious Cho was picking up on the fact that Thomas couldn't seem to do anything about the locks. She hadn't told him ahead of time because she wanted to see how he did encountering someone with a completely foreign fighting style. He was throwing more and more locks on Thomas now. "Get ready to call it, Jack. This won't last much longer."

*****

Thomas felt like he was moving through molasses. Cho, for his part, seemed to be getting faster. Thomas threw up another wall, but Cho was ready this time and dodged around it. Thomas met him with another fireball but Cho flipped above it, coming into Thomas's jaw with kick that once again sent Thomas flying. Thomas hit the ground and pushed himself up, feeling close to exhaustion. He couldn't take much more of this. Cho raised his hand and smiled at something. Thomas couldn't figure out till he tried to move and realized he couldn't. It was like he was incased in cement. Cho smacked his hands together, rubbing them with a quick motion that appeared to generate some kind of energy. He raised a glowing fist and charged once more at Thomas.

Thomas didn't know what Cho had done to his fists but knew it wasn't going to feel good. He didn't know that he could take much more, and one punch might floor him for good. He knew he had to move, but he couldn't. He was at a near panic when a thought occurred to him. Maybe there was another way to avoid getting hit. As a last ditch effort, Thomas tried turning his body into a gas.

Cho passed through him.

Thomas smiled as Cho spun around, an obvious look of surprise on his face. Thomas made a last ditch attempt to shape change, and to his surprise, he succeeded. He hit the ground on all fours, solidified once more and charged Cho before he could figure out what had happened.

Cho for his credit recovered quickly, but slowed just enough that Thomas's pounce caught him with full force. Thomas threw all of his weight into Cho's chest, claws first, raking down as Cho fell. Without hesitation Thomas buried his fangs into Cho's neck and ripped upwards. Had Cho been alive it would have taken out the full front of his throat. As it was, Cho flipped the two of them over, sending Thomas flying. Thomas landed on all fours. Cho flipped back up to his feet and produced a long staff.

Thomas didn't know how much more he could take. He took some heart, however, in the fact that Cho seemed to use the staff as much for support as in preparation for another attack. The two circled warily, both seemingly more interested at this point in being defensive. Thomas considered his options. He could leap at Cho. His speed was now greatly enhanced in his current form, and Cho's seemed to have slowed down tremendously. Yet he couldn't be entirely certain that wasn't a bluff meant to make him get sloppy. Thomas doubted he could take even one swing of that staff if it connected at full force. On the other hand if Cho was as weak as he looked, Thomas could take him down with one more solid attack.

Thomas's strategy was interrupted by a thunderous gunshot that appeared to take Cho by surprise as well. Jack and Charlotte appeared between the two, each with a raised hand. Charlotte had her pistol pointed at the sky.

"Alright boys, I think that's enough rough housing for one day, don't you?"

Thomas shifted back to human form and collapsed to the ground in one motion. He managed to keep a sitting position but could not manage anything more. Cho, for his part, leaned heavier on his staff. He looked at Thomas with what appeared to be genuine respect in his eyes.

"Thank you, Friend Thomas. You have taught me that I have much yet to learn. More than I believed myself to."

Thomas feebly shook his head. "I got lucky. You're good, Cho. You're really good."

Cho smiled, then he too collapsed to the ground.

Jack reached down and pulled his student up with a grunt, supporting him on his shoulder. "Luck is a good skill to have, Thomas me boy. But you held your own well. Both of ye did good. What say we get a drink?"

*****

Thomas looked around at his companions by the firelight. Jack sat across from him in his familiar lounge chair laughing with

Charlotte, who made good use of the rocking chair she had summoned for herself. Cho sat to his left on a blanket in a lotus style position, seemingly oblivious to the world.

Thomas for his part sat on the ground backed up against a surprisingly comfortable rock. Then again, as he considered it, it might not be so comfortable as it was just there. In his completely exhausted state, anything that didn't cause him to lose more energy was a winner in his book. He felt like he could sleep for days. Except, of course, he couldn't sleep. Sleep was something he was realizing he missed more than anything else. Just letting go with no possible consequences save a trip within his imagination would have been far preferable to this slow recharge. Or even the meditation that Cho now used, which Thomas remained reluctant to retry.

He had not really done so since he had been summoned to Shari. He realized that it was the complete letting go that scared him. Meditation was similar to sleeping in that respect, but here, if his mind took him somewhere the rest of him might readily follow. That made him very nervous, which made it difficult to let go and relax enough to actually meditate again.

"Tommy, honey. You still with us?"

Charlotte's voice shook Thomas from his thoughts.

"Yeah. Sorry. More drained than normal."

"I don't doubt that, sugar. That turning to gas thing you did was brilliant, but had to take a lot of energy."

"Yeah. Guess so."

"Meditate. You'll feel better soon."

Thomas started to object and let her know that he really didn't feel up to that just yet, but an appraising look from Jack stopped him. Thomas took his habitual deep breath. It really was silly to be so afraid of something very helpful just because of a bad experience during his first time doing it. As he reflected, he realized the experience hadn't even been that bad overall. He'd learned to take his Saber toothed cat form from that experience, and that had come in handy more times than he could count now. It had just been the visit with Shari that had really hurt. Seeing her completely break down and being unable to do a thing to even acknowledge her pain, much less try and make it better, had been more of a nightmare than he would have thought possible. That was what he dared not repeat. Still, months had passed since then, and while he suspected she still had bad moments, from what his Dad had said, she seemed to be doing a bit better. Surely she wouldn't be thinking of him at that very moment, would she?

Thomas gave in. "You're right. I should try to do that." He pulled his legs up, and sat up a bit straighter. He felt Buster get up from his place on the other side of the fire and trot over to lay his head in Thomas's lap. Thomas smiled and stroked his ears softly as he closed his eyes and relaxed. He opened his body to the ambient energy around him and let tried to let his mind go.

Twenty-Two

Thomas looked around at the plains. The last few teepees were almost completely erected. The village looked near completion. This would be home for the next few moons. Except... Thomas realized he didn't know why he knew that. He looked down at himself, and as far as he could tell, he was still Thomas Salazar. His clothes were still modern. This didn't seem at all like his memories of the cat or even of Irwan. "Are these memories even real?"

"Yes." Came a voice beside him that was both familiar and somehow different. "But they are not yours, Thomas. These memories are mine."

Thomas turned to see a Native American brave standing at his side. "Buster?"

"I was not known by that name in this time. I was Running Wolf."

"Running Wolf. Okay. Why am I here in your memory? For that matter, how exactly am I here in your memory?"

The past Buster shrugged. "The Great Spirit willed it to be. He now wishes to speak with you. Come with me."

Running Wolf began walking at a measured pace towards the village. He did not look back to see if Thomas followed, but Thomas quickly decided he had little choice but to do so. He wanted to know more about this mysterious figure that held enough power to send Buster to guard him. Now looked to be his chance, and he was unsure that chance would return if he chose not to take it.

Thomas hurried and caught up with Running Wolf, then matched pace to stay just behind him. Thomas wondered how real this was; if the many villagers moving about would see and react to him. He had seen enough westerns as a kid that he definitely wouldn't want to be seen as some kind of invading enemy, Being scalped, even if it couldn't actually kill him now, did not seem like it would be pleasant.

Thomas's many fears appeared to be unfounded. If the villagers noticed him at all they must have seen him as somehow one of their own. He wasn't certain whether they actually could or not. People seemed to walk around him, but no one ever looked at him. It was like they knew he was there and either consciously or unconsciously ignored him. Running Wolf received a cursory nod from some of the passing villagers, but even he had few people pay any more attention to him than that.

Thomas decided that was probably for the best. He followed Running Wolf as they weaved their way to the center of the village. There were maybe a hundred or so people in total, perhaps more given some of the children running about. The village was made up of about half of that number of teepees. If there was logc to the layout of it, Thomas wasn't seeing it.

Somewhere close to the center of the village, Running Wolf stopped in front of one of the teepee's entrances and pulled the leather skins that constituted the door aside. "You should enter."

Thomas nodded, took a deep breath, and ducked into the room.

The interior of the Teepee felt very cozy. Animal skins covered most of the ground area, with a fire pit in the center. An impossibly old Native American male sat cross-legged, staring into the fire. A couple of black feathers were woven into the man's almost white hair, which was split into two long braids that rested on a bear skin that draped over the his shoulder. Beneath the bear skin the old man wore plain leather breaches and a matching shirt. A couple of strange items appeared to be attached to the man's belt, but Thomas wasn't entirely certain from here what they were. Rattles maybe? The man puffed on an ornately carved pipe, and smiled kindly at Thomas as he entered. His skin was gaunt and leathery, showing a long life spent in the elements.

"Thomas Salazar. The young man with an old soul. It is good of you to come see me."

"I don't think it was entirely my choice."

The old man took a deep draw from his pipe, and then blew it out in a slow measured breath. "There is always a choice, Thomas Salazar. Just because you do not like the alternative does not mean it is not there."

Thomas shrugged, feeling somewhat uncomfortable in the older man's presence. "I guess. So… um… are you the Great Spirit?"

The old man let out a surprisingly deep and hearty laugh for someone who looked sort of gaunt. "To Running Wolf, I suppose I am. But I had a life just as you did. I was last known as Falling Dusk. I was medicine man to my tribe and spiritual leader of my people. Please. Sit. The skins are comfortable and the fire is warm."

Thomas warily did as the older man instructed. By all appearances, Falling Dusk seemed nothing more than a very old man enjoying a moment's respite in life. But something seemed out of place. The old man seemed too… vibrant… for someone as old as he seemed to be. Granted, Thomas supposed, the actual restrictions of an old body did not really apply here. Thomas realized that he had not actually met anyone in the afterworld who chose to show themselves as they were when they were older. Everyone he'd met since dying had chosen to display themselves as no older than thirty-five to forty at most. Falling Dusk looked as if he could be eighty. His movements, however, were as smooth as someone a quarter of that age.

Falling Dusk studied him as intently as he realized he had been studying the older man. "You have questions, Thomas Salazar." It was a statement, not a question itself.

"Yeah, I suppose I do. Buster… er… I mean Running Wolf. He says that you sent him to guard me."

"Running Wolf speaks true."

"Why?"

Falling Dusk took another draw from his pipe, studying Thomas once more. After a few minutes of silence, he spoke with a strikingly nonchalant tone. "It is my hope that you will be able to set me free."

"You're trapped somewhere?"

"I will be."

Thomas was growing more rather than less confused. "Okay, I'm not sure I understand."

The old medicine man smiled as he took another drag from his pipe. "No. I do not suppose you do. Here." The old man passed his pipe over. "Smoke with me while I explain."

Thomas took the pipe hesitantly. He had never so much as puffed on a cigarette when he lived. He'd seen too many people get addicted to them, and could never see where trying it would out way the health risks. He did remember in the movies he'd watched as a kid, however, that Indians often smoked 'peace pipes' to seal deals with others, so maybe this once it would be okay. "It's not like I can get cancer now, can I?"

Thomas closed his eyes and took a long drag from the pipe. He fully expected to erupt into a massive fit of coughing, but was pleasantly surprised when he didn't. A warm relaxing sensation filled lungs (or at least where his lungs would have been if he'd really been alive) and his entire body seemed to melt for a moment.

Thomas exhaled slowly and opened his eyes to see an axe headed for his skull. "Holy crap!"

Thomas fell backwards, and watched as a leather shield deflected the axe. The massive Viking looking axe wielder suddenly found himself the target of a tomahawk chop that shattered the big man's face. Thomas looked away in disgust and fear while trying to scramble up and away from the sudden onslaught. A firm hand grabbed his shoulder and helped steady him up.

"Do not be afraid, Thomas Salazar. These are memories. They are not capable of hurting you."

It surprised Thomas just how much the old Medicine man's touch calmed and reassured him. He stopped his attempt to run, and slowly turned his focus back to the bloodbath behind him.

A nasty decapitation made Thomas winced again. If he had still possessed a stomach he would have emptied it. The sight was brutal and savage. Six Vikings fought against over twenty Native American braves. The Vikings had better arms, but the braves had better numbers and seemingly more deliberate tactics. Both sides were equal in their savagery. Within minutes, the six Vikings joined three others of their kind face down in the dirt. Two more of the braves fell as well.

Falling Dusk pointed to two more bodies about twenty foot behind the battlefield. One of them was immediately recognizable to Thomas, and Falling Dusk confirmed what he saw. "There. There is where I died, Thomas Salazar. My apprentice and I were gathering herbs when the men with fire beards jumped us. We stood no chance. As it turns out, however, the noise of our death caught the ear of a near by hunting party, who exacted retribution for our fall."

Thomas studied the fallen warriors, instinctively trying to stay out of the way of the braves despite knowing they could not sense or touch him. "Wow. You fought Vikings."

Falling Dusk nodded. "Yes. Such things were not uncommon. But my people once numbered as sands on the beach. The intrusions of the fire beards were like the attacks of the bear. Dangerous to a small number who were in the wrong place, but insignificant to the people as a whole. So it was that I passed from that world to the next, just as you did, Thomas Salazar. However, unlike you, no one waited for me. I learned quickly how to make changes to my sanctuary; like you I too grew board with my safe surroundings. So I returned to the world of my people, what you will call The Prime."

The view shifted to a village, not unlike the one Running Wolf lead him through. Then it shifted to other scenes with native americans hunting or gathering, or walking and enjoying the scenery. Falling Dusk continued talking all the while. "For some time I watched over my people. I found that with work I could influence what my people did, and used that to protect them as best I could."

Thomas watched as the memory of the Medicine man whispered into the ears of a female Native, who seemed to then decide to change her course. A few minutes later, another group of Vikings passed through where the woman would have walked.

"I grew curious of these strange outsiders. Where did they come from? Why were they here?"

As Thomas watched, the memory of Falling Dusk followed the Viking raiding party back to camp, then boarded their long boat and remained as it set sail east.

"I studied these strange warriors for some time. There was much to admire in their spirit and tenacity, even if they did cause trouble wherever they went. They returned to their land, and I watched them there for a while. When a group headed out to sea again, I decided to travel with them. I do not know if it was fate or luck that I did, but the decision changed my afterlife, as well as the history of my people there after."

Thomas watched as the Viking disembarked from their boat near what appeared to be an English Church. Their visit was again short and brutal, and they killed everything that moved. Thomas felt sorry for the British monks as he watched them fall one by one. His sorrow turned to complete revulsion as he saw them bring out the head monk, clutching an ancient holy book from the monastery to his chest. What Thomas witnessed next he hoped he would somehow find a way to forget. One of the warriors drew a sword as he motioned for the monk to be thrown, chest down, on a tree stump. He cut the man's robes from his back. With seemingly surgical precision, he then began cutting into the man's back along his spinal cord as the monk screamed at the top of his lungs in horror and pain.

Thomas turned away, but he could not shut the excruciating sounds of torture from his ears. The laughter of the warriors mixed by the horrific screams of agony coming from poor monk. Finally the monk fell silent with a ragged gasp.

Thomas dared to look back and immediately wished he hadn't. While the Vikings had begun digging through the bodies of the corpses and as well as raiding the church, the poor tortured monk laid face down on the stump he'd been forced to lay across. His back had been split open on either side of his spine, and his ribs had obviously been broken away to make room to pull his lungs out through his back in some grotesque mockery of wings. It was the single most disgusting thing Thomas had ever witnessed in his life or death. "Oh god."

"No. Their god would arrive just after. There."

Falling Dusk pointed to the church. Thomas tore his glance from the mutilated monk to the church in time to see another shock. An eight-foot tall monk in long white robes, a red cape, and skullcap walked calmly through the chaos. As he passed each body he paused, bent down and took the dead body's hand. He then stood up, pulling the spirit from the body as if merely helping them to stand up. He then hugged the confused looking spirit, who slowly melted into the monk. When the lesser monk spirit disappeared completely, the larger monk moved on to the next body.

"What is that?"

"One of the last gods to walk the earth. I do not know who he was as a human, but he was, by this time, far more than any mere human could be."

Thomas watched as the God Monk continued to go to each body, collecting the spirit from each of the fallen. He moved last to the tortured monk. Thomas realized in fresh horror that the poor man was still alive, despite the grotesque shape of his body. The God Monk placed a hand on the man's forehead, and with a shiver, the victimized cleric finally passed on. The God Monk then collected him like the others.

Thomas shook his head. "I don't understand. If he was a god, why would he have allowed his people to be slaughtered like this?"

Falling Dusk shrugged. "I do not know. Perhaps he lacked the energy at this point to stop the fire-bearded warriors. This is unlikely. I believe the death fit his purpose, so he allowed it. He gained new souls, and the living remained fearful and open to his manipulations. Even the fire beards were not truly beyond his reach. Watch."

One of the Vikings, who seemed to have slightly better equipment than most of his peers, came over to the dead body of the tortured monk. He reached down and picked the monk's bible up. For a minute he looked like he was going to toss it, but the God Monk placed a hand on his shoulder, and the Viking immediately looked to reconsider. He looked at the book with an interest he did not have moments earlier, then stuffed it in a bag with some of his other loot.

"He would eventually convert all of the Fire Beards to his ways. It was what he did. He drove his people, the people of this land, to expand ever farther. I followed him for quite some time."

Thomas's view shifted and suddenly they were in a savannah. Judging by the people and the view, Thomas suspected they were somewhere in Africa. Falling Dusk remained at his side.

"Everywhere he travelled, he influenced events in the favor of his people and their culture. He also collected the souls of those who followed him. And with each soul he became more powerful."

"So, souls are power?"

"The River is possibility, Thomas Salazar. All that has ever been or ever will be comes from it. Each of us has a thimble full of that power innately. With that thimble full we can do wondrous things. This being…. This being had been collecting those thimbles for a hundred years or more now. He had absorbed all of that into his own body. He existed now as a small stream in and of himself."

Thomas watched as the view shifted rapidly. Each new scene showed various Europeans pushing further into new areas, subjugating the locals through power, influence, and plague. At the front of each event walked the God Monk. Sometimes he was subtle, whispering into the ears of allies and enemies alike then smiling as they carried out his bidding. Other times he seemed more active, pushing his ally's weapons to be harder, faster, and more accurate than they might otherwise have been, or causing his enemy's equipment to fall apart and their ranks to break in fear. With his most subtle strikes he would move ahead of his oncoming troops, sowing sickness and death so that by the time his armies arrived, those who might have stood against them were too weak to stand at all. All across Africa, Southern Asian, and Southeastern Asian, the scenes played out over and over.

"Wherever he went, his followers grew more powerful, and he as well. They would occasionally fight amongst themselves, and in those battles he seemed to merely stand by and watch, not interfering at all, but collecting souls of the fallen afterward. Occasionally he would leave the Prime, and I would lose him, but then he would return and I would easily find him once more. Wherever he went within this world, I followed. His energy was like a brilliant sun in the dreariness of the living world. Even when he teleported far away, it was simple to track him. He never noticed me. I was an accomplished hunter in my youth. In my death I thought I had retained that prowess, and my skills had allowed me to escape notice of the enemy I was growing to fear more by the day. I soon learned different."

Thomas watched as the past ghost of Falling Dusk stalked the God Monk. The pair were currently in a tropical area, and judging by the locals he suspected the location was somewhere in Southeast Asia. Something of the area looked familiar. A few minutes later he understood why as another spirit entered his view. A bald monk in orange robes walked calmly up to the ghost of Falling Dusk as the God Monk lead several groups of explorers out into the jungle. "Master Ardru."

The current Falling Dusk looked at Thomas quizzically then returned his gaze to the scene before them as Master Ardru tapped the past Falling Dusk on the shoulder.

"You need not hide. The tiger does not chase the mosquito unless it buzzes too close."

The Past Falling Dusk studied the ancient Buddhist. "You mean he could see me all of this time?"

"If he chose to. He does not. Those such as us are beneath him."

"I have heard stories from my grandfathers of times ages past when his kind roamed the earth. I though them tales to scare children."

"Once they were real. They became tales. Now, this one seeks to return to the old ways. Unlike days past, there are no others to oppose him."

"Can he be stopped?"

The old Buddhist nodded. "Yes. It will not happen easily, or without sacrifice, but it could be done."

The Medicine Man's ghost turned to study the God Monk once more. "If he is not stopped, what will happen?"

"There is little reason to ask questions to which you already know the answer."

"His ways will become all ways."

Master Ardru nodded sagely. "Yes. Even now he returns to the River to see his most loyal souls reborn into powerful positions. He influences them and they influence history."

A growing horror was obvious on the face of the past Falling Dusk. "He will find my people too." It was not a question.

"He knows of them already. He does not yet know of their riches. But as his victories grow here, he will send his people to explore. When they discover what your people possess, it will peak his interest, and that will be the end of your people's ways."

Thomas's view shifted again, and suddenly he was back in the teepee, pipe in hand. He exhaled, blowing smoke as he did. "Were we… here? Or there?"

"The spirit is all places. It is all time. It only matters where we choose to observe."

Something in the old Medicine man's comments brought Irwan's Buddhist studies to mind. He decided not to press the question in favor of other more important ones. "What did you do?"

Falling Dusk smiled, but the smile possessed a great sadness. "I returned to my people. I watched them. I had learned well while watching the last God. Take another puff and I will show you."

Thomas put the pipe back to his lips and once again inhaled. Again a warm feeling filled his chest. He closed his eyes as he relaxed, then opened them to find himself back in what appeared to be the American north east.

Falling Dusk remained at his side, and the ghost of the Medicine man's past played out once more in front of them.

"I took the souls of my people as I found them dying. I knew that the bald stranger had been correct. I was a mosquito and my opponent was a Tiger. My people were lambs, and if I were to save them then I must become the bear."

The ghost of Falling Dusk blinked from village to village, watering hole to battle ground. Each time one of his people fell, he was there to pick them up, talk to them, and in most cases pull them into himself.

"I was not the God Monk. I did not force my people to take my path. As they passed over I told them of my battle. Some declined to join, and those I allowed to pass onto the other side. Most, however, chose to join me. As they did, I felt my power and influence grow. It was an amazing feeling, but I realized while I was no longer a mosquito I was not yet even a cub, much less a beast. My enemy had a century or more head start on me in collecting power. Were I to follow his lead, I would not stand a chance of being at his level when he finally chose to conquer our lands. I mourned my people. Then I did what was necessary to give them a chance to survive."

Thomas watched as the ghost of Falling Dusk appeared in a village. He recognized the pestilence that appeared shortly there after as something like what the God Monk had used on his enemies. This, however, was far worse than what the God Monk had done. The God Monk had infected the warriors of his enemies to the point where they could not fight and had no choice but to accept subjugation. Falling Dusk infected all of his people: men, women, old and young. Those who contracted the illness did not last long.

Thomas watched in growing horror as village after village fell. With each death Falling Dusk would speak briefly to his victims, and in most cases, assimilate them. The surroundings changed. The woods of the North East gave way to the open plains, which gave way to swamp land, returned to grasslands, then rolling hills, mountains, and deserts. Each new sight brought new death. Few were spared. Most villages disappeared completely. Others had only tiny portions of their numbers still standing when Falling Dusk moved on. The death was on a level Thomas couldn't even begin to fathom.

"You… You killed them. You murdered your own people."

Falling dusk shook his head. "My people were dead already. Better by the hand of one of our own in defense of the remaining, than in complete subjugation of the last God and his minions. My people numbered as the sands on the beach when I began. I left one alive for each full moon in a cycle."

"One per full moon? So you…. You killed 27 of every 28 members of your people? You left like one thirtieth of your people alive?" Thomas tried to consider how much history might have changed if America had been populated by 30 times the amount of Natives as it was when Columbus first brought the Europeans to it. Would they so easily have conquered it? At least, would they if they did not have the God Monk at their forefront?

Falling Dusk looked forward, an emotionless mask on his face. "I did what needed to be done."

Thomas found himself once again in the teepee. He exhaled and tossed the pipe to the ground next to Fallen Dusk's side. "I can't believe you killed that many of your own people. Buster's people. Buster himself. You murdered them all, in some weird quest to save them? Was that really the way?"

"It was, Thomas Salazar. It remains the only way. The God Monk must be stopped. Even now he and his people sail for our lands. He will soon arrive and when he does, he will subdue and change all in his path. If I do not act, their lives will be lost, but so will their soul. Their way of life. Their past. I will preserve these things, at least for a time. I do not know how much time I have brought to my people but I know it is more than they would have had."

Thomas shook his head, trying to wrap his mind around everything he had seen and heard. Walking Gods. Soul collectors. Death and torture. Something else caught in his mind. "Wait. Even now? What do you mean by that? You must have defeated the God King like, what, five hundred years ago at least."

"For you, Thomas Salazar, that is the truth. For me, the events you speak of are yet to come."

"So I'm… I'm talking to you in the past? How the hell is that possible?"

The old medicine man remained calm and controlled. "All places, all time, Thomas Salazar. When you have drunk enough of the River, you may observe more than your present. Time becomes like flowing water. It is not easy to press against, but it can be done. So it is that I brought you here, in Running Wolf's dream. I will plant this in his mind so that when the time is right, you may retrieve it."

Thomas held his head, trying to wrap his mind around the timeline of this conversation. "I am way on the confused side. Is this even real?"

Fallen Dusk stood with the fluid ease of someone half the age he appeared to be. "It was, Thomas Salazar. I have seen some of my future. I will defeat the God King, but a price will be paid. My connection to the other side will be severed. My power will be reduce greatly, as likely it should, and I will become a shell of what I am now. I will, however, still hold many souls within me. Too many to safely release on my own. So I will be doomed to roam the earth instead. Cursed in victory over my enemy to a grim fate with but one possible hope. You."

"So past you is showing me more past you to convince me to find the future you with the current me and, what, kill you then?"

The old man nodded. "Set me free. You will one day know how to do that. I ask that you do so."

"I… I think getting rid of you may be for the best."

The medicine man walked slowly over to Thomas as he spoke, and placed a hand on the younger man's shoulder. Thomas felt the need to jerk away, but fought it. as the older man stated "I am sorry that your reasons are bitter, Thomas Salazar, but I understand.

Your actions are all that matters in the end. Your reasons for doing so do not. I will send a guardian to protect you until you are ready. I will have enough time between my battle with the last God and your birth to recover some power. I will use that to send Running Wolf to your side."

"But he'll still be the slave of the man who murdered him and his people."

"Until this time, he will remain tied to me. If you would like, as of this conversation I will turn him over to you."

Thomas considered for a moment. Buster had been a loyal companion his entire life. Whether he was following orders or not, he seemed to genuinely be a good soul. He deserved better than to be a slave. Trading him from one master to another wasn't right. Buster deserved better. "Free him."

The older man shook his head. "You will need him."

But Thomas wasn't going to give ground on this. If he accomplished nothing else, he would see this one thing done. "If I do, it should be his choice as to whether to be there for me. Bust... er... Running Wolf is my friend. I don't want him as a slave. If he wants to keep helping me I will gladly accept his help. I was never his master and I don't want to be now."

Falling Dusk picked his pipe up and took a long puff, obviously considering his course of action. After a few moments of silence, Thomas was beginning to think the old medicine man was going to keep Buster's soul for his own, but finally he spoke and relented. "I will do as you ask. Running Wolf's soul will be his own. His destiny will be his own. Your destiny may not be. I cannot see for certain how your path will play out. Choose wisely, Thomas Salazar."

Twenty-three

Thomas opened his eyes. Buster bolted upright from Thomas's lap, staring at him with a look that bordered on horror.

"Something is wrong, Thomas. I cannot feel the Great Spirit."

Thomas smiled. Falling Dusk had kept his word. "No, Buster. It's fine. Your job is done. You are free."

Jack and Charlotte ceased their talking and turned their attention to Thomas.

Buster cocked his head in confusion. "Free? I do not understand."

"I spoke to the Great Spirit. Your charge was to get me here to this point. You did so admirably. He rewarded you with your freedom."

Jack cocked his head. "Wait. When did you bloody well talk to anyone?"

Thomas looked up calmly. Apparently he hadn't actually left here, but that didn't really surprise him. He realized less and less was surprising him. "Just now."

Jack and Charlotte both raised their eyebrows at him.

"I'm guessing I probably didn't actually go anywhere this time."

"No lad. You just agreed to try and meditate no more than two minutes ago. You haven't exactly had time to go anywhere."

That did manage to surprise Thomas. He felt like he'd been gone for hours at least, possibly days. He was completely relaxed and recovered physically, though mentally... how many millions of people died because two people decided to become gods? How much was history changed by the will of two individuals? *That can't happen again. Whatever the cost, no one should have that kind of power.* Thomas shook off his revelries and looked up at his companions. "I definitely had time to go somewhere. And we have a lot to talk about."

Buster stood up, still looking wary. "Thomas. I wish to leave. Can I do so?"

"Buster, I told you. You're free. You don't have to ask my permission, or anyone else's anymore."

Buster looked at Thomas for a moment, then in a blink was gone.

*****

Thomas filled Jack, Charlotte and Cho in on the history he had picked up from Falling Dusk. He covered everything from his arrival in the Native American village to the horror of the Vikings, the havoc wreaked by the God Monk, and the mass genocide of Falling Dusk himself. Charlotte asked a few questions for clarification, but outside of that his companions merely sat back and listened with looks of horror and near disbelief. Thomas understood their reactions. A few months ago he would not have believed such things possible, much less that they had actually occurred.

When he finished his tale, there was silence. Cho looked deep in thought. He had not spoken since coming out of his meditation. He merely sat back, watched, and contemplated.

Jack, as usual had produced some kind of alcoholic beverage from somewhere. "Bloody hell. So European expansionism was pushed by a European god. Hard to believe, but it makes sense in a twisted sorta way."

Charlotte shook her head. "I can't believe that many Indians died before white people showed up. The world really would look different if those two fellas hadn't done what they done."

"Yeah." Thomas agreed. "It's insane. I mean, I was watching the highlights, but still. You wouldn't believe the devastation these two guys brought. The God Monk made sure his side won just about every encounter they came across, and Falling Dusk... Gods the man killed a million or more people inside of what couldn't have been much longer than a year or two. He made the Nazi's look like amateurs, and these are the people he claimed to like."

Jack nodded. "Reinforces why our Order was setup."

Cho finally interjected. "Perhaps it explains why someone would want to stop the order."

Charlotte cocked her head. "You think somebody's trying to make themselves a new god?"

Cho nodded. "It is a possibility not to be dismissed. The order's reason to exist is to keep this from happening. If one were to try and reach that level of power, one would not want people like us standing in one's way. "

Jack shrugged and took a drink. "Lad's gotta point. We'll wanna be doubly careful. I'll warn Leo to keep his eyes peeled for anyone seems strange. Figure he's doing it already but he should know about this. We'll be wanting to tell the others too."

Charlotte reached over and grabbed Jack's bottle and downed it. "I think we need more people too. If something like that's coming we're gonna need more than what we got to stop it."

"Aye," said Jack, producing another bottle. "Thomas, Lad, are you sure you made the right decision not taking on Buster's soul? He's a capable warrior. We get into a scrap with someone like that God Monk guy or this Indian you talked to, he could come in handy."

Thomas shook his head. "If we get into a fight with someone like the God Monk, we lose. Period. We're not anywhere close to his league, so let's hope we don't. Besides, Falling Dusk said that when he found out about the God Monk, he could track him anywhere, that his aura was extremely obvious. None of us have encountered anything like that, so let's hope that means nobody of that level exists. I kinda think if they did, Falling Dusk would have known and told Buster."

Charlotte wasn't so certain. "But you said the Falling Dusk fellow's still alive, and we having found him yet."

"He's apparently really weak." Thomas added. "I don't know what happened in his fight with the God Monk, but whatever it was he seemed to know it would leave him at a tiny fraction of his power."

Jack shrugged. "Might be the case. I still don't think letting Buster go was a good move."

Thomas expected this, but he stood his ground. "My mom always said if you love something, let it go. If it comes back, then you know it's yours, otherwise it wasn't meant to be. Buster's been a slave for hundreds of years now. A willing slave maybe, but even that's questionable. I saw what Falling Dusk was capable of at full strength. I don't think many people could tell him no even if they wanted. There's also… well…."

Thomas fell silent for a few minutes. Charlotte reached over and put a hand on his shoulder. "What is it, sugar?"

"Falling Dusk learned what he learned by watching the God Monk. I watched both of them. I don't fully understand everything I saw, but I think I could copy at least some of what they did. That… that really scares me. I don't want that kind of power. I might use it. I'm pretty sure Falling Dusk wasn't evil, and it wouldn't surprise me if even the God Monk thought he was doing the right thing, but so many people died because of their actions. History irreversibly changed because of what they did. Who knows what the world might have been like if they hadn't forced their wills on it? Taking Buster would have put me on that path. It would have confirmed I had the ability to enslave a soul. If I did that, would I stop there? Or would I justify one more? And one more after that?"

Thomas fell silent again. He replayed the death and destruction he had seen over and over in his mind. He couldn't let that happen again. He really couldn't be the one who did it.

After a few moments of everyone sitting in silence, Jack raised a bottle. "Let's hope, laddie, that you never have to make that choice. Buster's a good bloke for a dog. I'm sure if and when we need him, he'll be there for us even without you taking control of his reigns."

Thomas nodded his head in agreement. "Yeah. You're right." He wished he felt certain about that.

Charlotte stood up, and once again brought light back to the world. "One thing we do know is that we really need you two to be full members so Jack and me can track down some more recruits. You boys ready to up your game?"

Cho stood up and bowed his assent. Thomas forced himself to put
away his thoughts and stand as well. Maybe a good workout would
make him feel better. Take his mind off of everything going on.
Surprisingly he did feel completely energized for having only
apparently been meditating a couple of minutes. *"Maybe I should
give mediation a try more often..."*

*****

Buster stood outside the Great Cave. It felt like the Great Spirit
still slumbered within in the long hibernation. But unlike times
past, there was no contact from this vantage point. No instructions
on what should be done. Only the sense of a great power close by
betrayed any stillness and silence. Without that sense, Buster
would have sworn nothing was around for miles. Even then, he
might easily have missed it had he not felt such a deep connection
to it for so long.

Now that connection was cut off and he found himself cast away
from the one constant he had known for centuries. It was as if a
part of him had been ripped away.

Now, he was free. But free to do what? Running Wolf had done as
the tribe needed. As Running Wolf's soul, he had vague memories
of an epic battle, working in concert with other souls to do what
must be done. As Buster he had spent his whole life taking care of
Thomas. As Buster's Soul, he had continued that charge. Two lives
and two deaths had been spent in the service of others.

Now he realized he faced a choice. Thomas no doubt could still
use his assistance, and that was the final charge he had received
from The Great Spirit. But Thomas was also well protected by the
Order of the Shield. It was not likely his assistance would be
needed any time soon. He could go keep an eye on Thomas's
Shari. Thomas would no doubt wish that, however many other
souls were already doing that, and again there seemed little he
could actually do there.

Buster padded back and forth in front of the cave. He had never
had to make decisions such as this. For the first time in several
hundred years, Buster realized he really could do anything he

wanted. It was a disturbing feeling. He wasn't entirely certain he liked it.

There had been a few things that had caught his notice over the last few years. Perhaps it was time to follow up on those? With little other direction, Buster made his first truly independent decision and headed back out to the Great Path.

Twenty-four

"Okay sugars. Understand, while you need to be able to take care of yourselves, you gotta make a good team as well. We usually work in pairs, so, let's see how well you two can take care and help each other."

Charlotte walked past and Jack followed behind her.

"Right lads. You'll make a right proper team I'm sure. So now's the time to prove it. Here's your assignment. We're gonna drop you in an abandoned sanctuary. Normally Sanctuaries disappear when their owners leave but some stick around. This is one of those, and I'll warn you it has some... odd properties."

Charlotte nodded. "Odd's a good word for it. Now. Somewhere in that sanctuary. I put a bottle of Irish whiskey. Your job's to go in and retrieve it for us. Y'all got any questions?"

Thomas shook his head. Cho stood quietly.

Jack nodded. "Good lads. Now, let me set you straight on something. This test... it isn't a bloody training run. You do something stupid and you're buggered. You do something really stupid you could find your asses back in the River and I'd have to start me recruiting all over again. So, in case ye haven't figured it out..."

"... don't do anything stupid." Charlotte finished for him.

Thomas considered. He was certain that the test must be reasonably safe. He didn't think Charlotte and Jack would risk their unlives unnecessarily. Still, it was clear that whatever the order's usual training methods were, he and Cho were being placed on an accelerated track. Clearly their soon to be official jobs would be very dangerous, so there would be some incentive for him and Cho to begin thinking as if their lives depended on their decisions, since they soon would. Regardless there seemed little choice, outside of quitting, and after everything he'd been through that didn't even seem an option. "So how do we find this bottle?"

Jack created his favorite lounger and plopped back into it with an open beer in hand. "Dunno. Don't rightly care. Find it and it'll bring you back here. Don't and well… well let's not think about that, shall we lads?"

Cho bowed. "We will do as you have instructed."

Charlotte clapped. "Great! Okie dokie boys, I'm fixin to ship your asses away. Any last minute requests?"

Thomas and Cho both shook their head. Charlotte smiled and reached up and patted both men on the cheeks. On the third pat, the world flashed and shifted.

*****

The heat and humidity oppressed them like a sealed steam room. Thomas tried to cool the surroundings around instinctively, but met with pushback. He tried cooling himself down as he would on the Prime and met with the same resistance.

"Well this is obnoxious."

Cho nodded. "Yes. It appears we have as little control over our comfort as we did in life." He closed his eyes, and his dark top became damp. "It does appear we can work within the rules we had in life. Sweat does cool one down."

Thomas shrugged and soaked his own shirt. The light breeze did actually make it seem slightly cooler. It was still miserable, but slightly more bearable. Thomas took stock of their surroundings. They were obviously in a jungle. Beside that there was little to go on. Green blanketed every direction, with vines and other thick foliage making travel almost impossible. The sole exception existed as a machete hacked trail starting where they now stood and twisting off into the jungle ahead of them. "At least our path is well marked."

Cho nodded. "Let us hope that it is the correct path."

Thomas shrugged. "One way to find out."

Cho looked around nervously, obviously looking for hidden options. "Yes. But let us travel with care. This is a test. We do not know what surprises they have left for us."

Thomas couldn't argue with that point. The duo began trudging and picking their way along the path. While it was obviously a path, it was not a well travelled one. Fallen trees and low hanging branches made for a lot of ducking and climbing. The threat of some unknown danger lurking around each corner, or stalking them within the jungle's depths, made the journey slower and far more tense.

Cho walked with an impressive silence, his steps making no sound, his head steadily swiveling back and forth in search of hidden threats. Thomas for his own part banged his head on a few low lying branches and made enough noise for both of them, but so far as he could tell it attracted no attention.

Cho smiled back at him. "I think perhaps you misunderstand the concept of stealth, Friend Thomas."

"Sorry. I answered phones when I was alive. I've never really had to try to walk quietly."

Cho shrugged. "It is a good skill to practice, but likely unnecessary here. I suspect anything that is of a danger to us already knew we were here when we arrived. Still, better safe than sorry."

 Thomas continued his attempt to be quiet as they moved, but in the strange silence of their current world it sounded as if every step he took, every leaf he crunched or twig he snapped became amplified a hundred fold. The jungle did not possess the muted sound that his own sanctuary had originally had, but neither did it possess the usual sounds one would expect from such a lush think jungle. There were no birds chirping, no animals calling, no insects buzzing. Even the light breeze that occasionally passed through failed to create the rustling of limbs one would expect. It was just… quiet. Thomas supposed under other circumstances it could even be called peaceful, but as Cho had pointed out this was a test, and therefore he felt the silence resembled more the quiet before the storm than anything else.

The path before them zigzagged in a seemingly haphazard fashion. There were times when it seemed to spin around on itself to the point where Thomas felt certain that they would have crossed their own trail in the real world. Here that never happened. The more they walked, the more oppressive the heat and humidity became. Both men pressed on, forcing their bodies to create more sweat to counteract the steam room like atmosphere they were marching through.

Thomas briefly considered taking cat form. It would certainly be quieter, and the ability to pant might be cooler, though the extra fur certainly would not. It would also be a huge energy drain, which became the true reason he decided against it. If this had been the Prime, Thomas would have been concerned about dehydration. As it was, he merely hoped the energy they were exerting was not significantly more than they were naturally replenishing. It wouldn't do very well to finally encounter something dangerous and find themselves too exhausted to face it.

Cho, who had been walking about five foot ahead of him, stopped dead in his tracks as he rounded the next turn in the trail. As Thomas caught up to him he realized why. Three or four feet ahead of where Cho stood, the jungle ended at a ledge.

Thomas slowly approached the edge of the cliff and looked down. A ravine met his view, probability a hundred foot across and as far as he could see down. About halfway across a light grey haze started. It wasn't quite a fog. It didn't actually obscure his view of the other side, but it was noticeable. Cho looked over the edge and then down to the bottom before stating the obvious.

"I do not believe we will want to fall here, Friend Thomas."

Thomas peered over into the abyss below. "No. That first step would be a doozy."

Cho looked at the path behind them and then back at the ravine's opposite side. "I should be able to jump this. I have done further in training."

"I can fly us across." Thomas waved his hand, and his now trusted Pegasus appeared just behind them. "That should be safer."

Cho appraised the winged horse admiringly. "Fascinating. Yes, perhaps that would be a wiser plan. Can it carry both of us and still fly?"

Thomas patted Shadow on the side of its neck, then stroked its muzzle. The winged horse stomped its foot in anticipation. "Yeah. Shouldn't be a problem at all. Well, provided that haze isn't some kind of poison anyway."

Cho stared at him for a moment, then looked across and stared the other side of the ravine, then turned back to him. "What haze do you see, my friend?"

Thomas pointed to the other side. "About halfway across and then beyond. It's light, but look carefully, you'll see it."

Cho walked up to the edge, and strained his eyes, obviously looking closer. He then turned back to Thomas. "No, Friend Thomas. I do not see any haze."

Thomas looked back. The haze was light, but no lighter than it had been. "It's there, Cho. I see it."

"I do not doubt you, my friend. It concerns me that there is something there that you see and I do not."

Thomas pulled himself up on the Pegasus and offered a hand out to Cho. "What do you think it is?"

Cho took his hand and mounted behind him in a smooth fluid motion. "I do not know. But we should be very careful of it. Is there anyway around it?"

Thomas urged Shadow up to the edge of the cliff and looked left and right. The haze extended as far either direction as he could see. It also continued both up and down from this viewpoint, so he shook his head. "Doesn't look like it. Assuming our goal is ahead, anyway."

Cho was quiet for a moment behind him, and then replied. "It is. I sense my teacher ahead of us. It is likely not actually her but her creation."

Thomas pulled the reigns up, patting Shadow again on the side of his neck. "Well then, I don't suppose we have much choice but to go through it."

Cho took a tight grip around Thomas's waste. "Just be careful. It could be nothing, but…"

"I know, better safe then sorry." Thomas finished. He put pressure on the Pegasus's flanks and it leapt into the air, covering the first fifty feet in two flaps of its mighty wings. Thomas pulled it to a halt right at the edge of the haze. The Pegasus bobbed up and down as its wings pushed steadily against the air. The Haze before them seemed completely undisturbed.

Cho leaned slightly around him. "Are we in it, yet?"

Thomas shook his head. "No. But we're about to be. I take it you still can't see it?"

He could feel Cho shaking his head. "No. It is as clear ahead of us as it is behind us to me."

"Well then. Let's hope it really is nothing." Thomas again gave Pegasus a nudge and they continued moving forward. The horse pushed nose deep in the haze then disappeared. "Shit."

The two men plummeted. Thomas tried to stop himself, but quickly found that he could not. Not surprisingly, this world had strict laws on physics. Luckily they didn't appear strict enough to stop a winged horse. Thomas willed Shadow back into being. It was noticeably more difficult than it had been the first time, but it appeared above them, swooping beneath Thomas while carefully avoiding the dangerous haze. As Thomas landed back in the saddle with a grunt of effort, he reached out and took Cho's outstretched hand. Cho grabbed a hold then spun himself back up onto Pegasus's back. Thomas nudged the winged horse away from the mist, stopping about halfway back towards the cliff wall that now towered above them just as it continued below them. Below, the echo of rushing water was barely audible.

Thomas felt the need to let out a sigh. "Okay, so the haze is bad."

Cho tightened his grip once more on Thomas's waste. "So it would appear, friend Thomas. Is there still no way around it?"

"Let's find out." Thomas nudged the flying horse right and down. They flew for a few miles. As they dropped down they came across the source of the roaring water. A thirty to forty foot wide river roared in a snaking fashion back and forth across the chasm's floor. Sometimes it was in the haze, sometimes it was out, but as far as they went, the haze never disappeared and never allowed access to the far cliff. "Doesn't look like it this way. Let's try the other way!"

The horse winged around, again steering well clear of the haze, and began following the River downstream. After about five minutes the water's noise began to alter, becoming louder and of a noticeably different tenor. Within a few more minutes, the River merged with The River, and the rushing water altered quickly into rushing souls and the familiar flashing discs. Thomas pulled back to a hover and shook his head. "I don't think we're going to have much luck this way either."

"Turn back" Cho yelled over the roar of The River. Thomas nudged Shadow and flipped back around, following the River back upstream. They passed the Y where The River and the River split in two. They continued a few more miles following the regular river upstream, till Cho finally tapped him on the shoulder. "We're back where the original trail should have been. Is there a spot on the other side of this river that is not in the haze?"

Thomas searched below and located a place where the River curved far outside the bounds of the haze, leaving about twenty foot of its far bank outside of the haze. Thomas brought them down, with the winged horse touching down with a light crunch on the pebble-strewn shoreline. The water coursed by with a loud roar, though not anywhere close to the volume of The River a mile or two downstream. Both men dropped down, finding stable footing on the pebbles. Thomas, thinking back to the noticeable difficulty in summoning the Pegasus the second time, decided not to dismiss the Pegasus just yet. Instead it wandered over to the River and began drinking.

Cho stared at the far shore. "Where is the boundary of the haze?"

Thomas looked around and saw a small stick at the edge of the River. He picked it up and walked up to the edge of where the haze began and drew a line in the pebbles about ten foot in length. Afterwards, on a whim, he took the stick and pushed it into the haze. Nothing happened to it. "Interesting."

Cho walked up to within a foot of the line. He picked up a rock and through it over the line. The rock sailed forward, bounced a few times, then stopped. He looked over at Thomas for a moment, then bent over and picked up a handful of pebbles. He closed his eyes and pushed his hands together for a moment, then revealed the handful of pebbles had been combined into one large rock. He threw it like a fastball pitch over the line. It sailed across the line into the haze and immediately split apart into its original form, with pebbles bouncing in all directions as they hit the ground. "Yes. Interesting."

"So..." Thomas observed, "it appears to have little to no affect on anything from here, but it doesn't seem to like anything that's changed or created."

"So it would seem. I have a theory. Let us hope I am not wrong." Cho stepped up to the line. Before Thomas could say anything, Cho stuck his arm across the line into the haze. Thomas leapt forward and grabbed Cho by the back of his shirt and yanked him back. He half expected the Asian man's arm to be missing. Cho, however, raised the arm up, displaying absolutely no damage to it or the clothing covering most of it. "It would seem it is not entirely toxic to us either."

Thomas inspected Cho's hand for any sign of harm. There did not appear to be any, but he still could not approve of the method Cho had used. "Surely there was another way to test that?"

Cho shrugged as he pulled his hand back. "This is a test, not a suicide mission, Friend Thomas. Our objective lies within or past the haze. Logic dictates our masters passed through here unharmed."

Thomas could see the logic, but still didn't like it. "Maybe. What happened to better safe than sorry?"

Cho shrugged his shoulders with a feigned innocent look. "My wisdom does not always outlast my patience. My apologies, Friend Thomas."

The apology sounded completely sincere, and Thomas smiled despite himself. "Well, I can't fault you too much. Without you I would have probably flown full speed into that stuff. I hate to think what would have happened if I had gone fully inside this haze when my Pegasus disappeared."

Cho looked up at the cliff, which disappeared completely into the distance above them. "We would have had a long fall followed by a very unpleasant stop."

Thomas nodded. "That's one way to put it. So you think that stuff's actually safe for us?"

Cho shrugged. "I merely put my arm in, however I felt nothing unusual. I suppose as you said, 'there is one way to find out'." With that Cho walked forward. Thomas looked on nervously as Cho stepped across the line. Again he half expected Cho to vanish as soon as he crossed over into the mists, however it appeared those fears were unfounded. Cho looked down at himself, then back at Thomas. "I believe I am now fully within your haze, is that correct?"

Thomas nodded. "How do you feel?"

"Fine, but…" Cho reached down and scooped up another handful of pebbles. He pushed them together again and closed his eyes for a moment, but when he opened them and pulled his hands apart a handful of pebbles fell to the ground. "Yes. It is as I thought. I feel as if I am locked down. Unlike a normal lockdown I cannot see what is causing it. If you were unable to see this haze I would be very perplexed."

Thomas took a step forward into the haze. He nervously crossed inside of its boundary, however it contained no noticeable odor nor any feel to it at all. If not for the wispy smoke like look around him he wouldn't know that he had crossed the boundary… except… he turned to look and noticed the Pegasus was gone once more. "Well, that is annoying."

Cho nodded. "That would be an appropriate term. The wall before us is at least a kilometer in height, and we have no means of scaling it."

"Do you think we can just climb it?"

Cho shook his head. "Not without altering ourselves or creating equipment. We will either fall or merely run out of energy before we make it to the top. We cannot stop to rest along the way unless we find a natural ledge large enough. I did not notice any of those on the way down."

Thomas considered their options. "I could fly us up high enough outside of the haze, then hit the haze at an angle. If we are careful on our aim and continue to fall at the same trajectory we could hit the top of the cliff on the other side."

Cho adamantly shook his head. "No, friend Thomas. The height we would need to gain to guarantee such a fall could dissipate us on impact. There is also no guarantee that we would not alter trajectories and fall straight down as soon as we hit the haze."

Thomas had to admit that the man had a point, however he was quickly becoming frustrated and out of ideas. "Okay, then what do we do? Obviously there's some way around this crap."

Cho nodded, calm and unflappable as always. "I suspect there are many options. Some may be outside of our abilities." He paused, as if considering. "I wonder about one though. When I am locked down, I can still affect the lockdown itself. Since I can see it I can manipulate it. I can try to escape it. Can you do the same with this haze?"

Thomas shrugged. "I dunno. I can try I guess." Thomas closed his eyes. He tried willing the haze to go away. It didn't feel any different, and when he opened his eyes he saw Cho looking on hopefully, but the haze remained. Thomas frowned and stared at the haze closely. He willed it to blow away. For a brief moment it actually stirred slightly, but just as Thomas was about to get his hopes up it settled back and remained around them. Thomas took a deep, unnecessary breath, then concentrated on pushing the haze away from him. It stirred again and he redoubled his effort.

This time, it worked. Thomas managed to create a circle around himself with what looked to be about a five-foot radius.

Cho smiled as soon as it passed him, reached down and scooped up a hand full of pebbles, and easily pushed it into one large rock. 'Very good, Friend Thomas."

Thomas smiled and exhaled the breath he had been holding. "Thanks." As soon as he did, the haze slammed back around them and Cho's rock fell a apart. "Uh oh." Thomas concentrated again and the circle expanded once more. "Okay, good news is that I can get us a circle that's maybe ten foot across. Bad news is that I have to keep most of my concentration on it or it collapses."

Cho nodded. "Does this circle center around you?"

Thomas walked towards the cliff and back. "Yes. Seems to."

Cho nodded again. "We can work with that." Cho walked over and turned his back to Thomas. "Climb on my back."

Thomas almost lost the sphere, but managed to maintain it. "Are you sure?"

Cho turned and stated "Yes. Without the haze I can greatly alter my body's abilities. I am pretty certain that as long as you do not drop the circle, I can get us to the top. I warn you, it may not be an easy path. If you should lose your concentration before the top we will surely fall and we may not recover. Are you up to this task?"

In truth Thomas did not feel he was, but he saw no other way around it. He could quit, tell Jack he was a failure, and return back to his sanctuary to spend the rest of eternity there, but that didn't seem like a very appealing alternative either. He could not think of any other choice. "I'll try. Really though, I apologize in advance if I get us both back into The River."

Cho smiled as he turned back and presented his back. "As do I, Friend Thomas. Let us endeavor to see this does not happen."

Thomas took a deep intake of breath again then clambered onto Cho's back. It was weird. He had not done a piggyback ride since he was a small child, and then it was with his parents who at the time were far larger than he had been. Cho was around his same size. It felt extremely awkward, however Cho did not seem to mind or, for that matter, even really notice Thomas's presence. Thomas locked his arms around Cho's shoulders, and his legs around Cho's waist. He fought to keep his concentration on keeping the haze at bay.

"Are you prepared, friend Thomas?"

"As ready as I think I may ever be."

Without another word Cho immediately moved into a dead run heading for the cliff wall. The shock of movement almost caused Thomas to lose his concentration on the haze but he regained his composure fast enough to keep the now very dangerous wisps from closing back in on them. He again nearly lost concentration when Cho hit the wall and bounced straight up ten foot, grabbed a small ledge and tossed himself another ten foot up and left to another ledge. He then continued running nearly vertically using barely visible hand and foot holds to propel the two men up and leaping huge bounds when the options for holds ran out. It felt both exhilarating and frightening as hell. All the more so knowing that if Thomas lost his concentration for more than a second, both men would plummet back down to the pebble-strewn ground below for, as Cho had so eloquently put it, 'a very unpleasant stop'.

Thomas felt as if his energy were literally draining away. He hoped it was merely paranoia, but he feared it might not be. The more he pushed, the more the haze pushed back. He worried as Cho made another inhuman leap that the sphere encircling them might be shrinking. They had to be over a half mile up by now. Thomas grew afraid to even look up or down for fear that even the most minor of additional distractions might prove too much for him to handle.

The minutes pounded away in slow motion, and every jarring jump and upward scramble brought the haze bearing down harder on Thomas's concentration. He could tell now that it wasn't his imagination. The sphere now only extended a good two feet out. If Cho extended his arms as far as he could he would hit haze. Thomas couldn't be sure if that would be enough to drop them or not. He closed his eyes and pushed back, trying to extend the sphere back out to a safe distance. He couldn't tell if he was successful or not, but they kept moving inexorably upwards, so he took that as a good sign.

Finally, after a completely exhaustive eternity, Thomas felt Cho's pace and direction change. He opened his eyes to see Cho clambering over the edge of the cliff. "We… made it… Friend… Thomas."

Cho collapsed to the ground face first. Thomas rolled off of him, giving in to the haze as it too collapsed in. He hoped they could recover energy within this. He knew with certainty that he would not be able to hold it back at bay for sometime without a recharge. "Let's… let's not do that again… okay?"

Cho raised a thumb up, but aside from that did not respond.

*****

Thomas laid on his back for what felt like hours before being able to setup. He noted with a smile that he did feel his energy returning, and seemingly at much the same pace as the Training sanctuary. Cho already sat in his normal lotus position when Thomas looked over. Thomas decided to open himself up and meditate as well. Surprisingly, while he did feel energy coming in quicker, he did not ever drift away as he had during prior meditations. Perhaps no one else called for him, or perhaps the nervousness of being in potential enemy territory kept him from completely letting go of his body.

Whatever the reason, when Cho stood up, Thomas felt mostly refreshed himself.

"Are you prepared to continue, Friend Thomas?"

"Sure Cho." Thomas stood, suddenly missing the ability to truly stretch his muscles. "*It's odd what small things you miss.*"

"Our rest was undisturbed, Friend Thomas. We were lucky."

Thomas nodded. He hadn't really considered what would have happened if an enemy had awaited them at the top of their climb. They would have certainly been dissipated. Thomas would not have been able to stand after that climb, much less fight. "Very lucky."

"Is the haze still around us? It feels as if it might be."

Thomas looked around. They were certainly still in the haze, and from here it was impossible to tell how far it might extend. He couldn't even tell with certainty where it began across the chasm. "Yep. Unfortunately. Everywhere I look, it's still hazy."

Cho nodded. "We will deal with it then. You seemed to drain quickly holding it at bay. Better to save that strength in case it is needed."

Thomas shrugged. "No arguments from me."

Cho looked around all directions, obviously trying to discern any alternative paths or threats they might have missed. "We will need to be on higher guard. Our reflexes will not be enhanced. That will put us at a disadvantage in an ambush."

"You still think there's other living things here?" The thought made Thomas shudder.

Cho looked back at him, calm and matter of fact. "Tests come in many forms, Friend Thomas. We must be prepared."

Thomas shrugged, resigning himself to the ever present danger he now found himself in. "As you say Cho, better safe…"

"Than sorry. Correct, Friend Thomas." Cho smiled, then motioned Thomas to take the lead.

Thomas began moving forward. The jungle on this side of the ravine grew far less dense and the trail far more defined than it had been on the other side. Where it had been an impenetrable wall on either side of a barely manageable path there, here it was a well beaten, sometimes dirt trodden path navigating through less inviting surroundings. He could probably have struck out off the beaten path if he needed to, which somehow worried him. Before, he was certain that following the path was the best plan because there seemed truly no other option Here it felt like he might be just taking the easy way out, which immediately made it the more dangerous option. "Cho, you sure this is still the correct way?"

"No. I cannot sense the master anymore. I suspect it has to do with the haze rather than a change in her item's location. That would imply we are still headed at least the same general direction. Perhaps we should follow it a bit further before we…."

Cho stopped mid sentence and dropped to his belly. Before Thomas could react he saw a blur of motion and felt pain rip through his being. He looked down to see a spiked branch protruding from his chest.

"Son of a…"

Cho leapt up and turned quickly to him. "My apologies, Friend Thomas. I felt the trip wire just as I hit it."

Thomas pushed the limb back, forcing a six inch spike out of his chest. "*Gods. If I had been alive I would really be dead.*" As it was, he was merely in a great deal of discomfort. "Ugh. It's okay, Cho. I should have dropped when I saw you drop. Damn that hurt."

Cho knelt down to study the trip wire in more detail. "Apparently we will need to watch for booby traps."

Thomas pushed the fog away far enough to seal the hole in his chest. It was tough to do both, but he managed to do so with a noticeable hit to his energy. "Yeah. A few of more of those and we'll have to stop and rest again. If we're lucky."

The two continued forward, this time paying closer attention to their path. Three more times over the next hour Cho stopped and pointed out trip wires. The first two were pulled back limbs with spikes on them like the first one they triggered. The third would have smashed them between two very large tree trunks tied on either side of the trail.

Thomas shook his head, trying not to think of how that would have felt. "Damn. They're getting more vicious."

Cho looked around carefully, obviously trying to determine if he had missed anything else. "Indeed. We must continue with care that our existence may depend on our alertness."

"Yeah. It probably does." Thomas said wryly. He wished he had been joking.

They slowed their movement to what felt to Thomas like a near crawl, searching all directions as they moved slowly forward. They had moved for what felt like about an hour without seeing anything else when Cho suddenly stopped again. Thomas prepared to drop or dodge, but Cho just stood in place.

"This ground. It looks strange."

Thomas looked at the path ahead. It was hazy, like the rest of the trail had been, but it did not appear to him out of the ordinary. "I don't see anything."

Cho gestured behind Thomas right arm. "There is a long branch there. Please hand it to me, Friend Thomas."

Thomas did so. Cho took the eight-foot branch and began tapping the ground. On the third tap the ground collapsed completely in front of them revealing a pit a good five-foot wide, ten foot long and at least twenty foot deep. The bottom ten foot of the pit was covered in nasty looking ten-foot tall spikes, which for effect was littered with human looking skeletons.

Thomas let out a low whistle. "Good eye, Cho."

"Thank you, Friend Thomas. The color difference was subtle. I suspect whomever designed this did so to camouflage it with the haze that fills your vision."

Thomas shook his head. "Sneaky bastards. If you can't see the haze you're likely toast at the chasm, if you can see it you're spiked here."

Cho nodded. "Yes, friend Thomas. It appears these traps were well thought out."

Thomas looked at the pit. With the restrictions of this sanctuary along with the haze, there was no way they could actually jump across, but there appeared to be room on either side that they could walk along the edge. Apparently Cho felt the same, as he began carefully making his way along the left side of the pit, using the branches sticking out of the jungle to help keep him from falling. Thomas took the right side and began doing the same. He was half way across when he felt the snap.

"Fuck!" Thomas could feel the movement of the giant trunk whizzing towards him. He knew he couldn't dive anywhere but the pit. Instinct took over. Thomas slammed the anti-haze sphere out as far as he could, let go of it, transformed his own body from his chest down into a solid oak tree with deep roots, then grabbed the sphere before it completely collapsed back in on him. The trunk

slammed painfully into his unyielding form, bouncing off and then
hitting him a second time with far less force. Thomas looked over
his left shoulder in time to see Cho, who stood outside the sphere's
protection, take a crushing blow to the chest from a second trunk.
The trunk carried him over the pit's edge and no doubt would have
dropped him onto the pit's spiked bottom had it not also crossed
him over into the sphere's barrier and out of the influence of the
haze. Cho obviously felt the shift, and managed to push himself off
of the trunk. Like a trapeze artist crossing from a bar to his partner,
Cho spun around and reached out for Thomas's hand. Thomas
grabbed it, his deep roots giving him the stability he needed to
keep the both of them from tumbling into the pit's gaping maw.

"Thank you, Friend Thomas. I do not think I like this place."

"Yeah." Thomas pulled Cho back up to solid ground. "There's an
understatement." Thomas redoubled his grip on the sphere holding
the haze at bay. "Can you push this trunk off me?"

Cho did so, easily pushing the large piece of wood around him.
Thomas let his body change back to normal, then stumbled to the
other side of the pit. Luckily no more trip wires presented
themselves. Thomas collapsed when he reached the other side,
letting the haze slam back around him. "Gods I can't take much
more of this place. Give me someone to fight any day over this
crap."

Cho sat down next to him. "Rest, Friend Thomas. I'll keep watch
in case your wish is granted."

Thomas smiled in spite of himself. "Thanks, Cho."

Twenty-five

"I'm worried about them, Jack. It's been too long."

Jack was worried too, but it did no good, so he sat back and had a drink. "It'll be all right lass. Hell, you didn't get out of there for another day, and you had me guiding you."

Charlotte leaned over the bar she had created and slammed another shot. The room resembled a pretty close recreation of the saloon in Charlotte's own sanctuary. It was quite a bit busier than Jack would have preferred it, but it kept Charlotte calm (by Charlotte standards, anyway), and that was worth the extra hassle.

"Yeah, well. I still don't like it."

Charlotte did not do 'sit and wait'. She always needed to be in the middle of things.

"Charlotte, lass, it was your idea."

"Don't mean you have to go with it. You're fond of telling me when I have a dumb idea. Why didn't you do so here?"

Jack snickered. "Cause, lass, unlike many of your other ideas, this one was good."

"I would break this bottle over your head if it wasn't a waste of good booze. And ineffective."

Jack laughed heartily. "Glad to know me hard head is good for something. Relax. You were right. These lads are good. Maybe the best we've seen."

Charlotte was more nervous than Jack had seen her before. "Yeah, but the final run is always done with a mentor and student. Never two students. What was I thinking?"

"That desperate times call for desperate measures." Jack shrugged. He took another drink then reached over and poured Charlotte a shot. She slammed it back like water then studied the glass in her hand intently. Without a word she threw it against the wall, snatched the bottle from his hand and downed half the remainder.

"Still don't like it."

The door suddenly flew open, revealing a very fidgety and out of place looking Italian. Not someone Jack had expected to see. "Leo! What the bloody hells brings you here?"

"Jack. I think I found it."

"What?"

"The ones, Jack. The ones who are taking our people. I've noticed a pattern, Jack, one that wasn't there before. She's not perfectly clear just yet, but I'm close. Very close."

Jack stood up, dismissing his drink. "Bloody hells. It's about time we caught a break. Notify Heather, Jacob and Huang. I want 'em on standby the minute you find this bastard. I want em going in hard 'n heavy."

Charlotte slammed her bottle down. "I'm going too."

"You sure, lass?" Jack knew the answer as soon as the question left his mouth. Charlotte didn't do waiting around, and with everything that had happened, she would most certainly want in on this.

"Damn sure. Can't stand this waiting, and I've got one hell of a score to settle with this rat bastard."

Jack considered. It would be good to have her in case something happened and he did need to go in and rescue the boys, but he kept telling himself the odds of that were small. It was time to put his money where his mouth was. Besides, if this person (or people, he couldn't rule that out) could take out two members, they might actually be able to take three. Four would steady the odds. More would be better. "Alright, lass. You go do what you need to do. Soon as our wee lads get back from their walkabout I'll bring 'em in too."

Charlotte smiled. "Hell, Jack. By the time you and those boys get there we'll have em hog tied and have half their fingernails pulled out. That is, assuming Leo here can do what he says."

The small Italian suddenly looked a bit nervous. "I'll a do my best, Charlotte."

Jack laughed. "I'd do better than your best, laddie. Last thing you wanna be stuck with is a bored Charlotte looking over your shoulder."

Leo suddenly nodded even more nervously. "I'll a do what I can Jack. Hurry when you can."

*****

"Have you had enough rest?"

Thomas wanted to tell him no, that he would use another few days rest. Or at least an hour in his own sanctuary, but the truth was he was concerned about how much time they had taken already. "I'm fine. How about you? You took a nasty hit back there. You good?"

"Yes. Thank you, Friend Thomas. I am fine."

"No thanks to me." Thomas still felt bad that his mistake had nearly cost his partner dearly. "Sorry about missing that last trip line."

Cho shrugged. "It would seem we are even, Friend Thomas." He smiled and looked around. "Let us make certain neither of us tips that scale."

Thomas smiled. "Good plan."

"I remember seeing you do that once before, in our first battle together. I was unaware that one could turn into a plant. Or partially turn. That was an interesting revelation."

Thomas shrugged. "If it's any consolation, Jack didn't seem to think it was possible before I did it, either. I certainly didn't know it could be done till I sort of accidentally did it. Guess I shouldn't be surprised. Jack says that in theory anything over here is actually possible."

Cho stood and extended Thomas a hand. "Wise words. The more I learn here the more questions I discover."

"Yeah. I know what you mean." Thomas said, using Cho's hand to pull himself up. "Shall we see what other nightmares this place has for us?"

The two set out once more. They set a pace that was measurably slower than it had been before. Thomas was concerned that if any of those traps caught them off guard it might prove more than they could recover from. The heat and humidity also remained a distraction. It felt as if several days had passed, but the time of day never changed. It always felt like mid afternoon, the most obnoxiously sweltering time of day. There had been no reprieve since their arrival. Thomas thought briefly about the warm ice covered sanctuary Jack had once told him about. Maybe he would do the opposite when he returned to his own sanctuary. Still green and lush, but forty degrees in temperature. Maybe fifty. At least for a little while.

Cho stopped, holding up his hand. Thomas cursed himself silently as he realized he'd let himself get distracted and had stopped paying close attention. As he stopped carefully over yet another trip line he was thankful that Cho seamed to be able to stay more focused. He shook his head and tried to redouble his concentration. That worked so long as he constantly reminded himself not to think of anything but his surroundings.

They passed three more tripwires and an additional pit looking trap over the next hour. With all but the last trip wire Cho was the one who kept them from wandering into the trap. The last was actually located about head height as opposed to lower where they'd been watching for the others. It happened that Thomas's eyes had drifted from the trail just in time to keep Cho from touching it.

Thomas had accepted that he'd wandered into hell, and it had taken the form of an endless, booby trapped jungle trail that he would in all likelihood never escape when the cave entrance suddenly appeared ahead of them.

Suddenly was the correct term. One moment there was a seemingly endless trail ahead of them, then the next step they were only twenty paces from a mound of rock slightly taller than either of the two souls with a black gaping cave entrance in the center of it. Out of curiosity Thomas took two steps backwards. To his horror not only did the cave entrance disappear, but Cho with it. He rushed back forward, and was extremely relived when both immediately came back into sight.

Cho for his part appeared not to have noticed Thomas's test, being instead focused on a slow and cautious approach to the cave. Given what they had gone through, Thomas decided that was the correct response to have, and focused himself on the cave as well. Cho stopped when he reached the edge, giving Thomas a chance to catch up to him.

"Dark. That could be trouble."

Thomas shook his head. "No." He took two steps into the cave and produced a torch. "The haze ends at the entrance. Looks like we can use our will to change things again."

"Let us hope that is a blessing and not the sign of a new unknown danger."

Thomas had to smile. "Cho, anyone ever tell you what an optimist you are?"

Cho smiled back as he stepped forward and produced a large lantern. "No, Friend Thomas. But they did tell me I was good at spotting sarcasm."

Twenty-six

Thomas and Cho slowly made their way through the twisting cave. Thomas was relieved that the obnoxious heat of the jungle was quickly fading into a damp coolness. The temperature plummeted to an almost uncomfortable low fifties, though with the fresh memories of the outside still on his mind he was willing to ignore the discomfort for now. The walls were damp but smooth, and the path seemed to move at a slightly increasing slope downward. For now, the footing was sure, but Thomas quickly grew concerned that the moistness of the walls could make for very treacherous walking if the path continued to steepened. Judging by their hike through the jungle, he had little reason to suspect this would be remain easy.

The torch light and lantern created an odd sort of shadow dance on the cavern's walls. The interior of the cave stayed between ten and fifteen foot across. As best he could tell, the inside looked like it was created to appear natural, as if some vast underground river had carved it out over time. He had visited a few caverns in his childhood. They generally smelled like bat guano in the outer areas, and gave way to strange and foreign looking stalactites and stalagmites. This one was different. Just as with the jungle, there were absolutely no signs of living creatures within it. Thomas gave a small bit of thanks that that included any odd bugs and spiders that he secretly expected to find in the dank depths. The path also remained smooth, with no growths from ceilings or floor. Thomas was a bit surprised to realize there wasn't even any moss or lichen on the walls. Rock and water were their only decorations. "At least it'll make trip wires easy to see." He thought with a shrug.

"DOWN!" The warning echoed through the cavern as Cho tackled him, both men crashing to the floor as a hail of arrows shot across the hallway from discreet holes in the walls.

"Thanks Cho." Thomas sat up and looked around. "What happened? I didn't see any trip wires or anything."

Cho picked his lantern up from where it had fallen and examined the floor. "There." He pointed to a spot about three foot behind them that was a perfectly circular indentation in the ground. "One of us must have stepped on the plate."

"A plate that shoots arrows? What are we invading an Aztec tomb?" Thomas asked incredulously.

Cho's response was typically matter of fact. "The creator of this sanctuary seems to have had a love of adventure stories."

Thomas stood up and retrieved his torch, looking at his surroundings with new vigilance. "Guess it's too much to ask that the traps be predictable. I just hope we don't trip a rolling boulder."

Cho looked at him quizzically. "Do you feel that is possible?"

Thomas shrugged his shoulders. "Depends on just how clichéd this place gets in its attempts to dissipate us."

*****

Half an hour of walking resulted in three more pressure plates. Without the mist, Cho seemed far better suited to locating them than before. The path continued to slope downward, and the slope continued to steepen. As Thomas had feared, footing started to become treacherous. The angle of the incline at this point was only slightly less severe than the average staircase, but smooth and damp. Thomas caught himself from slipping several times, and even Cho was starting to slow his pace further, having to concentrate as much on footing as watching for hidden dangers. Finally, the grade shifted again, and Cho stopped, staring downward.

"We are unlikely to walk beyond this."

"Can you still sense the thing we're after?"

Cho closed his eyes, then nodded. "Yes. It feels closer. It also feels like we are going the correct direction."

Thomas carefully stepped forward. While there was no actual water pouring out, the ground seemed to seep just enough to keep it slick. The wetness along with the grade made it look almost like a water slide instead of a path. "Hmm."

Thomas tossed his torch out. It hit the ground and began sliding. It quickly picked up speed, and continued sliding ever downwards till it disappeared out of site. "Well, we know it goes a ways down there. Do we slide?"

"I do not like it. We cannot avoid any traps if we are not controlling our movement."

Thomas considered for a moment, and then produced a small sledgehammer and a large steel spike. As Cho watched on he tapped the spike into the progressively harder force. Each pound echoed loudly through the cavern, but to his relief the spike actually sank into the stone floor neatly. He looked up and smiled at Cho. "Wasn't sure that would work."

Thomas then reached down and reshaped the spike so that it had a circular eye at the top. He then produced a long, lightweight rope and tied it off to the spike, then handed it off to Cho. "See if you can use this to keep yourself from sliding too far."

"Okay. Will you do the same?"

"Maybe. But for now…" Thomas dropped down to all four paws as he morphed into his saber-toothed cat form. "I'll try four legs."

Cho raised an eyebrow at him, but said nothing. Thomas realized that the only other time Cho had seen him in this form, Thomas had savagely attacked him and ripped out his throat. That probably made this form somewhat disconcerting for him. To Cho's credit though, it seemed to barely faze him. He nodded quickly, then grabbed the rope and began moving. Thomas shook his thoughts away as distractions and tested his footing.

His paws were wet. That was annoying. But so long as he measured his pace, he felt comfortable in keeping his footing. He noticed a familiar scent in the air. He thought through what it could be and realized it smelled like part of the Training sanctuary. Given the direction, he suspected he smelled the item that Charlotte had created. That was a good sign. It meant Cho had been correct about them being on the right path.

Thomas began his measured movement downward. Cho had chosen to stay on his feet but walk backwards, using the rope to support his weight and keep him balanced. This kept his descent slow and measured, but it obviously made keeping an eye for the unusual measurably harder. This meant Thomas now became the primary scout. Luckily his new vantage point actually put him in a far better position to spot things out of place with the floor. Within a few minutes he had already spotted the next pressure plate and growled back a warning to Cho. He wondered why he hadn't thought to take this form as soon as they hit the cave.

Cho had tied the lantern to his waist, It rocked with each step, causing the shadows to dance again, but it cast enough light that Thomas could easily spot the ground ahead a good twenty foot. Even with that, it was his ears that first noticed something new.

Whoosh…..whoosh……whoosh….

Thomas stopped and growled. "Something up ahead."

"Do you know what it is, Friend Thomas?"

"No." Thomas began slowly padding forward again. "But we will find out soon."

After a few more minutes, it was obvious Cho could here it too. A few more steps and Thomas got his first glimpse of what was causing the sound.

Whoosh……whoosh……whoosh….

A huge pendulum swung at an even pace across the path, with a large and sharp looking blade marking the end of it.

Thomas stopped and growled. "You have got to be kidding me."

"What is it, Friend Thomas?" Apparently his eyesight did not yet go as far as Thomas's now enhanced vision.

"Blades." He could tell by the sound that this was the first of several. "Big ugly swinging blades."

Thomas continued forward, and quickly confirmed what his ears had already told him. They stopped about five foot away from the first blade. By now Cho's lantern made a very clear view of what they were looking at. Five blades, each about three foot apart, swung in alternating directions. Each released from its respective side at the same time so that all of them started and stopped at the same time.

Thomas sat down on his haunches, less annoyed at the wet ground now than what he saw ahead of him. "I hate this place." He growled.

Cho studied the newest obstacle. "I agree, Friend Thomas. I will not miss this sanctuary when we leave."

"If we leave." Thomas grumbled.

Cho smiled down at him. "Now it is you who gives into pessimism. Do not despair. The masters would not have assigned a task that they were not confident we could pass."

Thomas growled under his breath. He knew Cho was correct, but he did not care. His energy was feeling noticeably lower, his haunches as well as his feet were soaked, which amplified the cool temperature. There was nothing about this place that wasn't designed to instill the utmost misery.

He sighed. Cat form always made him less patient. He tried forcing the cat's instinctive personality back and focused on the path ahead. Cho was correct. There was a way through this. Despite the feeling that this entire place existed as one big death trap, others had apparently made it through successfully. If they could, then chances were high that he and Cho could as well. "Suggestions? Can we stop them?"

Cho studied the swinging blades, edging slightly closer to them. He then shook his head. "No. Perhaps we could create something, but they have much weight and appear well made and sharp. However…."

Thomas waited for Cho to finish his statement, but the Asian seemed intent on studying instead. "However what?"

"Sorry. I was timing the movement and playing through the options. I am certain that if we move quickly at the moment the blades cross the center, we can make it to the other side."

"And if we miss?"

"If we are lucky, it will hurt very badly." Cho shrugged.

Thomas sneered. "That's reassuring."

"That is not all."

Thomas cocked his large head sideways and stared at Cho. "What else?"

Cho sighed. "The grade steepens more here. With the speed we will need to make it though these blades, we will be unlikely to be able to stop our momentum once we start. We will be at the mercy of the trail."

Thomas growled instinctively once more. "That sounds stupid."

Cho nodded. "Agreed. But I do not see another way through. We may have to trust the fates to this one."

Thomas did not like that idea. If there were any actual fates in control of anything, they had not been kind to him thus far. They had already killed him once. Would they hesitate to do so again?

But at the same time, he saw little else in the way of options. "Do you believe this will work?"

Cho remained silent for a few minutes, then looked back at him. "It is the best option I can come up with."

"That's not as reassuring as I would like."

"I know, Friend Thomas. As it was my idea, I will go first."

Before Thomas could say anything, Cho took off at a dead run, hitting the first blade just as it passed the center of the path. He was through three of them as they hit their zenith, and dove forward as the final passed the center, barely making it beyond its reach. "IT Woooorrrkkked."

Cho and his light quickly began fading. Thomas hissed a curse and before he could think about what he was doing pushed himself forward into a sprint. This body was well designed for short bursts of speed and he easily cleared all five before they could complete their downward swing. He slammed his paws into the other side, but to no avail. As Cho had feared, the already steep decline grew steeper and slicker, and despite his scrambling he found himself spinning down the cavern floor. Thomas tried sinking his claws into the floor, but something stopped him. Whether it was the design or more mist had appeared, Thomas couldn't be certain. The light was too dim and he was moving too fast.

Cho was well ahead of him, but luckily his enhanced eye site meant that even this far from Cho's bright lantern it was clear enough for him to see a little. He heard a hissing sound and pushed himself low, ducking beneath what sounded like a series of shooting arrows. He noticed Cho's lantern ahead make a strange bouncing movement, and within a few moments saw why. Several sharp blades were pointed up at him from the ground. He knew he couldn't stop himself, but he was fairly certain they were low enough he could clear them. He forced himself into a crouch as he slid, and when he was within a few feet he launched himself using his powerful hind legs, easily clearing the deadly protrusions. Suddenly, however, the entire room cavern went pitch black as Cho's light disappeared.

"Shit." Thomas had just enough time to contemplate what a stupid idea this entire thing had been before the light reappeared below him, replacing the ground. He was falling.

"SHIT!" Thomas screamed through his saber teeth as his paws flailed for anything to slow his fall. When that failed, he instinctively tried to stop through force of will. As before, it didn't work either. He tried reaching into the nearest wall, but it was smooth and unforgiving. He considered his Pegasus, but there was definitely no room for the winged horse here, and it would only....

He hit the water hard. He felt it swallow him up and he sank fast. Thomas panicked. He hated water. Being damp was bad but being wet was horrible! He flailed with little result till he realized he was still in cat form. He morphed back, strangely calming a bit, and fought his way back up to the surface, gasping as he finally broke the surface. Cho appeared a few second later next to him, raising his still burning lantern out of the water.

"Are you okay, Friend Thomas?"

Thomas wiped the water from his eyes. "Yeah. Just went pretty deep there. Kinda freaked me out I guess. "

"Friend Thomas, remember, we are dead. We cannot drown."

Thomas stared at Cho for a moment, then flushed with embarrassment. "Yeah. I guess not. Sorry. I guess… I guess I panicked there for a moment."

"Do not worry. You were not alone in that feeling. But it appears we survived." Cho looked around, and Thomas noted what he suspected his friend was noting as well, their air pocket did not go very far. 'Though it would seem our path now takes us underwater."

"Well, that will be weird." Thomas stated in agreement. "But I guess, as you said, we can't really drown, so why not?"

Cho sank back beneath the water's surface. Thomas fought the urge to try and take a deep breath, then stopped swimming and let himself begin sinking. Surprisingly, he did so like a rock.

Thomas and Cho hit the floor of the now flooded cavern after about thirty foot. Thomas was surprised, but there didn't seem to be any additional pressure on them. He had tried scuba diving once, and had trouble with his ears hurting after just ten foot or so down. This felt different. Very different. First off, there was no feeling of floating. It seemed as if he were weighted heavily enough that he sank comfortably to the floor with roughly the same amount of weight that he would have had on land. He also had no internal pressure. The visibility around him was pretty clear, and he could see to the edge of Cho's admittedly more subdued light range. He had no mask on, but his eyes didn't sting.

He took a test step forward, and here he did meet with resistance. He pushed himself a few feet, and it genuinely felt as if he were trying to push through a wall of water. The mixed sensations of really being in water but not was extremely disconcerting. He also had to fight the urge not to take a breath, despite knowing full well he didn't need one. He wasn't sure, however, what would happen if he did take a breath. Would he start coughing uncontrollably? Or would his lungs just fill up with water and give him another odd but harmless sensation? He wasn't certain and he decided he really wasn't interested in finding out.

Cho put his head down and began pushing forward. Thomas fell in line beside him. The resistance of the water was annoying but otherwise seemingly harmless. As a test he pushed himself forward and began to kick, finding he could swim with about the same speed and far less resistance than walking. After seeing Thomas do it, Cho quickly joined in, and the two were now moving at a much more steady pace.

"This is weird." Oddly, Thomas was able to talk underwater. His voice was muffled, and it sounded pretty much like he would have expected to sound if speaking underwater, but he could do it.

"I agree." Cho's voice too was oddly muffled but understandable.

"At least we don't have to worry about pressure plates like this."

"Correct, Friend Thomas." Cho nodded, trying to keep his lantern as steady as possible in front of them. "So I expect we will find all new traps to challenge us."

Thomas shook his head. There was no reason to chide Cho for his pessimism here. Thomas knew it was just a statement of fact. This entire sanctuary, if that was even an appropriate name for this nightmare of a place, existed for no other obvious reason than to push peoples' abilities to their limits. There was no reason to expect this part of the path would be any different than the jungle or the cavern paths had been. There was no choice but to be vigilant for the underwater spears, nets, or giant sharks that would no doubt leap out at them when they least expected it.

Thomas and Cho swam on in silence. Like the cave, there was no sign of plant life anywhere to be seen, and like both the cave and the jungle, no signs of animal life either. The sphere of light from the lantern showed brightly in the exceedingly clear water. It seemed obvious it was meant to be freshwater and not salt, though the light sediment at on the floor looked more like the white sand one would expect to see on the ocean's floor in beautiful blue water photographs.

Thomas wondered if that would be where the traps would come from. If they had been actually walking on the floor, there would be absolutely no way of detecting any hidden pressure plates. But what would be the odds that someone would walk across the bottom when swimming seemed to offer less resistance?

Trip wires seemed an odd choice for the same reason. With a good thirty-foot vertical area to choose from, where would you place trip wires to ensure they could be hit? Unless maybe there was a trip net. That thought seemed plausible. A large but thin trip net, like a giant underwater spider web. But it would have to be huge in that case, assuming that the realm stuck to real world style physics here like it did above, and lack of water pressure aside, it certainly seemed to.

Cho suddenly flew backwards with an audible "Ugh!". Thomas stopped swimming himself to see what happened when he felt a punch to his own gut.

"Ouch! What the hell?" Another blunt slam to the side of his head sent him reeling sideways. Thomas spun around but nothing seemed out of place. Cho doubled over as if he had been slammed into. He lashed out widely, but seemed to only connect with the water all around them. Another punishing blow cracked into the back of Thomas's head, sending him spinning towards the sand below.

Thomas tried shrinking into a more protective ball, glancing around for their hidden assailant. There was no trail of movement, no signs of life. There was no evidence whatsoever that there was anyone or anything in the water aside from Thomas and Cho. But as Cho began spiraling downward as well, it was very clear to Thomas they were certainly not alone.

"Cho! Where is it? What is it?"

Cho touched down on the sand and again lashed out wildly. "I do not know, Thomas. It is like the water itself is attacking us."

Thomas took another blow to the stomach, doubling him over in pain. "Ug. Whatever it is feels like it's using a damn lead pipe." Thomas tried lashing out himself, but to no avail. He was underwater punching water. There seemed no feeling of connection. "This sucks, Cho!"

"Agreed, Friend Thomas." Cho spun so that his back was against Thomas, both men keeping a constant look around them for their enemy to appear. It didn't, however blunt force slammed into

Thomas's nose with sufficient force to smash his head back into Cho, causing both men to scream in pain. "We must do something, Friend Thomas. We will not last long in this assault."

"Yeah. Agreed. What the hell do we do?"

"Can you push the water back like you did the mist above?"

Another blow swept Thomas's feet out from beneath him, however the water slowed his fall enough that it allowed him to catch himself and stand back up. "I don't know. I'll try."

Thomas focused, imagining a large pocket of air around them. At first nothing happened, but then slowly the water began receding from them. Within a few moments, there was a ten-foot wide half circle surrounding them. The water seemed to push back with a brick load of force. Thomas dropped to a knee, but held the circle still.

"Look, Friend Thomas. It is the water attacking us!"

Thomas looked out with an effort that made him grunt. At the edge of the circle, a tentacle of water lashed forward a foot or so in then pulled back, lashing in a few seconds later at another point of the air sphere. The size of it, with a diameter near the size of a bowling ball, left no doubt it was responsible for the beating Thomas had been feeling. "Great. How do..." he doubled down his focus on the air sphere as it continued trying to crush back in on them, "... how do we stop it?"

Thomas felt his knees buckle, as it seemed like the water creature slammed into the air sphere itself. For a brief moment he thought he could see through his own hand. "*Is this what they mean by dissipating?*"

"I do not know, Friend Thomas."

Thomas grunted again as the sphere tried to crush back in on him once more. "We better figure it out fast. I... I don't think I can last much longer!"

Twenty-seven

"I thought you had em found, Leo!"

The small Italian visibly flinched, and spoke in a reassuring voice, "I thought I did too, Charlotte. But the science, she is not exact here."

"Well it damn well should be. I'm tired of waiting." Charlotte paced back and forth in front of Leo's pool. Huang, the mountain of a man, sat in his plain brown pants and tight fitting shirt with the sleeves ripped off sharpening a knife that could probably slice the whetstone in half if he wanted it too. Charlotte bit her lip and tried to ignore the scraping sound the blade made with each pass. It grated on her nerves, but she knew that was only because of her frustration at having to sit there doing nothing. The more frustrated she became the more she wanted to take it out on everything around her. But the near seven foot tall Chinaman had many more annoying habits he could be exercising, so Charlotte forced herself to ignore him.

Heather pushed her bright red hair out of her eyes as she continued her typical past time, juggling. She was dressed in black leather pants with a dark halter top covering assets that Charlotte swore got curvier with each year since Heather's death. "Better hurry Leo. You know our resident cowgirl's got a metric assload of impatience."

"I am going as fast as I can go." Leo replied exasperatedly in his thick accent. "Distracting me, it is not making the job easier."

Charlotte gritted her teeth and continued pacing, only the slow *snick* sound of Huang's blade and the occasional distant bird call broke the silence. It was wrong. It was all wrong. She reached out instinctively and traced the bond to her comrades. The three here were quick to trace. Jacob could be felt just on the other side of Leo's small cottage. The large black man had never been one for being social, and Charlotte suspected that being on a nonstop set of missions with Heather had tested the lengths of his patience more than he probably would have thought possible. He had earned some alone time.

Jack's link was easily traceable, leading off towards the Training sanctuary. The fact that he was still there and there were no new links to Cho or Thomas told her the boys had still not returned. That worried her, but she forced the worry down. There was no time for worry now. She reached out for the other links she had known, but felt no others. John, Roberto, Dominique, Marco, all gone. It was as if they had never been there.

That was unsettling, especially with Dominique. He had been her partner for the past fifteen years, and with the way some of their missions had gone, dealing with Sanctuaries where time passed so much slower, it felt like five times that. Dominique had been her companion, her love, and more of a friend in death than anyone had ever been for her while she had lived. Now he was gone. The frustrating part was that she didn't even know how. She had taken a break to train Heather, just as she had done several times before. Jack said she had a good feel for training new recruits, and the truth was she enjoyed the break from the missions. It always felt good to do a little something different now and again. But if she'd known…

She had felt the link to Dominique sever long before Jack came to tell her what happened. Despite his protests she had made Jack take over Heather's training while she did a personal search for Dominique and Marco's trail. There was nothing. No way of knowing where they'd gone or what had happened to them when they'd gotten there. She had made a good many threats against Leo during that time, and the poor little Italian had no doubt believed she would carry them out, but in the end he couldn't help her find the trail either. They had gone on what should have been a routine mission, then vanished without a trace, tossed back in the River for all she knew.

They had not been the first either, but they had been the closest to Charlotte. They had been the ones she had worked with since dying those many years ago. Now John and Roberto were gone too. Two more souls she counted on the short list of people she called 'friends'. Again, no trace, nothing but frustration. It brought up the misery of losing Dominique all over again, and she had to constantly fight herself to keep from taking it out on Cho during his training. In the end, that was why she had decided to have him start training with Thomas. She really didn't trust herself to be his sole mentor anymore.

Now though. Now there was hope. Now after all of this time, there might actually be a trace, a way to find out who or what was responsible for ripping her friends away from her, and make them pay. She would find whatever did this. When she did she would rip piece by piece off of them until they told her what happened, where her friends were. If they could be rescued, she would do it. If they had returned to the River, she would make certain the creature responsible did as well. She might even throw it into the Glacier of Gods and Monsters, just to make certain that only the tiniest piece of it ever saw life again.

The only thing standing in her way was Leo locating them. "I swear by every god that ever existed, Leo, if this is a dead end and you got my hopes up I will dissipate you. "

Leo spoke as if he were trying to remain calm. "That knowledge, Ms. Charlotte, I knew it before I contacted you. I am close. Please, miss. Be patient just a little longer."

Snick. Snick.

Patient. She had been patient. She had not taken Huang's knife from him and thrown it through Heather's juggling balls. Or Heather for that matter. She had not gone after Thomas and Cho despite knowing that they should have been back, and that something bad very well might have befallen them. There were too many traps, the water elemental far too dangerous. They should not have been forced to make the test alone. But she had let them go as Jack had insisted, and she had been patient. Now was not the time for patience. Now was the time for action. And she was fast losing her care as to what form that action took. Either she went and drug Thomas and Cho out of the Test sanctuary, she beat the crap out of whatever enemy Leo could find, or she would take her frustrations out on her companions. Something was going to give. Something had to.

"There. It is there." Leo spoke with a mix of relief and excitement.

Huang paused in mid slice over the whetstone. Heather let her juggling balls drop, each one disappearing after a couple of bounces on the ground, and Charlotte rushed over and looked down into the plane that Leo's pool had opened up.

"You're sure that this is it, old man?"

"Yes, Ms. Charlotte. I feel it. It is the same as the others went into. But I cannot get a very good reading on it. And the gateway, I do not know if I can hold it for long."

Charlotte turned to Huang. "Grab Jacob. It's time we let this bastard know who it's been fucking with."

Twenty-eight

"Hold, Friend Thomas! Here!"

Thomas felt the weight of the sphere lesson from his position on the sandy floor. It still felt like he was shouldering twice his own weight, but it no longer felt like he was being stomped on by an angry elephant. "Than… thank you, Cho."

"No problem." Cho's grunt showed that it obviously was a problem. "Since I can see your sphere this time I can reinforce it. I… I do not know how long I can help though."

"We better get out of here then." Thomas grunted.

"Can you move, Friend Thomas?"

Thomas managed to get one knee up into an upright position. "I think so. As long as you're helping anyway. Let's go, Cho."

Cho reached his arm under Thomas's and helped him up. The two men did their best to support each other, and began stumbling forward. The sandy bottom did not present the best footing Thomas could hope for, but it was stable. Thomas just hoped there were no traps hidden beneath the sand. It was all he could do to hold the water monster at bay. A well-placed trap would end him for certain this time.

Each step was more excruciating than the last. One particularly powerful blow brought both men to their knees, but they struggled and pushed forward once more.

"*This is it.*" Thomas thought, despair starting to drift in. "*This is how it ends. I'll return to the River. I'll never… I'll never meet my child…*" That idea was too much to bear. "*NO….*" He had abandoned Shari once. He would not do it again. He would be there to watch over his child. And when Shari finally crossed over to this side, he would be there to greet her. This would not… this could not… be the end. Jack would not have sent the two of them on a suicide mission. This would soon pass.

Those thoughts gave him strength. They kept his legs moving, even as Cho's began to falter and slow. "Stay with me, Cho! What would Charlotte do to you if you gave up now?"

It was the best Thomas could think of, but it must have worked. Cho put his head down and pushed forward, much more steady than he had been. Thomas concentrated on keeping the air bubble whole, and placing one foot in front of the other. The rhythmic pounding of the water monster on the sphere's exterior, occasionally protruding into the sphere itself, faded into the background. Left foot. Right Foot. Left Foot. Right Foot. Left Foot. Right foot.

Then it happened. Looking back, Thomas wasn't certain if it happened suddenly or if he had just been so busy concentrating that he'd failed to see its approach, but with a suddenness that shocked him, Thomas suddenly broke through the water's surface. Quickly he pushed forward, dragging Cho with him. The air sphere dropped as a dark underground beach came into view. Thomas felt a crushing blow slam into his back, sending him flying out of the water and rolling along the beach. He turned to see Cho stumble onto shore, narrowly ducking a watery tentacle as a large humanoid shaped section of water stood for a moment above the lightly lapping waves, then crashed back down becoming one once more with its surroundings, leaving the two men gasping in silence.

"We... we did it... Friend Thomas." Cho squeaked.

"*Yes we did.*" Thomas thought, before the darkness swallowed him completely.

*****

Thomas wasn't certain how long he was out. He had not thought it possible to sleep here in the land of the dead, but that was the closest explanation he could find to the experience of suddenly realizing he had completely lost consciousness. There had been no dreams, no visions, no recognition of anything around him or memory of anything transpiring. There had only been the black nothingness that engulfed him until he fought his way out of it with the same determination he had used to walk out of the water.

He had expected to see Cho in his familiar Lotus meditation position, but when he finally forced himself to sit up he instead saw the small Asian lying face down in the sand. For a moment he panicked that the man might be dead, then realized that he was, but in the same way as Thomas himself. If Cho had actually died in this reality, he would have disappeared. There would be no body left face down.

"Cho." Thomas reached over and shook the small man's shoulder. "Cho, you still with me?"

Cho slowly stirred. "What?" Oh. Sorry, Friend Thomas. Where are we?"

Thomas looked around. "An underground beach. Looks like we survived the water. God I hope we don't have to leave that way."

"I do not think we will, Friend Thomas. I am not certain I could if we do."

Thomas forced himself to stand and look around. Behind him the underground lake lapped gently at the sandy shore. The tranquility of the sound formed a harsh juxtaposition to the memory of the terror lurking within it."

Ahead the beach continued into the darkness. Thomas raised a torch high, the light from it penetrating the darkness with a far brighter radiance than it would have had in the real world. Ahead, about fifty foot in, the sandy beach ended in a slick, damp, under ground wall. The only break in the smooth wall was a one-foot diameter round hole about eight foot above the sand.

Thomas turned to Cho. "Trap?"

Cho nodded, still obviously not fully recovered from their ordeal. "Probably, Friend Thomas. But I sense our objective that direction. It may be our only option. "

Thomas shrugged. He was getting very tired of this test. "One way to find out, right?"

Before Cho could say anything, Thomas took off on a dead run for the wall. He pictured himself running up the side, and was almost shocked when he found himself doing just that. When he was high enough he pushed himself into the hole, expecting to find the gaping teeth of a monster or the spiked edge of some kind of trap waiting on him. Instead he was laying on a smooth floor of a room just on the other side.

Shocked, he laid there for a moment, waiting for the inevitable trap to spring. But nothing happened. After waiting long enough to feel certain there would be no immediate trap, he pulled his legs through the hole, spun around and reached down for Cho. "Umm... strangely enough it seems safe."

"I would ask that you never do that again, Friend Thomas." Cho reached up and grabbed Thomas's hand, and used the leverage to easily pull himself up.

Thomas stood up and surveyed the room. The room was a large circular chamber. The walls curved into a massive dome, stretching up fifty foot or more to a circular opening, allowing a bright beam of sunlight to peer down onto a pedestal in the center of the room. On the pedestal sat a bottle of what looked to be a dark brown whiskey. Thomas smiled. "Bout damn time."

Cho, for his part, was apparently still wary. "Yes. But does it not seem too... exposed?"

Thomas surveyed the surroundings. The floor was smooth and clear, made from what appeared to be solid carved stone. There was not so much as a particle of dust on it. The path between them and the alter was completely as absolutely clear. Cho was right. It was entirely too easy. "What's the catch? I don't see anything."

"Nor do I, Friend Thomas." Cho said, inspecting the floor closely. "That concerns me, greatly."

Thomas took a small step forward. The ground did not collapse. The domed roof did not cave in. No invisible monsters lashed out at him. He took another step, and again absolutely nothing occurred.

"Okay, now I'm really worried."

Cho reached down and scraped the floor. As Thomas watched, Cho rolled up a section of the stone as if it were snow, forming a bowling ball size stone sphere of stone. He then pulled the stone back and in an under hand motion rolled the stone lightly across the floor towards the pedestal. Thomas watched with anticipation as the ball slowly wound its way across the flooring, each turn failing to bring any unexpected calamity. Finally the stone bumped gently against pedestal. Nothing happened.

Thomas shrugged. "Maybe we're over thinking this?"

Cho looked over at him, then back at the round stone against the pedestal. "I do not know, friend Thomas. I do not like it, but perhaps you are correct. Perhaps the final test is that there is no test."

Thomas took another step towards the whiskey. Again, nothing stopped him. Slowly he continued his path. He could hear Cho a few steps behind him. To be as safe as possible, Thomas tried sticking as close as he could to the path that the stone had taken, just in case it had been merely luck that it had found the path between tripwires. Whether it had or whether there were no traps to trip he wasn't certain, but in the end he found himself safely next to the pedestal and just inches away from his goal.

Thomas circled around slowly until he found himself on the exact opposite side of the bottle as Cho. "Well?"

Cho shook his head. "I do not know, Friend Thomas."

Thomas reached up, his hand mere inches from the bottle of whiskey. He flexed his fingers, looking closely for any possible trap he could see. There was none to be seen. It was a bottle of whiskey on a block of stone in a beam of sunlight in the middle of a large cavernous room. All signs told him that was the extent of what there was. His mind screamed that there had to be more, but his sense could find nothing.

Finally, he couldn't stand it. With one smooth motion he snatched the bottle from its resting place. All was quiet.

Except....

"Look out!" Cho tackled Thomas, knocking him and the bottle to the side just as a section of ceiling collapsed where he had been staying.

"Damn it! I knew there had to be something!" Thomas kicked Cho to the side and rolled as another chunk landed where they had just been lying. A cursory glance showed a huge piece had collapsed in front of the opening in the wall they had entered from. "Damn it!"

"Thomas! There!" Cho exclaimed with a sharp finger point.

Thomas followed Cho's finger, sliding to the side once more as another chunk of ceiling fell. Just on the other side of the growing sun circle in the center was a slight shimmer. Something that wasn't there a moment ago. "A Portal! Go Cho, GO!"

For a brief moment it occurred to Thomas that this too could be a death trap, but at this point he cared little. He had already died once. What was once more? Better than staying in this plane of hell.

Cho reached the portal first and dove through. Without pause, Thomas followed, flinging himself through as another section of ceiling crashed down behind him. He rolled to a halt, pushing himself to his feet in preparation for the next assault. He was met with clapping.

Twenty-nine

"Well done lads. Well done indeed! I knew you had it in ya."

Thomas took a deep sigh of relief as he recognized his surroundings. He was back in the Training sanctuary. "Jack! Thank the gods."

"Gods have nothing to do with it, laddy." Jack exclaimed, clasping a hand on both men's shoulders. "You two could only make it back here if you used incredible team work and ingenuity."

Cho sat down. Thomas wasn't entirely certain he could keep himself from collapsing completely. "That test SUCKED Jack! It was horrible!"

Jack smiled. "Aye. But you made it."

Cho pulled himself into his preferred lotus position. "Thank you for your praise, Master Jack. That test seemed rather more… extreme."

"Well, to be fair it was for you two." Jack snatched the bottle, and poured a healthy dose of the contents into three glasses he pulled from the ether. "But you two did as impressive a job as I had expected."

Thomas stared at the glass in front of him as Jack handed one down to Cho. "Could we have really died there, Jack?"

"Oh, aye." Jack nodded. "It's a dangerous place to be certain."

"Have people died there?" Thomas wasn't certain if he wanted to know the answer to that or not.

Jack picked his own glass up, but did not drink from it. "Aye lad. So I'm told. Used to be the test was conducted as you took it. I've been told many trainees did not make it out. A hundred or so years ago somebody decided we should test new recruits a wee bit more safely. Since then it's been one new recruit and one older hand. The older hand keeps the new recruit alive and pulls em out when they get too close to getting themselves dissipated. Truth be told I think me and Charlotte are the only two in recent history that made it through first go. Well, till you two."

The full extent of the danger they had been in sunk into Thomas's mind. "Good gods, Jack! Were you trying to get rid of us?"

"Nay lad. I had faith in you. Times are bad, and they're getting worse from here. You two are one of the strongest pairings I've seen since I died, but you'd normally be in training another year at least afore we let you go. We don't have time for that. I needed to know you were as ready as we need you to be. I was pretty sure you were, but now…" Jack raised his glass, obviously instructing the other two to take theirs and do the same, "now we know. Congratulations lads. Training's over. You're full members as of now."

Jack tapped his drink against Cho's and then Thomas's glass, then downed its contents. Cho followed suit. Thomas paused for a moment before did the same. "No more training? You're serious, Jack."

"As a bloody heart attack, mate. You past your final exam. There's more to learn to be sure, but I'll tell you this much, there's always more to bloody well learn. But you know the basics. Well beyond it I'd wager. You two are forces to be reckoned with."

Cho's smile was as broad as his face. He bowed to Jack. "Thank you, Master Jack! Master Charlotte, is she around? I must thank her."

Jack shook his head. "She's off on a mission. Point of fact, I'm going to join her in a moment. If you lads want, you can too. Leo thinks he's found the bastard that's been targeting our people. Charlotte and the rest of the crew went to deliver a bit of well deserved payback. More the merrier I think. "

Thomas set his empty glass down. "Let's go then. What are we waiting on?"

Jack smiled. "Aye lad. But one more lesson first. Come here, both of you."

Cho and Thomas stepped forward, standing side by side across from Jack. Jack knelt down, and as Thomas watched closely, reached down into the ground of the Training sanctuary itself. To Thomas's surprise, the ground looked like it took on the consistency of pudding. Jack pulled his hand back, and while not so much as a speck of dirt remained on his hand, he pulled up what appeared to be a brilliant sapphire blue cord. When he stood, all signs of Jack's typical mirth disappeared.

He spoke in a very serious, somber tone. "Tell me true lads, and I want you to think hard before you answer. Do you wish to join our organization as a full member, or do you wish to take your knowledge and walk away? If you accept, you'll be expected to follow the orders given you, do what you can to keep rogue souls from taking on souls and Sanctuaries that are not theirs to take, and give everything for the greater good of the Order, up to and including your very existence. If you choose to walk away, now will be the time. I'll be disappointed, but I'll get over it. You'll not be hounded in any way, and your existence will be yours to do with as you will. Think well, and answer knowing you will not be able to retract what you say."

Thomas paused. The unusual weight behind Jack's words made him wonder for a brief moment if he should go forward. The test had been horribly bad, and in all likelihood he would have to do worse now. Could he do that? Would it be better to walk away, be his own soul, and take his new knowledge to explore what was out there?

"No." He thought. The cause of the order was just. He thought back to Falling Dusk and the God Monk. People like Jack's order stood to keep creatures like that from rising again. They may be the only things that kept such creatures from regaining power. That could not happen again. What kind of world would he be leaving to his child if he walked away and something like the God Monk walked again?

Cho bowed. "I made my decision when you first contacted me, Master Jack. That decision has not changed. I will pledge my existence to The Order."

Jack nodded. "Thomas?"

Thomas nodded his head. "I agree. No point in changing my mind now. I'm in."

Jack smiled. He then took the beautiful blue cord and pulled it apart, somehow forming two identical glowing blue cords, each leading back into the ground below. "Well then. Know that this sanctuary is not just where we train, it is what connects us. Through it, we are one. From here forward, we are family. You need not worry of being alone, you will always be able to find those of us connected." Jack placed a hand on the left shoulder of each man. As he did, the brilliant blue cords flashed brightly.

Thomas felt an icy blast of feeling as the cord fused with his shoulder. He gasped as fresh sensation flooded into his body. New energy, new feelings, it was amazing and frightening at the same time. Jack's hand, at first there to hold the cord to his shoulder, now served to steady him. It alone stopped him from dropping to his knees.

"Take a moment, lads. Let it sink in."

Within a moment the cord flashed even brighter, then disappeared from view. It was not, however, gone. Thomas could feel it pulsing, calmly and strangely comfortingly, at his shoulder. He felt very alive, suddenly. Not quite as much as when he stood in his own sanctuary, but very close. "Wow. That's intense."

Jack smiled. "Aye. And it's more. I want you to close your eyes. Reach out mentally through the link. Follow it."

Thomas did so. As he focused his attention on it, he realized that he could trace it easily back down and into the sanctuary itself. From there, the cord seemed to branch out. Two of the paths seemed short. He traced the first and realized it lead to Cho, whom he could sense as excited and happy. Thomas followed the other path, and it lead to Jack, who felt very proud, though somewhat nervous as well.

Thomas followed one of the longer paths, this time searching for Charlotte. He found her link as if he'd known all along how to do so. She felt far away, but he could sense her. She was angry, focused, and slightly... scared? Thomas followed another link. This one belonged to....

…no one. The link was gone. "Jack?"

Jack's link suddenly grew dark and angry, with a flash of fear as well. "Come on, Lads. We've got work to do."

Jack put a hand on both of his former apprentices' shoulders and suddenly the world shifted again.

Thirty

The view through Leo's pool had been empty grasslands. Charlotte had not been entirely certain he had found the correct path, but Leo was adamant. The energy signature fit. This had to be it. So she had lead the charge through the door.

She had immediately realized two things: Leo had been correct and his view had been wrong. While the view from Leo's side had been clear grasslands, as soon as she stepped through she found herself in something altogether... different.

Hell.

There was no doubt that this represented someone's vision of Hell. Sulfur stung her nose. The grassland burned away, replaced by a harsh wasteland that assaulted the senses as both too hot and too cold at the same time.

Heather's description as she touched down seemed as apt as any Charlotte could think of. "Wow. This place sucks big ass donkey balls."

Jacob, in his blue jeans, tight black t-shirt and combat boots, sniffed in disdain while Huang just grimaced quietly. Charlotte quietly mused that Jacob's response to hell looked the same as his response to almost every other sanctuary he found himself in.

Charlotte took stock of their surroundings, looking for anything moving. Nothing did except the slight breeze whipping the stench of sulfur into their nostrils. "Heather, can you go up and see if you can spot anything?"

Heather, like Jack and Leo, had managed to uncover a flying past life.

"Sure, Shar. Hang on." She leapt into the air, her body shrinking and altering into the shape of a black cockatoo. She swept up into the air in a circular motion, gaining height while staying close to the others. Her lazy circles widened as she climbed, reaching a couple of hundred foot before diving downwards and swooping back into human form.

"That way." She pointed. "Some kind of movement, but I can't tell specifically what from here. "

Charlotte shrugged. "That way we go then."

"One more thing, Shar. Maybe nothing, may be something."

"What?"

Heather looked about uncomfortably, something Charlotte did not normally see her do. "I could see for miles in all directions. I didn't see the River."

That was somewhat strange. Usually the River was the one easy to find landmark in any sanctuary. But Charlotte had been in a few where it had been more tricky, so that didn't mean a lot. "I've seen it underground a few times. Could also be an illusion covering it. It's here, of that you can be sure. We'll probably stumble across it soon. Let's go."

They began walking in the direction Heather lead them.

No one spoke for the first few miles. Charlotte kept her eyes on the horizon, searching for any form of danger. Even Heather walked uncharacteristically quietly. Surprisingly to Charlotte, it was Jacob who broke the silence.

"Yo man, something is seriously wrong with this place."

Charlotte forced a smile. "Not used to being in Hell, Jacob?"

"Come on, Cowgirl. Give a brother some credit. You know I've been in some shit looked worse than this. But...the feel. Something ain't right here."

Charlotte concentrated on her surroundings. As much as she wanted to make fun of Jacob, he had hit on something that she hadn't realized had been nagging at her since they arrived. Something was off. The plane seemed more vast, more empty than it should.

Huang apparently felt it too. "Bigger than it should be."

"Come on guys." Heather apparently wasn't comfortable with where the conversation was going. "It's just another sanctuary with just another wacko soul who's figured out some trick for making it feel different. Happens all the time. Jacob, remember that Bedouin sanctuary with its endless desert? This is probably the same."

The tall black man seemed unconvinced. "Dunno bout that short stack. That one felt normal, we just had trouble spotting the loop. This one... this one don't feel looped. It feels big."

Heather was undeterred. "Just a trick I'm telling you."

Charlotte held up her hand as something moved on the horizon. "That's enough for now. I think we found your something, Heather."

Heather stopped and produced a pair of binoculars. She scanned the horizon.

"I don't see anything... wait." She scanned quickly one way, then another. "Something black keeps flying through my field of vision, but the bastard's moving fast."

She lowered her scan somewhat, then paused. The contorted look on her face made it obvious she'd found something. "Ewe. Gross."

Jacob stepped up and uncollapsed a long telescope and stared through it, then handed it off to Charlotte. Charlotte followed the direction Heather still stared at. There in the middle of the wasteland stood a rock with a man chained over it, his naked chest pointing to the sky. The man's stomach had been split open, and his intestine poured forth where black birds fought each other over the best places to peck. The man yanked at his chains in a way that showed he was definitely alive and definitely in agony, or at least thought he was.

Charlotte handed the telescope to Huang. "Well, someone here appreciates the classics."

Heather looked back, a bit whiter than normal. "Not much light shining through from him. I guess. Either way it's kinda sick."

Charlotte nodded her head. "So, best case? It's a creation by whoever created this sanctuary. In that case we're dealing with a black-hearted bastard but at least they're taking out their fantasies on nothings. Worst case, it's the owner of this sanctuary and we've got a powerful rogue soul with a vendetta from hell. I can think of a few other things in between those options it might be as well. Won't know till we ask. "

"Fantastical." Heather said sarcastically, dropping her binoculars, which disappeared before reaching the ground.

Jacob shrugged and continued walking. "Let's go. Ain't no point sitting round here. I wanna get this done, kick some ass, and get the fuck out of here."

The group continued forward quickly, but slowed its pace as the scene ahead became fully visible to the naked eye. The whimpers of the man on the rock slowly started breaking through the sound of the sulfurous breeze. Charlotte shuddered despite herself as she saw the man's predicament up close. An endless stream of blood pouring from the man's abdomen stained the ground around the boulder black. Two large crows were playing tug of war with a long piece of small intestine, while other smaller black birds sat on his chest pecking down at what appeared to be his stomach. The man's face was dried and crackled, like someone who had spent days in the blistering sun with no liquid to parch his thirst. His whimpering sounded like someone who had been in excruciating pain for so long he had lost the ability to articulate it through scream.

Jacob hurried his pace, and began making wide flailing motions with his hands, an obvious attempt to scare off the birds. "Shoo, birds. Get the fuck out of here."

The birds, probably close to twenty of them in total, squawked in near unison and took off, but did not go far. Instead they formed a circular black cloud about fifty feet above the man on the stone, who desperately tried to raise his head but appeared too weak to do so.

Huang stepped forward, producing a long pole arm with a massive axe head on the end of it. With a speed that would have seemed impossible of such a big man in the living world, Huang crashed the axe down twice, shattering the chains holding the man's arms down. He spun the axe around, then brought it down on each of the chains binding the man's legs. The man didn't move.

Heather stepped forward and gently placed a hand on his forehead, obviously trying not to look down at the mess below his chest. "It's okay. We're not here to hurt you." She closed her eyes for a moment, then opened them and looked over at Charlotte with a touch of sadness in her eyes. "This is a full soul. It's not a projection."

Charlotte sighed. She had been hoping for the opposite but had suspected as much. She produced a canteen and gently poured a small amount on the man's lips. He weakly took it in, gasping at it as if it were a source of life itself. "There there. Can you pull yourself back together?"

The man closed his eyes, and some of his insides slowly made their way back into his body. Charlotte could tell the man wouldn't be able to do much more than that on his own. "Heather, can you give him a boost? Just a slight one. We don't know what else is here, so I don't want you over doing it."

Heather nodded and placed a hand back on the man's forehead. The man gasped, and suddenly his intestines quickly pulled back into his body. Heather lost a bit of color as the man's stomach sealed itself up, his face cleared, and his body regained a more natural tone.

Jacob yanked Heather's hands away. "Whoa, Red. Don't you know the meaning of 'slight'?"

Heather flashed a small embarrassed smile. "Sorry… there was just… so much damage…. It was hard to stop."

"Who.." the man, obviously still weak tried to sit up, "…who…are… you?"

"We're here to help. Is this your sanctuary?"

"They…" the man tried to stand, but tumbled to the blood soaked ground. "They took it."

Jacob helped the man to his feet. "Yo man, you mean they changed it? This was it but now it's like, corrupted, right?"

The man shook his head weakly. "They took it. Said I didn't… didn't deserve it."

Jacob looked up at Charlotte. "Any idea what this fool is meaning?"

Charlotte shook her head. "No. I've never really heard of someone taking someone's sanctuary. Maybe they were lying to him?"

"Took... took it. Added it to hell. I don't deserve it. I don't deserve it."

Heather raised an eye at Charlotte. "I think they broke him."

"I think that was their point." Charlotte mused. "Sir, do you know of any other Sanctuaries you can go to for now? Or can you make it to the prime?"

"Don't deserve it. Don't.." the man jerked upright with a speed that caught everyone off guard.

Before anyone could do anything he flew backwards out of Jacob's grasp, slamming back first back into the boulder with an audible 'crack that sounded like broken bones. The man let out a blood-curdling scream as the chains lashed out once more and locked onto his limbs. The man's scream intensified as an invisible knife sliced deep into his torso, tearing a gash from sternum to groin then left side to right side.

The birds dove and swarmed, seemingly multiplying. Everything became a blur of black pain as Charlotte lashed out in all direction trying to clear a path out of the madness. Within moments the black blur subsided, and the entire scene was gone. Once again, the crew were back in a desolate wasteland, surrounded by nothingness.

Jacob wheeled about as if looking for something to hit. "Yo man, that ain't cool. Did he teleport or did we?"

Charlotte shook her head. "I don't know. But we need to find him. We can't leave him like that. Heather, can you go up and take another look? Maybe we're just back where we started."

"Sure."

"NO."

Charlotte whipped around to the source of a new voice.

"THOSE HERE ARE OURS. YOU CANNOT HAVE THEM."

The only way to describe what stood behind them was a demon. It was about seven-foot tall, with curved horns, cloven hooves, and a chest almost as broad as the creature was tall. Gnarled clawed fingers dangled from the end of arms that seemed far longer than they should have been, dangling down close to what would be considered the creature's knees, though those were backwards, adding to the mess of the creature's appearance.

Its voice, however, sounded human. Or, Charlotte corrected, humans. It sounded like five or more voices speaking in complete unison.

"WE HAVE NO QUARREL WITH YOU. YOU MAY LEAVE IF YOU DO SO NOW."

Charlotte shook her head. "Um… Don't think we can do that. Not without that soul back there anyway."

"HE BELONGS HERE. THOSE WHO ESCAPED PUNISHMENT IN LIFE CANNOT DO SO IN DEATH. RETRIBUTION WAS PROMISED. GOD HAS SPOKEN. YOU HAVE NO SAY IN THE MATTER."

Jacob produced a long metal baseball bat, then started tapping it against his hand. "Look homey. Cowgirl here says we're taking the soul, we're taking the soul. Your god can kiss my ass if he wants to stop us."

"YOU ARE LIKE THE OTHERS. YOU WERE GIVEN YOUR CHOICE AND YOU CHOSE THE SIDE OF EVIL. YOU MUST SUFFER THE CONSEQUENCES OF THAT CHOICE."

Charlotte had had her suspicions, and now she accepted them as confirmed. The thing might be referring to any number of 'others', but she knew with certainty what it meant. Dominique, Marco, Roberto, John, likely even others. This is what they had met. This creature is why they were no longer here. A fury burned brightly in the pit of her stomach, tempered only slightly by the fear of what this thing must be capable of to have taken on all of those members and won. It would stop here. If she had to die again to take this thing down, so be it.

Heather apparently reached the same conclusion. "Um… guys? I think this is the bastard we've been sent to find."

"Well then. This is for Marco." Jacob raised his metal baseball bat and charged forward with a screaming war cry. "DIE Bastard!" He slammed the bat into the creature's stomach with force that should have carried the bat through the creature and out the other side.

The creature let out a loud howl of anger, but instead of falling it reached out with its massive clawed right hand and grabbed Jacob by the head, picking him up like a rag doll. Before anyone could say or do anything, the creature raised Jacob high in the air. Jacob kicked and pulled at the creature's hand, then burst into a flash of light. When the light subsided he had vanished. To Charlotte's horror his link suddenly disappeared as well. Jacob was truly gone.

"Bastard!" Charlotte pulled out a pistol and began unloading into the creature. Huang pulled a massive war axe out of the air and charged. "Don't let him grab you!"

Huang ducked underneath the creature's grasp and brought the axe into the creature's midsection near the same spot Jacob's bat had hit. It sank in, causing the creature to scream once more. Heather meanwhile had pulled out two thin rapiers and had joined the battle herself, sliding nimbly between the creature's legs and poking holes wherever she could. The creature wailed in anguish.

Huang brought the axe around again, slamming it into the creature's back. The demon spun, and as Huang ducked another outstretched hand, he stepped right into a cloven hoof that appeared to connect with the force of a kicking horse. Huang flew backwards some ten feet, landing on his back. A moment later he was back on his feet and charging again.

Heather ran up the creature's back, flipped onto its shoulders, and buried her rapiers into each side of the creature's neck. "That's for Jacob, Assmunch!"

The demon wailed in pain, but reached back and snatched Heather off of its back with its extraordinarily long right arm. Huang tried redirecting his axe towards the creature's right arm, but in doing so was caught off guard by a back hand from the creature's left that sent him flying into Charlotte. By the time the two recovered their feet, Heather had ceased to exist.

"No!" Charlotte continued to unload her pistols into the creature. Each shot connected, but she wasn't certain whether or not they were causing anything more than an annoyance to the creature. Huang charged once more, but this time the creature was ready for him. A feint grab obviously caught Huang off guard, as he ducked into another cloven kick that sent him spinning once more. The creature caught Huang's axe as the huge Chinaman started spinning away, and with inhuman speed sent it flying towards Charlotte. Charlotte tried to duck, but the tumbling blade caught her in the shoulder, putting her on the ground again.

Charlotte looked up to see the demon stomping towards Huang, who was standing up much slower.

"We can't win this." Charlotte realized with horror. The horror immediately turned to determination. If she was going down, she at least wanted this creature to pay some price for it. There was no defense like a good offense. Charlotte poured much of her energy into creating a grenade. More than she probably should, as she noticed her hand fade for a second. A few hits from this demon would probably dissipate her at this point, but she was beyond caring. Most of her team was gone. If she could go down avenging their deaths, it would be a worthy end to her afterlife. She would embrace the River and be reborn.

Another massive backhand sent Huang flying again, and that's when Charlotte saw her opening. "Hey! Assmunch!" Heather's name for it seamed as good as any. "Why don't you pick on somcone half your size?" With that she let the grenade fly.

Thirty-one

The world reappeared with a complete onslaught against Thomas's senses. His nose was hit with a sulfurous smell that was borderline nauseating. His skin burned from a wind that felt like it was coming off of a frozen fire, some how molten hot and icy cold at the same time. A massive explosion slammed his ears, swinging his attention to his left where a massive creature modeled off of the Devil himself clawed its way out of a pit.

Jack already moved at a dead run for the creature. Cho sprinted on a slight tangent, heading for a kneeling form that Thomas immediately recognized as Charlotte. Another soul, a large Chinese looking man, slowly stood and hefted a huge wicked looking axe on the other side of the huge pit in the ground. Thomas didn't recognize him, but knew instinctively he was one of theirs. The connection running to him showed a mix of rage, fear, and exhaustion wracked the stranger's body, along with an impressive streak of determination.

Two things were clear to Thomas. There were far fewer members of their Order than there had been even a few moments ago, and the Devil was the cause. That was all he needed to know for the moment. He shifted forms, ignoring the new assault on his olfactory senses, and charged forward.

A scream that his mind barely registered as Charlotte's called out from his right. "Don't let it grab you!"

Thomas didn't plan to let it touch him. The creature was now on its feet and focused on the charging Asian and his axe. It didn't notice until it was too late the crashing of Jack's cricket bat into its legs, sweeping it off of its cloven hooved feet. Jack brought the bat down, bashing into the creature's head as the large Chinese guy tried lopping a horn off with the axe, burying it deep. Thomas, seeing an opening, launched himself forward and felt the satisfying sensation of his six inch front teeth sinking into the demon's throat. He yanked backwards, ripping it out, gratified at another kill.

With a surprising scream, the creature flailed out wildly, sending Thomas and the others flying. Thomas looked up to see the creature rise to its full seven and a half foot height and bellow loudly at the sky. "WE ARE RETRIBUTION! WE CANNOT BE DEFEATED."

The large Asian man was already charging again. Thomas leapt to his feet to do the same, but before he moved he saw why Charlotte had screamed her warning. The demon stood firm as the large Chinese man leapt into the air and brought his wicked axe crashing down. It bit into the Devil's shoulder, and continued slicing till the creature's right arm lay on the ground. The creature barely blinked as it grabbed the man's head with its left arm, raised him up, and then with a flash, dissipated the man. In that moment, Thomas realized there was nothing left of the man, not even his link.

"Huang!" Jack leapt back into the fray, dancing around the creature with speed Thomas had never seen him use. The Devil, who suddenly had both arms again, reached out to grab him, but each time he did, Jack was in another spot bringing the bat down again and again with bone cracking force. Cho was now there as well, moving at his insanely inhuman speed and landing punch after punch on the tall demon while deftly dodging its grasp. Charlotte opened fire with a pair of pistols. For a brief moment Thomas could swear he could see through her.

Thomas considered his options. He could leap back in, but Jack and Cho seemed to be having a hard time already dodging both the Devil and each other. He stood back up into human form and changed the ground directly beneath the creature into soft mud. He smiled as the creature's hooves sank deeply, bringing the creature down to its reversed knees. Thomas immediately changed the ground back to something far harder, trapping the creature and reducing its movement. The demon screamed and flailed, but Jack and Cho easily ducked its blows and continued landing their own. Charlotte was walking closer, pouring more of her energy into each shot she took, and now screaming loud obscenities with every pull of the trigger.

Thomas summoned a fireball, and looked for an opening to release it into the creature's chest. This fight couldn't go on much longer.

"NOOOOOOOOOOO!"

Without warning the creature brought its arms down into the ground. The world exploded and Thomas felt himself fly backwards, crashing hard on his back. He fought the exhausted feeling that threatened to overcome him and pulled himself up. The creature was out again and as Thomas watched the demon stepped over to where Jack was picking himself up off of the ground. With speed it should no longer possess, it snatched Jack up and held him high. "No!"

Cho rushed forward, but was met with a backhand that sent him flying. Thomas unleashed a fireball at the creature, but before it hit a flash erupted from its hand. As the ball of fire connected with its chest, sending it flying backwards into the charred pit behind it, Jack dissipated. Thomas felt his link to Jack drop into nothingness. "No! JACK!"

This creature had too many tricks. It was too strong. Thomas knew with certainty that if they didn't change the rules, they would lose the game. They couldn't take it with all of its power. Could they do it if no one had power? Thomas wasn't certain they could, or that he could make it happen, but as the creature crawled back out of the pit he knew he had to try. He closed his eyes and pictured the grey haze that had been their bane in the Test sanctuary. He opened his eyes to see the haze forming around the demon. It screamed.

"NO! WE CANNOT BE DEFEATED. WE ARE RETRIBUTION. WE WERE PROMISED!"

As Thomas watched, something odd happened. First the land within the haze, which now covered a twenty-foot circle centered on the Devil, sprouted grass. The wasteland itself seemed to melt away. The Devil screamed again, then fell to all fours. As Thomas watched, it too began melting, and large chunks fell to the ground and rolled away. Thomas watched with a mix of fascination and horror was the chunks themselves took the form of bodies. Within minutes, the demon was gone completely, replaced by seven bodies, the youngest of which looked to be five years old, the oldest not more than fifteen or so. Only two of the older ones managed to stand up. The others disappeared into wisps of smoke.

"WE weRE PromISED." Both still spoke as one, but their voices were no longer in perfect unison.

Charlotte stood just a few feet outside of the boundary of the haze. She seemed to fade even further as something appeared in her hand. "Yeah? Well, I made a promise too. Here's me fulfilling it."

Charlotte lobbed what looked to be a grenade into the haze, between the two remaining souls. Thomas expected it to dissipate with the fog, but it didn't. The force of the resulting explosion once again sent him flying backwards onto his back. When he looked up again there was no trace of the demon or the souls that appeared to make it left in the fog.

Cho was already making his way quickly across the grass within the haze's boundaries to where Charlotte had fallen to the ground. The faintness of Charlotte's connection worried him enough that he forced himself up to rushed forward too.

Cho was lifting Charlotte head from the ground when Thomas arrived. Charlotte was literally fading. He could see Cho's arm supporting her through her body. "Good job… boys…. I knew we trained you well."

"Stay with us, Master Charlotte. Friend Thomas and I will get you back to your sanctuary."

"No Cho. I don't have the energy to survive the trip."

"Master Charlotte!"

"It's okay, Cho. We took out the threat to the Order. I'm willing to die doing that. I just wish we'd left you more of…" Charlotte closed her eyes, and for a brief moment, was only partially transparent, "more of it to work with. Promise me you two will rebuild it. Leo will help you."

Thomas knelt down. He felt completely helpless. He knew there had to be a way to help Charlotte, but he didn't know what it was. In her own sanctuary she would quickly recover, but here… he knew here in an unknown sanctuary the energy she was expending keeping herself whole was more than she could be pulling in. She didn't have much time left.

Cho wasn't buying into that. "We'll bring Leo. He can recharge you enough that you could make the trip. He'll…"

"Promise me, Cho."

Thomas knelt down and placed a hand on Charlotte's fading shoulder. "We promise, Charlotte. For you and Jack and all the others. We'll rebuild it."

Charlotte smiled faintly. "Thank you, Thomas. Cho? I need one more… one more favor from you."

Tears were visible on Cho's face, something that surprised Thomas. He had not thought about the dead crying. "What is it, Master Charlotte?"

"Give me a drink of that Saki you loved."

Cho smiled sadly, then reached down and produced a small cup of rice wine. He propped Charlotte up slightly higher, then helped her to take a small drink.

"Ahh. That is good."

And with that she was gone. Thomas felt the link to her fade and disappear. Cho stared at his now empty arms, heavier tears streaming down his face. "Master Charlotte! Master Charlotte… no… Master… no…" He collapsed next to where Charlotte's body had a moment again been, sobbing intensely. Thomas wanted to help him, but he had no idea what to say. He felt strangely numb.

Jack was gone. Charlotte was gone. He reached back to the Training sanctuary and followed his link out from there. There were now only two paths aside from his own, Cho's and Leo's. No one else was left. No one.

"My condolences on your loss, Thomas."

Thirty-two

Thomas looked up through misty eyes to see an older man in a black suit with a high collar standing beside him. "Brother Coughlin?"

"Yes my child. Tragic. All of this fighting. Pointless."

"What are you doing here?"

"Watching. You were very impressive mind you. I would be remiss if I did not congratulate you on how far you've come since our first meeting those few months ago."

"You… you were here the entire time? And you did not help?"

"Not my place, dear boy. Even if I had, who would I have helped? Your companions? Or the poor children they attacked?"

"Poor… Poor children?" Thomas stood, a flash of anger and confusion simultaneously rushing through his mind. "They didn't look too poor to me."

"Have you the ability to read souls, Thomas?"

Thomas wasn't entirely certain what he meant, but he felt pretty sure that any interpretation would come back to the same answer. "No. Least not that I know of."

"Not surprising. It's not a common ability. I have it. I can tell things about souls by looking at them. I know your friend down there was a factory worker in his native Vietnamese village till he died of a heart attack when he was 63. He had few friends and no family by that time. It was a lonely life, but it could have been worse. I know your friend who just passed lead a rough life spent proving herself to others. She was born the only child of a man who desperately wanted a son and made no secret of it. Her mother died in childbirth, leaving her to his not so tender raising. She felt she constantly had to prove herself acceptable, and the sad fact is that she did. That resulted in her taking a risk she knew she shouldn't take to try and prove she could ride a horse no one else would dare ride. The resulting broken neck killed her instantly. But her life was nothing compared to the misery those children endured.

Those children belonged to a village in Africa. A local warlord felt slighted when they did not produce the amount of tribute he felt he deserved. He decided to make an example of them. For three days, his men visited unspeakable atrocities upon those children and their families. One by one each was raped, tortured, mutilated, and then killed while the others were forced to watch. Anyone who closed their eyes to the madness had their eyelids cut off. They were the last to be murdered.

The warlord went on to live a long and happy life on the suffering of others, dying in his sleep at the age of seventy of a brain aneurism. He woke up to find himself in a world where he could recreate all of his life's greatest moments whenever he wanted, and where he could spend an eternity in the same level of bliss he lived in. These children banded together to see that that would not happen. They visited upon him the fruits of the horrible garden he had sewn when he was alive. They saw to it that God's righteous vengeance was delivered, and that the man who escaped punishment in life did not also do so in death. That was their crime. For that, your friends attacked them. Even when the children asked your friends to leave, and gave them a path to do so, they refused. These poor souls who died suffering, were forced to endure the horror of battle once more at your hands. Would you have had me join in with that?"

Thomas stared at him in silence, trying to process what he'd been told. "But... they were a monster…"

Coughlin's lips tightened with a look of sad acceptance. "They were what they had been made to be."

Thomas sat back to consider. Were his people in the wrong? Did they die in vain? Could all of this have been stopped with more conversation? Then he thought back to Falling Dusk. He had meant well too. He started out with the intent of protecting his people from an enemy they might not have been able to stop, and in the process killed most of them himself. Had the God Monk started the same way? Trying to do what he felt was right? These kids had banded together, in a similar fashion to what to what Falling Dusk and the God Monk had. Would they have stopped here? Or would they have continued growing, doing what they felt was 'right' at the expense of everyone else.

Already their power was exponentially more powerful than they likely would have been on their own. Thomas suspected Jack could have taken all of them out individually on his own. That might be just his faith in what Jack was, but he had little doubt it was true. But together they had been powerful enough to withstand most of the assault from the Order, and take out five of the seven of them. If Thomas had not been exposed to the grey mist recently, it might very well have taken out all seven of them and continued its path.

"Thomas, I have asked you twice. I ask you once more. Join me. There is great work to be done out there. Your ties to your group are now severed. You will be responsible for rebuilding it in whatever image you see fit. Your friend will follow your lead; I can read that in his spirit. Let us protect the weak and be the standard bearers of Justice. We will do what must be done, taking the path God has laid before us, no matter the obstacles."

"Do you still believe in God, even after all you have seen over here?"

Brother Coughlin stood straight and tall. "How can I not? You have seen the River. All thought, all belief, all that is comes from it. Do you believe that when souls return to it, that thought goes away? Is it not logical to believe the River itself has its own consciousness? That it gives of its own life that we may have ours? What else would you call something like that if not God?"

Thomas wasn't really certain what he thought of the River. But if it did have a consciousness, he wasn't entirely certain it was interested in anything other than collecting the experiences of life. He had yet to see anything to even hint that there was a 'path laid out before him' by the River. "I don't know, Brother Coughlin. This path of yours, does it include becoming like them?"

Brother Coughlin smiled. "I would hope my path does not result in my becoming a demon, but in the end I will accept whatever fate God has in store for me. It is his will in the end that matters, not mine. Perhaps with you on the same path, you can help ensure such needless violence as today never occurs again. You can help see to it that while the guilty receive their just punishments, the innocent receive their eternal rewards."

He dodged the answer. That gave Thomas all he really needed to know. Brother Coughlin would walk the same path that Falling Dusk and the God Monk had without hesitation. He might very well have already started on that path, though Thomas did not get the sense of raw power that he got from the other two, so he suspected that if he had started on that path, he had not collected even a fraction of the souls the other two had. With any luck he never would.

"No, Brother Coughlin. I cannot walk this path with you. I have seen where it leads, and trust me, it's not a good place. You won't find God's will. Just death, destruction, and enough power to corrupt even the purest of intents."

A look of deep sadness passed over Brother Coughlin's face. "I see you have made your mind up. I am very sorry to hear that."

"Do not collect souls, Brother Coughlin. Release any you've already taken."

"Goodbye, Thomas."

Thirty-three

Thomas looked up to find himself back in the Training sanctuary. Cho knelt next to him, his face still stained with tears, but with a streak of determination that Thomas could sense through their mutual link to the sanctuary.

"How… how did we get back here, Friend Thomas?"

"Brother Coughlin must have sent us back."

"Who?"

Thomas looked down and offered a hand for Cho to stand up. "The man I was talking to back in the other sanctuary. "

"Friend Thomas, I know I am burdened by grief, but I do not recall you speaking to anyone else."

That was odd. Thomas considered for a moment. "Cho, your last life, was it in Vietnam?"

"Yes, Friend Thomas."

'Were you a factory worker?"

Cho looked at him with a hint of confusion in his eyes. "Yes. Did Master Jack tell you that?"

"And you had few friends or family?"

Cho shook his head. "Virtually none. What time I spent away from the assembly line was usually spent watching Kung fu movies out of China. I…. I did not make friends easily when I was alive. How do you know this?"

Thomas nodded his head. "Brother Coughlin. Cho we may have a bigger problem on our hands than we ever suspected. "

"Okay. What do we do about it?"

Thomas frowned. "I don't know yet. Get some rest Cho. Go back to your sanctuary if you need to. I think I may need some time in mine. Come to grips with our loss as best you can. I'll contact you soon and we'll get started on rebuilding the team."

Cho nodded. "I will stop in and tell Friend Leo of our loss. I am certain he knows by now, but he should hear it regardless."

"Thank you. And Cho?"

"Yes, Friend Thomas?"

"Be careful out there."

"Thank you, Friend Thomas. You too."

Cho disappeared. Thomas looked around the world that had been his primary residence for the past six months or so. It felt strange. On one hand it seemed like it had been just yesterday that he had woken up dead. On the other hand it seemed a lifetime ago since he had actually drawn a real breath. He had always thought life was kind of odd, but it seemed it didn't hold a candle to death. He still couldn't believe Jack was gone. Or Charlotte for that matter. The thought of their loss threatened to overwhelm him for a moment, but he beat back the feelings and sealed them away, just as he had with his father when he was much younger. There would be time to mourn them later. If he broke down now, he might not be able to move forward. So he put his internal walls up and took one last look around. Jack would push him to 'bloody well keep moving'. For now there seemed little else to do.

"Thanks Jack. I'll make you proud."

Epilogue

Jacob pulled himself by sheer force of will from the black oblivion that threatened to engulf him. Slowly, he became aware of his own body. With an immense amount of effort, he managed to force his eyes open, then shut them again quickly as sunlight filtering in through the limbs of a light wooded canopy assaulted him. He felt like he had been run over. Every part of his body ached in a way that it had not done since before he had died.

With some effort, he fought to open his eyes once more, slowly allowing them to adjust. He tried to sit up, but failed. He literally had no strength for it. He tried digging his way through the cottony fog that engulfed his mind. He wasn't certain where he was or how he had gotten there. All he knew for sure was that he was outdoors in a forest somewhere on the ground on his back. He was also becoming painfully aware that there were some uncomfortable sticks and rocks underneath his back, but he still couldn't summon the strength to move. He reached out to his peers to see if any of them might be close by.

The strands all met with dead ends. The shock threatened to put him back under. He checked again just to be certain, but there was no mistaking it. Everyone else was gone. Wherever he was, Jacob was truly on his own to deal with it. Heather, Jack, Charlotte, all of them were gone. A white-hot fury exploded in Jacob's core, consuming the exhaustion that paralyzed him and giving him the strength to force himself up to a seated position.

"Oh hell no. Somebody's gonna pay for this."

END OF BOOK I

####

Thank you for reading Waking Up Dead! If you enjoyed it (and I hope you did), please take a moment to leave a review of your thoughts with your favorite retailer so that others can get turned on to these stories. Stay tuned as the adventure continues in my next book, The Glacier of Gods and Monsters. - Zabe